THE SUN, THE STORM, & THE SHADOWS

HEARTS OF MAYA: VOL 1

MIKAYLA D. HORNEDO

Copyright © [2023] by [Mikayla D. Hornedo]

All rights reserved.

No portion of this book may be reproduced in any form without written permission from the publisher or author, except as permitted by U.S. copyright law.

The characters and events portrayed in this book are fictitious or are used fictitiously. Any similarity to real persons, living or dead, is purely coincidental and not intended by the author. While this story was inspired my Mayan Mythology, it is not a retelling of any of their stories.

Dedicated to all the readers who can feel underrepresented in books like this. This one is for you.

Contents

1. Chapter 1　　　　　　　　　　　　　1
   Xio
2. Chapter 2　　　　　　　　　　　　16
   Camila
3. Chapter 3　　　　　　　　　　　　27
   Xio
4. Chapter 4　　　　　　　　　　　　34
   Camila
5. Chapter 5　　　　　　　　　　　　40
   Xio
6. Chapter 6　　　　　　　　　　　　47
   Camila
7. Chapter 7　　　　　　　　　　　　56
   Xio
8. Chapter 8　　　　　　　　　　　　73
   Xio
9. Chapter 9　　　　　　　　　　　　82
   Camila

10.	Chapter 10 Xio	90
11.	Chapter 11 Camila	100
12.	Chapter 12 Xio	111
13.	Chapter 13 Camila	128
14.	Chapter 14 Xio	139
15.	Chapter 15 Camila	148
16.	Chapter 16 Xio	159
17.	Chapter 17 Camila	174
18.	Chapter 18 Xio	181
19.	Chapter 19 Camila	191
20.	Chapter 20 Xio	203
21.	Chapter 21 Holt	217

22.	Chapter 22 Camila	226
23.	Chapter 23 Xio	239
24.	Chapter 24 Cree	258
25.	Chapter 25 Camila	269
26.	Chapter 26 Xio	276
27.	Chapter 27 Camila	290
28.	Chapter 28 Xio	305
29.	Chapter 29 Cree	315
30.	Chapter 30 Camila	322
31.	Chapter 31 Xio	332
32.	Chapter 32 Cree	341
33.	Chapter 33 Holt	350

34.	Chapter 34 Camila	355
35.	Chapter 35 Xio	361
36.	Chapter 36 Camila	370
37.	Chapter 37 Xio	377
38.	Chapter 38 Xio	386
39.	Chapter 39 Camila	394
40.	Chapter 40 Cree	402
About Author		411
About the Author		

Pronunciation Guide

Xiomara/Xio – Zee-oh-ma-ra / Zoh

Camila – Ka-mee-la

Ixchel – Ee-shell

Kinich – Kee-nich

Itzamna – Its-am-na

Chaac – Ch-ak

Alux – Ah-loosh

Zuma – Soo-ma

Xibalba - Zee-ball-bah

Estrella – Ehs-trey-ah

Possible Triggers:

This story contains: grief, mentioned abuse, sexual scenes, and violence.

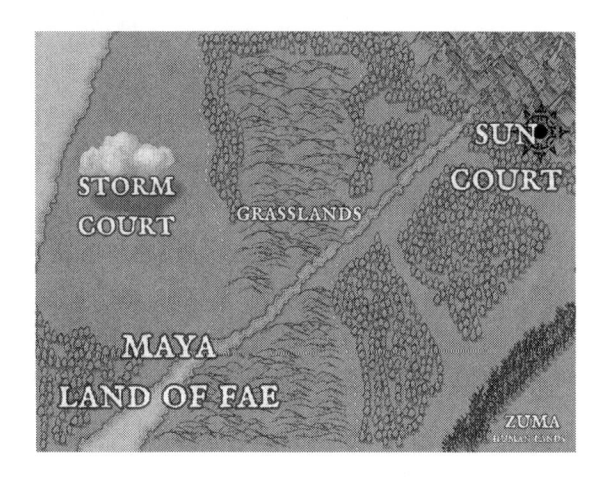

Chapter 1

Xio

Well, this wasn't going as planned.

I dodged the sword that the guard was swinging to kill, but he didn't know who I was.

Nobody did. I didn't even know who I was.

All the same, he underestimated me. Probably because I was a woman. He didn't know I could use his own weapon better than him.

Misogynists practically grew on trees here in Zuma.

I dodged again, staying on the defense, letting him continue to underestimate me. I could use that to my own advantage.

He had no real skill, just swinging his sword with all of his strength in the same formation over and over. I should have expected this from Lord Wayward's guards.

He never was very astute, influential sure, but an idiotic bastard.

The guard went in for another strike, but I anticipated it. I twirled around him and slashed the back of his legs, causing him to fall to the ground.

I didn't kill him. As skilled as I was with a blade, I never actually killed anyone.

I just stopped them from killing me first.

Death just seemed so final. I didn't think I should have that power over anyone.

Well, no situation made me feel like I should yet.

Our plan to steal from Lord Wayward was solid. We planned to go in during a guard change, slip into his treasury, throw everything we could into the bags we brought, and escape back out over the garden walls.

We had help from a couple of the servants in the estate who were looking for their own way out of the village and revenge against the Lord.

With that being said, we weren't expecting this guard to be where he shouldn't have been. I dealt with him quickly while Camila grabbed the bags and brought them over to the wall. I positioned my sword in my hand blade up and brought the hilt down against his temple. After I ensured the guard was unconscious, I met Camila at the wall and threw the heavy loads over.

If this was the only guard to see us, we would have plenty of time to get out. Not to mention he didn't see our faces since we had our hoods up and scarves over the bottom half of our faces.

Camila climbed up the wall with the skill of a thief, and straddled either side of it before making her way down.

She tried to shimmy down the other side, but the wind blew stronger than expected, and her hood flew right off her head.

Exposing her hair, her very noticeable, very unique hair.

Camila's hair was streaked with gold, like spun threads of pure gold running through her curly brown hair. While many people here in Zuma had blonde hair, hers was much more distinctive.

We heard a shout from the other side of the wall that sounded like a servant, but nothing else came from it.

Camila decided to take a lap around the estate to see if that shout we heard would turn into the full force of Wayward guards coming for us.

I ran to our home with the stolen goods and waited. I slammed the rickety door, dropped the satchels of gold, and jumped up and down with slightly premature excitement.

If we pulled this off...I needed to wait until Camila returned.

I didn't even feel bad for the Lord. That bastard deserved it.

He treated the people in our village like they were less than him and his noble family. He always seemed to find a way to make the villagers' lives more difficult than necessary.

Being the Lord of the village came with far too much control over the people. He held the influence to stop everything we needed to survive.

He raised our taxes, made food less available in our markets, and caused some people to lose their homes altogether.

Just because he could. Forcing people to have to come to him for help or work.

He got off on the power of it.

Not to mention what happened to my sister, who just happened to be in his line of sight during one of his especially cruel days.

I looked around our house, which honestly was more like a shack, thinking that we might finally be able to upgrade to a slightly larger shack.

This had been our home for nearly ten years, and I wasn't sure how much longer it would stay upright. The floorboards were starting to decay, and there were some areas in the house that I was sure would collapse any day now.

The walls were chipping, and the fireplace was one missing brick from caving in on itself. We'd been saving for the last five years in hopes that we could find a better place to live, and this last job put us right at our goal.

I paced the room. Camila should have been back by now, and that fact had anxiety festering in my gut.

I couldn't wait any longer and decided to look for her myself, but as soon as I opened the front door I saw Camila running full speed towards our house.

Either she was just trying to get back fast to avoid any other eyes, or we needed to run like hell. I jumped out of the way as she ran through the door and stared at me with wide brown eyes.

"They know it was us. One of the servants told the guards that they saw a girl with curly brown and gold hair slip over their walls."

Damn Camila and her weird hair, both of us stood out amongst the crowd. My bright gold eyes and her gold streaks of hair were not common attributes around here.

Not to mention the Lord was pretty familiar with this curly brown-gold-haired girl.

"We have to get out of here immediately. They could be here any minute," I huffed.

She nodded and grabbed our bags from the closet. Fortunately, this wasn't the first less than moral thing we'd done, so we always had a plan to run in place.

Thankfully up until this point we'd never been caught, so we never had to use our emergency bags.

I knew that we aimed too high with this one. Stealing from the highest-ranking person in our village was not going to be easy. Camila was confident that it would be the last time we had to steal, so I agreed, knowing she wanted revenge.

I wanted revenge for her.

"What about the gold?" Camila asked through panic.

"It's too heavy. We'll have to leave most of it," I responded quickly. Her facial features turned from panic to anger. The realization that we would be coming up mostly empty-handed boiling her blood.

"Take out what won't slow us down and throw the rest of it under that floorboard over there," I said, pointing to a particularly wiggly board. "If you move the table over it, they might not ever find it."

Her face split into a wicked smile as she stuffed our bag with a few gold coins and tossed the rest under the planks.

That would be worth the extra few seconds needed for our escape, hopefully.

After strapping the dual daggers on her waist, Camila handed me my bag and sword. These weapons were the most expensive things in our possession, but we never even thought about selling them.

Something about them felt right, and neither of us had even brought up the idea to try and pawn them off, even when we needed the money.

I finished sheathing my sword across my back and throwing my bag over my shoulder, not even bothering to close the door behind us.

We would never be coming back here.

I took one last look at our little shack and sighed. It was never a place I thought I'd miss, but all of the memories my sister and I had made here all hit me at once, and I felt a pang of sadness.

I shook that off because there was no time for sentimentality when we needed to run for our lives.

We started to move, but the sound of horses and shouting came from the direction we were heading. We turned around, but more guards were coming from the other direction.

I looked over at Camila, and she cursed as we looked around for another escape route. The commotion had caused everyone to stop and stare, making it even more challenging to get away alive.

"We're going to have to run into the forest," Camila suggested.

"You mean the Cursed Forest?"

"Oh, come on, you don't really believe in that myth, do you?" she responded with a hand on her hip.

Well, I kind of did. Everyone said there were evil spirits lurking in the forest and that there was a reason no one ever ventured into it.

One of our neighbors, Marie, even said she had a cousin who went into the forest last year hoping they could find something to hunt, but he never returned.

At this point, our options were: definitely get apprehended by the guards barreling at us, or go into the creepy forest that may or may not kill us. So *'may or may not'* was the better option.

"No, you're right. It's our only option," I replied.

We turned toward the forest, and I prayed to any Gods listening that we would survive. If there were any Gods listening, they surely never did us any favors before.

But, dire needs.

We ran as fast as our feet could carry us toward the forest. The thud of my feet against stone quickly turned to the crunch of dead grass beneath my feet. I looked down to see that everything near the forest was utterly dead. Even the air seemed to have a deadly quality.

My sister scrunched her nose up at the perishing land, but we had no choice but to keep running. We jumped over the gangly tree roots and dodged the flaking black trees that seemed like they, too, should have been dead. But they shot so high in the sky we couldn't see where they ended.

We made it deep into the forest before we heard the horses stop and the guards curse. They sounded close, so we listened and hid behind a wide dark tree.

"The forest is too thick. We can't keep riding. They're as good as dead if they made it this deep. I don't want to end up dead for some thieving rats," I heard one guard with a raspy voice say.

"They stole a good chunk of his gold. They must be punished, and the gold returned. Man up, this is just a forest," another responded.

Camila had both her daggers in her hand as we waited to see what they would do. It only sounded like two of them came into the forest so we could fight it out if it came to that. I reached back for my sword and heard the sound of footsteps on the brittle dead ground get closer.

I inhaled a deep breath and slowly exhaled as I shifted my mind into the weapon I'd trained myself into. My sister was doing the same with her eyes closed as she tried to listen for their location.

She opened her eyes abruptly and threw one of her daggers in an arch around the tree, and the sound of pierced flesh and a scream reached us before we jumped from behind it.

The dagger was sticking from the man's neck while he fell to the ground in agony.

I focused on the guard charging for me and let my sister finish handling the other. The man's sword was smaller than mine, and my confidence grew even greater at the joke of a guard.

He swung with more finesse than I expected, and I took a step to the side to avoid the slice of his blade. The armor the guards wore was gaudy and stiff, and they didn't even wear helmets. The Lord was more focused on the look of his guards than their well-being.

It made his moves much less fluid than mine, and as he turned to me and lifted his arm to strike again, I focused on the area of armor-free body exposed by his movement.

I immediately went on the offense and brought the sword across my body in a great swipe that cut through his side, exactly where I was aiming for.

He wailed as blood started to spray profusely from the wound. I told myself I wouldn't kill unless necessary, but I had to protect my sister and me right now.

The guard was hunched over, gripping his side, and I quickly placed my foot in the center of his back and kicked as hard as I could. He went tumbling down to the ground rolling over to try and find his weapon, but he was too late.

My blade had already found its mark.

Slightly higher than where I cut previously, with my advantage standing above him, angling my blade between his armor for his heart was no hard task.

I watched as blood filled his mouth and the light left his eyes.

My first kill.

My hands began to shake slightly before my thoughts turned to my sister.

I whirled around quickly, but Camila was already beside me, wiping the blood off her daggers. The look in her eyes confirmed that she was in the same exact situation I was in.

We'd both come close to killing before, Camila closer. She always ran hotter than me. Angrier than me. As if the whole world was at fault for everything wrong that happened to her.

She'd be able to cope with this, so I would have to try as well.

This was for our protection. If we didn't kill them, they would have killed us.

Undoubtedly.

"Those were the only two guards that made it this deep in the forest. We need to find a way out of here before they start to look for those two," I said, pointing my chin toward the deceased.

"I see some light through there. It looks like a way out of the forest. With luck, we can find somewhere to camp for the night," I followed her finger to where she was pointing.

Off in the distance was a small opening at the forest's edge where light seemed to sparkle through.

"Okay, let's get out of here."

We began to move, and I could see the wheels in Camila's head turning. She always tried to hide any feelings that made her feel vulnerable so I'd have to coax any of her genuine feelings about the situation out of her.

"Camila," I started.

She knew where I was going and quickly cut me off.

"One thing off the bucket list," she mumbled with a shrug.

I tilted my head to the side and gave her my best, *'really?'* look that she knew very well.

"It had to be done, Xio. They would have killed us. I'd never let anything happen to you," she said confidently.

We were always there for each other, no matter what. I'd protect her just as fiercely as she'd protect me.

It had just been me and her for as long as I can remember.

We both woke up in our shack nearly ten years ago with no idea what happened or where we came from. The only things we knew for sure were that I was sixteen and she was fifteen, we were sisters, and we would have to fight to survive from that point on.

Anytime I tried to remember anything before that, I got a splitting headache and grew highly fatigued.

We tried to ask the people around us if they had seen anything around the time we woke up, but no one knew a thing. They told us that the shack had been vacant for years but had no information outside of that.

I gave up on it quickly and decided that whatever happened before didn't matter, and the only thing that mattered was our future.

Camila wasn't so easily deterred, and I often caught her staring off into the distance with a scowl as she tried to remember anything she could.

We made our way toward the clearing, and I couldn't shake this feeling deep down that we shouldn't be here. Everything in the forest seemed to scream to turn around and return to wherever you came from.

I looked up at the lamented trees and decided the faster we got out of here, the better. The clearing didn't seem that far when we spotted it, but it felt like we'd been walking for hours.

The little light that came from between the trees was slipping away, and if there was anything this forest emanated, it was that you definitely didn't want to get caught in here after dark.

"We're going to need to pick up our speed. The last thing we need is to be stuck in this forest after dark," I exclaimed.

A snap and a clicking sound started from somewhere behind us as if we needed more proof of what I suggested.

Camila looked at me with wide eyes, and we both began to sprint. We were just a few strides from the clearing, and I felt deep relief that there was still a small amount of light for us to scout the area and set up camp.

As we exited the forest, a strange prickling feeling covered my entire body.

"Did you feel that?" I asked.

Camila scratched her shoulder blade. "Yeah, this forest is weird. Maybe it's just our bodies running out of adrenaline after that eventful little evening."

I chuckled and surveyed the area. I expected more dry, brittle grass or another poor village like our own.

But as I took in my surroundings, I was in awe.

Wherever we ended up felt like the opposite of the Cursed Forest. Everything was so green and bright, even in the dim light. There were rolling hills with trees peppered throughout the landscape.

There seemed to be more forest in the distance, but nothing like where we came from.

This one was full of life.

I pointed towards a large tree with decent coverage in case someone decided to follow us through the forest after all.

"Let's set up our camp there, and we can figure out our next move in the morning," I suggested.

This felt like an entirely new world. Camila's brow was lined with confusion as she tried to digest our new surroundings. If someone had told me this existed just past the Cursed Forest, I would have laughed in their face.

"What I need in the morning is a bath to wash the feeling of death off of me from that forest," she said jokingly.

Our near-death experience didn't seem to change my sister's sense of humor, not that this was our first dangerous experience.

We always tended to find ourselves in situations that caused us to run, hide, or fight.

Whether it was one of our clever little jobs or just a regular evening in the village pub, we surely didn't live a quiet, serene life.

I threw my pack down on the soft grass and pulled out the bedroll and tent. I turned to find my sister lying in the grass with her eyes closed.

I threw the stakes to our tent where she was sprawled out.

She huffed a laugh before sitting up. "Fine, I'll help."

"Yeah, you better help. I'm not your mother," I responded.

That was true and untrue since it had been just us. We both took on maternal roles for each other. It definitely didn't mean I was going to build this tent myself when she was perfectly capable of helping.

She grabbed the stakes and started pounding them into the earth as I finished setting up the bedroll and taking out our supplies.

"Shit, we don't have any food for the night," I muttered.

We stocked these bags full of food and essentials the first time we realized that our way of life may one day lead to us having to run with a moment's notice.

After Lord Wayward raised our taxes and food became scarce, we figured we could use the food from our bags and replace it another day since we'd never actually used them.

My sister shrugged. "Not the first time we went an evening without eating."

Camila began to try and get into a comfortable position to sleep, and finally found one after a few moments and closed her eyes. Before I could lie down beside her, she was fast asleep.

I looked down at my sister's slender sleeping figure. She looked so much like me that most people we met thought we were twins.

Her bronze skin was slightly lighter than my warm brown skin, and her hair wasn't as curly as mine, not to mention those gold streaks in her hair.

I had a curvier figure than her with what she referred to as *'birthing hips,'* but everything else about us was precisely the same.

The fullness of our lips, the almond shape of our eyes, and the curve of our noses were identical. I pulled the thin blanket over her shoulders and laid down beside her.

I closed my eyes and decided that nothing had really changed for us.

We would continue fighting to ensure we both survived.

Whatever tomorrow brought, we would face together, like always.

Chapter 2

Camila

The sun spilled over the mountaintops. I raised my face to it and soaked in the warmth and energy that only this time of day gave me. I looked over at my sister, who had the same calm smile on her face as she, too, took in the sun. Someone yelled for us to come back inside for training, what kind of training I had no idea of, but I could hear the authority in their voice that had me on my feet immediately.

"I'll race you," I said to Xio, raising my eyebrows in a taunting manner. Xio nodded her head. "On three!"

"One...two..." I ran before Xio got to three and boomed a laugh as I left my sister behind and started running toward the large white figure that was just out of focus. I was filled with such joy that I felt like it had to be spilling out of me as I looked behind at my sister's angry face.

I blinked out of my dream and panicked for a moment as I had no idea where I was. The events of the previous day started to come back to me, stealing from Lord Wayward, running for our lives, the Cursed Forest, setting up camp outside of said forest in a strangely alive land.

Killing that guard.

The fact I felt so little about it worried me more than anything. There was a shock initially, watching the life slip from him.

But, I recognized the guard. He was there that day in the village.

He gave me the scars across the back of my thighs.

That was part of the reason I didn't feel bad about killing him.

He deserved it.

Even so, one would think that some inkling of regret would surface for taking a life.

I always felt a bit broken, but this proved even further that something was wrong with how I was made.

I could see Xio was struggling with it more than I was, and I was worried this would dim some of the light she always burned so bright with.

I looked around the tent and realized that she wasn't there and sprang up off my bed roll. I busted through the tent flaps and ran right into my sister, standing just outside the tent.

"Oops, sorry. I woke up, and you weren't there. I started to panic."

She rolled me off of her laughing. How she was laughing this early in the morning, I didn't know.

"It's okay. I would have done the same thing. I just stepped out of the tent before you decided to tackle me to the ground," she smiled, dusted the dirt off of her, and then offered me a hand to help me up.

She was such a morning person. It was disgusting. We were alike in so many ways, but I needed some time to wake up before I was offering up smiles and laughs.

I shrugged, turned around to see where exactly we were, and gasped in a breath.

I had never in my life seen so much green.

There were rolling hills with long wispy grass that danced in the wind, the flowers were colors I didn't think I'd ever seen before, purple, yellow, pink, and blue but somehow just *more*. The sheer amount of them was astonishing.

Daisies, orchids, marigolds, tulips, and roses all intermingled with each other. The tree we set up camp near was broad, and the branches hung down with wisps of leaves and flowers dangling from them. They moved and swayed in the wind just as the grass did, sending a slight whistling noise around us as the wind blew between the branches.

I could also hear the sound of rushing water somewhere nearby and turned to tell my sister we needed to find the source of that sound.

She had her face turned to the sun, so much like in the dream I had that it made me stumble a step.

I had these dreams often that felt like they could be memories. I never knew how real they were, and when I asked Xio about them, she always said that she didn't remember anything like that happening.

I knew she was trying to live in a mindset of looking forward, but how could you move forward if you didn't know what was behind you?

"Do you hear that water? I need a bath and drink before I even start to think about what to do next," I said.

"I think it's coming from over there," she said, pointing past a large tree covered in blue blossoms, and we made our way toward the sound.

I looked up at the blue tree and saw flashes of sparkling light, I blinked, and they were gone making me feel as if I imagined them.

I shook my head and kept walking. No time to start having delirious hallucinations now. I was clearly very dehydrated.

We made our way through some shrubbery near the large tree and found the source of the rushing water.

I raised my eyes to a huge waterfall and pond covered in lily pads and vibrant vegetation. The water sparkled in the sun and was so clear I could see every colorful rock nestled in the bottom.

I slid off my shoes, and the soft sand that surrounded the water seeped between my toes. I had never seen anything like this place.

It was almost magical.

Whoever made up the lies about the forest must have been trying to keep people away.

I heard a splash and looked over to see my sister in her underwear swimming in the pond with a smile stretched across her face.

I finished taking off my own clothes and jumped in beside her. The cool feel of the water rushed over my skin, while a warmth tingled under it that I savored as I swam over to the waterfall. I needed water, and I didn't really care where I got it at this point. I opened up my mouth and drank as much of the fresh water as I could in one go.

Xio's laughing caught my attention, and I turned toward her to find her barely breathing with her finger pointed at me.

"You look like a drowning rat, guess the guards were right when they called us thieving rats," she said jokingly.

I splashed water on my sister, and we fell into a very child-like battle of not wanting to be the last one to be splashed.

I won said battle and taunted her while she climbed out of the pond, and grabbed the blanket we used last night to dry off with.

"Whatever, we'll see who wins our next pointless competition," she said while trying to squeeze the excess water out of her hair.

We truly were very competitive people, always making small competitions over the most mundane things. Who could finish their food first, who got the last hit in a fight, who made it back to the house first after a trip to the market.

"We both know it'll be me again, as always," I retorted.

But honestly, we were split pretty much down the middle on who won in our rivalries. I dragged myself out of the water, and my sister threw the blanket she was drying off with at me.

I instantly regretted being the last one out of the water when the cold wetness slapped me across my body.

Xio laughed. "Who's the real loser now?"

I huffed and ran my fingers across the strange scar on my shoulder that was oddly itchy. Both I and Xio have a scar on our shoulders. A half circle with a line extending from either end of it.

The lack of our memories made it hard to know what it was or where it came from. Judging from our relationship, I'm pretty sure one of us dared the other to brand it on ourselves or something else as ridiculous during the time we couldn't remember.

I finished buttoning my pants and grabbed the wet blanket to head back to our camp. Everywhere I looked, there was something more alluring. I noticed some plants with buds that resembled butterfly wings on the path. I ran my fingers over the soft purple petals, the wind blew, and the petals started to flap in the breeze giving the illusion the flowers might jump right off the ground and shoot into the sky.

Everything about this place made me want to explore and see what other wonders might be behind the next tree. I approached our tent and hung the blanket on a branch in hopes it would dry before we needed it again.

"We're going to need to find something to eat at some point today. I think we should pack up and head down that way to see if there's anything we can hunt," I said, pointing in the opposite direction of the pond.

"There should be some supplies for snares in one of our bags, we can set them up to catch some small game. I left my bow and arrow at the house, so I won't be able to take anything big down for now," Xio responded.

I nodded my agreement and began to throw all of our things in our packs, pulling out the small snare supplies from Xio's pack and setting them aside.

My sister was a great archer, but we couldn't do much without the weapon, so we'd need to keep an eye out for some sort of village that might have a shop we could buy from.

I strapped on my pack, and we began to walk over the rolling hills, the long grass brushed our shins as we tried to find a good place to set up our snares.

The light of the sun covered the land like a heavy blanket. It seemed to make everything come alive. The wind and the sun joining together to bring life to the plants and the flowers.

We watched for any sign of animals, but it was hard to focus with so much beauty surrounding me.

After finally finding a promising spot, we set up the snares and went to hide between some trees so we wouldn't scare off whatever unlucky animal about to become our lunch.

I saw that sparkling light I did before, but these seemed to be small figures floating away from us.

I had the sudden urge to follow whatever this hallucination was and stepped toward where they were leading me, but Xio grabbed my arm.

"Where the hell are you going? You just turned around without saying anything with a blank look on your face."

I shook my head and decided that I definitely needed to eat as soon as possible. I went to follow her back to our hiding spot but saw a plume of smoke rise up above some trees off in the distance.

"Do you see that smoke?" I asked. Because, at this point, who knew what I was hallucinating and what was real.

She gasped and nodded her head. "Do you think there are some people who can help us figure out where we are?"

"It's worth finding out," I said with a smile, more so thinking that where there were people camping out, there was probably some food and supplies we could…acquire.

We were accustomed to sneaking around and trying not to be seen, so we quietly made our way over to the camp. Avoiding any fallen branches or particularly crunchy vegetation.

Xio was distracted, picking at her fingernails with anxiety.

"You want to talk about it?" I asked.

I didn't need to clarify. She knew I was talking about the guard.

"I know what I did was to protect myself. It just feels wrong to play executioner. Not to mention they were only chasing us because we stole from them," she responded.

That was the first thought that came to my mind when I saw the look in her eyes after she killed him. If she blamed me and my plan to steal from the Lord.

"I don't blame you, Camila," she exclaimed, pulling me out of my spiraling thoughts. "We both made that decision. We both deal with the consequences. The Lord is not a good man, and neither were those guards."

"Trust me, I know," I hesitated, "he was *the* guard."

"The one from?" she said, looking down at my legs.

"Yes," I responded quickly.

"Well, then he deserved it. Fuck both of them."

"It's in bad taste to curse the dead, Xio," I said jokingly.

She chuckled, and I watched some of the weight on her shoulders start to lift. Not all of it. I knew she'd still need time to work through it.

We slowly approached the source of the smoke and crouched down behind a fallen tree.

We peered over the trunk to see if there was anybody around, and my eyes landed on what must be their food supply: a pile of dried fruit and nuts, dried meats, and some sort of oat bars.

My stomach growled as if to remind me of just how hungry I was.

"Nobody is here," Xio whispered while surveying the area.

I heard a screeching sound come from nearby and jumped slightly. My gaze took to the sky, but I saw no sign of anything.

"It must have been a bird. You stand watch. I'm going to go grab their food," I said.

"*This will be the last time we steal,*" Xio said mockingly, reminding me of what I said yesterday before we stole from Lord Wayward.

I laughed because what else was there to do, I really believed yesterday would be the last time, but here we were.

"Shut up. I'm hungry, and I can't wait for whatever the snares catch, if they catch anything at all," I muttered.

She threw her hands in the air in. "I'm just saying. I don't see anyone around. Hopefully, they're far enough that they won't be back anytime soon. Just try and be quick about it. I really don't want to get caught again."

"Oh no, I was planning on taking a leisure stroll down there and hanging out for a little bit. Maybe take a little nap?" I said sarcastically.

She nudged my shoulder the way she always does when I was being especially annoying and nodded to go ahead.

I took one last look around and jumped over the tree trunk. Whoever was camping here definitely wasn't in the same situation as us.

Everything seemed to be in pristine condition. Their tents were thick, and their supplies were all shiny and new.

They looked well off enough that they could go buy more food. I made it to their supply and shoveled it into one of the satchels nearby.

I only took half, a little more than half. I closed the satchel and placed it on my shoulder.

A shadow loomed over me, and my heart stopped as I heard a voice purr behind me.

"Well, what do we have here?"

Chapter 3

Xio

I had no idea what happened.

One moment, there was nobody at the camp, and the next moment there was a hand around my mouth, and I was being pulled against a rigid body.

I saw a vast form standing over where my sister was crouched down, and I began trying to scream for her, but no sound made it out with the hand squeezed tight against my face.

I threw my body, kicked, and punched, but whoever was holding me didn't even stumble as they carried me like a rag doll down to the camp.

They set me down next to my sister, and we both grabbed for each other.

I tried my hardest to put myself between my sister and whoever these people were, but she tried to do the same, and we just ended up right next to each other. Damn our natural protectiveness.

She couldn't have just let me have this one?

The camp owners turned around from where they stood with their backs turned to us. The moment they faced us, the air caught in my lungs.

These men were huge, my sister and I were average height, but these men towered over us and made me feel very, very small.

The one who grabbed my sister crouched in front of us and smiled with straight white teeth.

He had warm brown skin a few shades darker than mine and black curly hair hanging just past the tops of his ears.

I noticed his eyes were the color of clouds in a thunderstorm as he locked his gaze with mine. Something about him seemed to scream power and authority, and I looked away from him and at my sister.

She seemed to feel the same as me and let out a breath of defeat.

"You are aware it's fairly rude to steal from someone's camp when they aren't there?" he asked with a voice as smooth as silk.

A shiver ran across my skin, he somehow made this question sound sexual, and I cursed my body for responding the way it was.

"Well, we weren't planning on being here when you realized the food was missing," Camila said sweetly with her mouth pursed, and he laughed.

He put his hand out to try and help me up, and I refused.

Instead, Camila and I helped each other stand up. I brushed the dirt off her body and my own and looked back at the two men who ruined our meal.

We were a little bit in the wrong here, but I wasn't going to let any sign of remorse show right now.

I looked up at the man who tried to help us up, and his stare was already on me in a very intense, assessing look. He looked over at his partner and said something I never thought I'd hear pointed out.

"They're human," he muttered with a line of confusion running between his brows.

"That's impossible," the other man responded and stepped out of the sun, giving me a clear view of his face and body.

He was just as beautiful as the man who made the weird comment about us being human.

He had deep tan skin covered in tattoos that ran from his fingers up to his neck. His eyes were dark and turned up slightly at the corners, and shaggy black hair fell to his brows and oddly pointed ears.

My breathing stopped abruptly.

There were old stories told in our village about a magical land where the people had pointed ears and special powers. Camila and I always laughed and figured they were nothing more than fairy tales told to children.

Now here I stood in front of a pointed-eared man. The other one ran his hand through his curls, flashing us the sight of the pointed tips of his ears.

"Humans aren't supposed to be able to make it through the barrier. There has never been a case of them surviving as far back as our history goes," the curly-haired man replied, his brow still tight with confusion.

"Well...we are definitely humans and definitely alive. Care to share whatever the hell you are?" Camila retorted.

I looked at her with raised eye brows and she just shrugged.

"We're Faerie. You're in Maya, the land of the Fae," the tattoo man said.

"Well, that's impossible. Fairies aren't real. We live in Zuma...land of the...humans," Camila responded, snorting slightly at the mere suggestion of such a thing.

Tattoo man smiled a smile almost as perfect as the curly hair man, but the right side of his mouth seemed to not want to cooperate with the other side leaving his smile just a little lopsided.

I wondered why he was smiling in such a devilish manner as enormous shadow wings curled out from behind him.

I cursed and fell back, taking my sister down with me. They were terrifyingly incredible, the shadows forming something resembling black bird wings stretching out behind him as the sun shined behind him.

We fell hard on our butts as I looked up at this man, something between horror and awe.

"Yup, definitely human," the curly-haired man said, laughing at his friend.

He reached down to help us up, and this time I allowed him, still stunned from what I had just witnessed.

THE SUN, THE STORM, & THE SHADOWS   31

"I'm Holt," curly hair man said, "and that's Cree," he said, pointing to his friend.

I wasn't sure where to go from here.

I *was* sure I must have bumped my head back in that forest, and I was currently in some coma dream.

I pinched the inside of my arm forcefully and winced. This was real.

"I'm Camila," my sister said, and I raised my eyebrows at her again. "And this is my sister, Xiomara," she followed up.

My sister was always a bit more risk-prone than I was. She honestly believed we could get ourselves out of anything we got into. Maybe that streak was going to end now that we were apparently in a land full of fairies and magic.

"I go by Xio," I exclaimed.

"How did you make it through the barrier?" Holt asked.

"We didn't see any barrier. We just ran through a forest and saw a clearing we followed," I said, leaving out the fact that we were running from guards after stealing from them as well.

Holt and Cree looked at each other, speaking in some sort of wordless language, were they mind readers? Nothing was impossible right now.

"That shouldn't happen," Cree said with his arms crossed across his chest.

"Yes, you mentioned that. So can we be on our way, or are we just going to keep going back and forth about what is and isn't possible?" Camila said.

She gave them her most intimidating look, a look that always made people, or humans, back down where we were from. This just made Cree smile and laugh.

"Well, you stole from us, so we're going to have to take you as our prisoners," he said with his muscled arms still across his chest.

"Prisoners?!" we both yelled at the same time.

"Yes, that's how things work here in Maya. We'll let you eat some of that food you tried to steal, but after that, we'll have to restrain you to ensure you don't run off," Holt said, locking eyes with me. "We're going to have to take you back with us to my palace and figure out what to do with you then. My father will be inquisitive about how you made it across the barrier."

"I'm sorry, did you say palace?" Camila asked.

That bit of information ran right over my head while I was stuck in Holt's gaze. He released me from his intense stare, looked at my sister, and chuckled.

"This is Prince Holt of the Storm Kingdom," Cree said with pride, making me believe they were very close.

A freaking fairy prince in a land of magic where men can grow shadow wings.

"And you're going to take us to the dungeons of your castle for stealing some stale nuts?" Camila inquired, her voice laced with venom.

I wasn't sure what angle she was playing at if she was trying to get them to let us go.

"We really didn't mean any harm. We were just running because," I hesitated, "well, we had no food. Yours was just sitting out here, and we figured it was just a gift from above, but you can keep it. And if you could just let us get back to..." I trailed off.

I didn't know what angle I was playing here, either. But I definitely didn't want to be taken captive by these terrifying men.

Holt and Cree laughed at us as if letting us go was the craziest thing they'd ever heard.

"Not going to happen. Go ahead and eat up. We'll tie you up when you're finished," Cree quipped.

He looked at my sister like he was really looking forward to doing so, and she flipped him her middle finger.

I wondered if that was as offensive to a fairy as it was to a human before Cree bared his teeth at her in confirmation of my question.

"Fuck you," she muttered before turning around and shoving some of their food in her mouth. I watched as she scanned the area for our weapons with the threat of death in her eye.

While we were human, we were no damsels in distress.

We would fight our way out of this.

Chapter 4

Camila

Night came fast, and the stars twinkled high in the sky. They were so bright here they seemed to watch and judge you.

I was pretty sure the stars were squinting at Xio and me, judging us for our last failed thievery attempts.

Honestly, I should probably stop suggesting to steal from anyone for the rest of my life.

These last two times had put us in some serious shit. That shit being tied to my sister in a mystery land, around a fire with the two biggest men I'd ever seen.

I looked over at Xio, her face a picture of calculation as she tried to figure out how to get us out of the situation I got us into.

"So, maybe you can just drop us off at the closest village? I'm sure we're just going to slow you down with whatever you guys are doing out here?" she said, looking at Holt.

"Again, it's not going to happen. I suggest you stop asking before we decide to gag the both of you," Cree said with clear annoyance between bites of the deer he and Holt were eating.

Holt laughed at the suggestion, and I rolled my eyes and tensed my jaw.

"You said we're in Maya? And you're some kind of prince in this fairy magic land?" I asked.

"Yes, you're in Maya, and I'm some kind of prince in this *Faerie* magic land," Holt replied mockingly.

"Where's your palace?"

"We're on the far east side of Maya. Storm Palace is on the far west side. It's going to take nearly a fortnight to get back there."

That was more than enough time. We could escape before they threw us into whatever dungeon cell they had planned for us.

"What kind of magic do Faeries have?" Xio asked, clearly, catching along to my idea of gathering information.

"I forget that humans don't know much about Faeries," Cree said, rolling his eyes.

Holt didn't seem to mind our questions as much, he spoke to the both of us, but his gaze fell on Xio more than on me.

"There are different types of magic. All Fae have increased speed, senses, and strength compared to humans. Most also have healing and force magic," he said, pushing out some kind of power from his hand that knocked over some of the logs in the fire we were sitting around. "Some of us have more, given to us from the Gods. We're referred to as Descendants. Those of us who are Descendants have special magic that coincides with the God or Goddess we come from. All royals are Descendants. I am a Descendant of Chaac, the God of rain. So my powers are a little more elemental," he said, again, demonstrating with a little tornado of water in his hand.

I peeked at my sister, who seemed just as in awe as I was.

"So, where do you get your little shadow wings?" I asked Cree.

He looked at me with disgust, clearly not very happy about the use of my word *'little.'* He seemed reserved, like he didn't really want to answer our questions. We sat silently for a few moments, assuming he wouldn't answer.

"I don't know. The Gods are gone, so I've given up figuring it out," he shrugged, picking up a stick to poke the fire.

"The Gods are gone?" Xio asked.

"Yes, hundreds of years ago, Itzamna, the great creator of our world, grew angry with the other Gods for them becoming more loved than he was. Itzamna tried to kill all the other Gods, and the fight was so intense that he ended up dying himself. My father and I are the only remaining Descendants we can trace, other than whatever kind of mutt Cree here is," he laughed.

"What happened to the others?" I asked.

I sounded slightly more intrigued than I would have liked, and cringed at myself internally.

"There was once—" Holt started.

"History lesson is over," Cree said abruptly, cutting off Holt. He stood up and walked away from the fire towards the two tents they had set up when we found their camp.

I didn't even have time to think about the sleeping arrangements.

Are they going to tie us to a tree?

"We'll take this tent," Holt said, pointing to the navy tent on the left. "And you two can share the other tent."

"Don't get any ideas of running off in the middle of the night," Cree said, looking at me.

Clearly, seeing I'm the one who makes all the wrong decisions between Xio and me.

"We will catch you, then we'll have to tie your feet too, which will slow us down even more. You've already cost us a day on our trip," he finished.

Holt laughed at his friend, and I shot him a look saying exactly how I felt about the humor he found in Cree's statement.

Xio growled and tried to stand up to walk toward the tent.

She must have forgotten that we were tied together because she only made it a foot before falling on top of me. Holt laughed and tried to help her, and Xio hissed at him, causing him to back up with his hands in the air.

After a few failed attempts, we figured out how to stand and walk together and made it to the tent.

"Sweet dreams," Cree said, but his tone definitely did not display that he cared about what kind of dreams we had.

We stepped into the tent finding a bed roll on the right side thicker than the ones we had brought. There was a plethora of supplies to the left, and we made our way over to them before the flap of the tent was ripped open.

Cree stormed in, realizing he had left the items in here before Holt offered us his tent. I placed my foot over a small knife before he began grabbing his things.

I stood with my chin high, and my eyes narrowed until he left without a word.

Once I felt he was far enough, I moved my foot, and Xio's eyes went wide as she realized what I had done.

I raised my eyebrows at her smugly

"How did you—" Xio started.

"Shut the fuck up and go to sleep!" Cree yelled out.

Xio shook her head, advising me not to say anything else, and I nodded.

I grabbed the knife, and Xio helped tuck it into the inside of my sleeve. We figured out how to lay comfortably while tied together, and I sighed.

I mouthed the words *"I'm sorry"* to her.

She mouthed back, *"not your fault,"* which it definitely was my fault, but I knew my sister would never hold it against me.

I didn't deserve her. She always went along with my plans and helped me pick up the pieces if they ever fell apart. I closed my eyes and began thinking of every single way we could escape these fucking men.

The knife would certainly help, but our captors looked to be trained killers.

Not thinking about where we would go quite yet.

That would be a problem for when we successfully escaped.

Chapter 5

Xio

Somehow we both managed to fall asleep last night.

The last few days had been draining, so I shouldn't have been surprised. I woke up before my sister, like I always did, and tried to shift to sit up without waking her.

This, of course, was not possible since our wrists were tied together and I ended up waking her.

"Hey," I whispered.

"Hi," Camila said in a voice thick with sleep.

Today I didn't wake up confused about where I was. It seemed like my body was starting to adjust to the odd predicament we found ourselves in.

I heard the grass rustle outside our tent and looked over at Camila, waiting for her to wake up enough for us to face the day. I knew she needed a few minutes to be alert enough to make our way outside the tent, so I stared at her until she felt my gaze.

THE SUN, THE STORM, & THE SHADOWS

"Alright, alright, I'm up," she groaned.

She used her core to sit herself up since her hands were bound, and we helped each other stand up and exit the tent.

I opened the flap, and I looked across the camp to see Holt staring at me, seemingly still intrigued about how two humans made their way into his land.

"Good morning," he said, with a look on his face I couldn't quite decipher.

"Yes, good morning to you. We could hear your snoring all night, so we didn't get much rest," Cree barked from the other side of the camp, taking down the tent and packing up the supplies.

"Neither of us snores, so I'm sure it was some sort of magical beast sleeping near your tent," Camila barked back.

My sister was always quick-witted, but sometimes it surprised me how fast she could serve a witty retort.

"One of you certainly does, and I feel like I can make an educated guess on which one it is," Cree said with a smirk.

Camila rolled her eyes and guided us to sit on the log we had been sitting on the previous night near the fire.

"What's on the agenda, Sir Prince?" she asked Holt.

"We're making our way back to the palace. We're following that path," he said, pointing past our camp to a worn path on the other side of some bushes.

He finished packing the items around the fire and strapped his packs to a horse tied to the other side of the large tree next to his tent. I didn't even realize they had horses until now. I've always loved horses, and these horses fit right into every other beautiful thing in this land.

Holt's horse was a massive dark gray stallion that matched his eyes, and he had white spotted feet that made him look like he was standing on clouds. His mane was light gray, and I could tell Holt took great care of him by how shiny and groomed his coat was.

Holt caught me staring at his stallion and smiled.

"This is Thunder," he said, patting the side of his neck. Thunder turned his head towards Holt, looking for more affection, and he obliged.

Cree stormed past me, snapping me out of whatever hold Holt and Thunder had on me. He walked around Thunder and guided his horse from around the other side of the tree.

Cree's horse was pretty much what you would guess his choice of horse would be. Another tremendously big stallion, but his coat was all black with not a spot of white on him. He also affectionately patted his horse's neck, which was a weird sight. Cree didn't give me the impression that he would care too much for animals.

"This is Night," he said, not directing his comment at either one of us but continuing to strap his pack to Night.

I looked around, wondering if they were going to bring another horse from around the tree, but there was none. They were traveling alone. Of course, they didn't bring another horse with them.

So that means...

"You'll be with me," Holt said to me.

"Unfortunately, you'll be with me, Viper," Cree muttered with his gaze on Camila.

"Can't we just walk beside your horses?" Camila asked with as much poison as the animal Cree suggested she was.

"That would double our trip time, and again, you've cost us a day, so up you go," Cree responded.

"You're forgetting something," I responded.

I lifted our wrists in the air showing that we weren't going to be able to be separated just yet. Cree pulled a knife from somewhere on his body. I had no idea he had any weapons on him and looked at my sister, telling her to keep that in mind while she rode with him. He flipped the knife in his hand and gave us no warning as he brought it down between our wrists, missing the sensitive flesh so close to where he cut.

The rope snapped, and our still bound wrists jerked towards our bodies.

"Asshole!" Camila yelled.

She stomped her way towards Night while Holt and Cree shared a laugh. But with our hands still bound together, we couldn't mount the horses ourselves.

"Do you mind?" Holt said to me.

He held his hands out, suggesting he would lift me up on the horse himself and I laughed. Clearly, he didn't realize my body was made of pure muscle from my years of running and training with my sister.

"You can try," I laughed.

He seemed to find the challenge in this and came up behind me and placed his hands around my waist. I gasped a breath while his strong hands gripped me, and I found myself on top of Thunder.

I looked down at him, confused as to how he managed that.

"We aren't humans. I told you we're stronger."

He wasn't exaggerating when he listed it as a power of the Fae.

I looked over at my sister, who seemed to be in some sort of argument with Cree, most likely arguing that she didn't need him to help her on the horse. She tried to jump up without success, and he sighed.

He grabbed her and threw her onto Night, not quite as gently as Holt placed me on Thunder, but definitely not as hard as he could have handled her. She cursed at him as he jumped up on the horse behind her.

There was as much space as possible between them without him falling off the horse like he genuinely thought she was poisonous. These two bickered like they'd known each other for years, and I found it just a little bit funny.

At this point, I needed to find any sort of humor I could, given that we were prisoners here.

A hard warm body behind me snapped me out of my thoughts as Holt mounted the horse. He didn't seem to think I was poison as he ended up with his chest to my back.

I looked over my shoulder shooting him a look to tell him to back the hell up, and he chuckled and scooted away from me, taking the reins from around my sides.

"I'll have to hold the reins if we plan on getting anywhere. Let me know if you get uncomfortable," he whispered in my ear, and I rolled my eyes.

I wrapped my wrists around the saddle horn so I wouldn't have to try and hold onto him at any point in this ride.

This ride, that could take weeks, he said.

I definitely needed to try and figure out how to escape as soon as possible.

If I knew my sister, she would be doing the same thing. I looked over at her, and she must have felt my gaze because she snapped her face towards me with a deep scowl lining it and I offered her a small smile, all I could give her at the moment.

Holt brought Thunder to a gallop, and Cree followed suit. We found ourselves on the path Holt pointed out earlier, and I tried to mark all of my surroundings in case I needed to remember them for the future.

Unfortunately for me, there didn't seem to be any landmarks. Everything around us was just trees, plants, and flowers. The landscape was a thing of beauty, but that wasn't going to help me figure out how to get back to Zuma. If we figured out how to escape.

I sighed louder than I meant to.

"Everything okay up there?" Holt asked.

"Oh yeah, just peachy," I responded, and Holt laughed.

"So, why were you and your sister running so fast that you didn't realize you went straight through a magical barrier?"

"That information is on a need-to-know basis," I responded.

I wasn't sure why he thought I would have any desire to tell him about my life.

"My bet is on you stealing from the wrong person since you two seem to be such poor thieves," he said matter-of-factly.

"We are not poor thieves!" I barked

"But you are thieves?"

I could hear his smile through his tone without even having to look back at him over my shoulder.

"That's not what I said!"

Holt seemed to find this just as funny, the vibrations of his chuckling meeting my back.

"You didn't need to, Xio," he purred.

That was the first time he said my name, and I didn't like how it made me feel. A shiver ran through me, once again, and he must have felt it because he continued chuckling to himself.

"We're going to make this a silent ride," I responded sharply.

"Whatever you say, Prisoner."

We carried on in silence for the following hours until night started to fall, and they started looking for a place to make camp.

Chapter 6

Camila

This man was insufferable, truly insufferable.

There was probably a word that rang truer than insufferable. Unendurable? Impossible? Intolerable? Whichever was the most extreme case of insufferableness was what I would call Cree.

He tried to hold onto the reins without touching me, which some part of me appreciated, but every time he dropped them, he cursed at me like it was my fault he couldn't keep his grip. I told him I had to relieve myself, and he said I could hold it until we made camp. Every time I accidentally slid back due to the speed we were running and touched him, he told me to stay in my spot.

Me, the person whose hands were quite literally tied, like it was my fault they didn't just let us go when we suggested it.

Which I again suggested, and he said something about remembering promising a gag the last time I mentioned it, so I stopped trying to reason with him.

My sister looked like she was having just as much fun as I was, and excitement grew within me when I realized that the sun was going down and we would have to stop to make camp soon.

That, and the fact that that meant we would finally be able to eat. The only meal these two seemed to partake in was dinner.

Do Faeries not need to eat food throughout the day? Where do they get their sustenance...blood, small children?

"This looks like a good spot," Holt yelled out, and Cree hmphed an agreement and pulled the reins to slow down Night to a stop.

He jumped off his horse, and before I could even try to get myself down, he grabbed me and placed me firmly on the ground.

I bared my teeth at him, and he rolled his eyes while unpacking their things to make camp. I wandered over to my sister to see if she thought of any way to escape on the trip here.

"Anything?" I asked.

"No, I even tried to memorize landmarks or something so we could make it back to Zuma if necessary, and everything was just more of the same," she said.

"Ugh, I know. I tried to peek into Cree's satchels to see if the weapons were still there, but I couldn't find them. I don't even know where they put our packs after they grabbed us. Our weapons have to be somewhere here. I don't think they left them at the camp," I responded.

"No, you're right. I looked back when we left, and nothing was left behind," she pointed out.

Thank God, if they had left those weapons behind, I would have needed to kill them myself.

"Okay, so the first part of the plan, try and find out where they are keeping our weapons. There's no way I'm willingly leaving those behind. They're basically extensions of our bodies at this point," I responded.

My sister and I had trained with our weapons since we woke up at the shack. Something within us knew we'd need to use them one day, and that we needed to prepare as much as possible for whenever that day came.

It seemed like maybe that day was coming soon.

We never really took ownership of them, but we both knew that the daggers were mine and the sword was hers, again, just a weird feeling.

Cree pulled me out of my thoughts as he shouted for us to stop whispering and come over to the fire if we wanted anything to eat. We both rolled our eyes and stumbled over to where they sat.

A full day riding a horse left my legs sore, and my sister seemed to feel the same as I watched her limp to the stumps they laid out around the fire. I discreetly rubbed the inside of my arm, ensuring the knife was still safely lodged in my leathers.

I had no idea how they set all this up as quickly as they did.

"Magic," Holt muttered.

As if that was enough explanation.

I decided not to try and give any brain power to figuring out that conundrum as all of my thoughts needed to go towards escaping. I plopped down next to my sister and looked at Cree as he took the food out to divide between us.

"I'd like more dried meat than nuts, please," I said and immediately grimaced at my choice of words.

Holt and Cree busted out laughing, and Cree threw my serving of food at me.

"You'll get what we all get," he responded, thankfully ignoring the obviously embarrassing comment I had just made.

"We're coming up on a village soon. We'll refill our supplies. If you have other suggestions on what you might like to eat, please let us know," Holt said with a sarcastic smile.

I rolled my eyes rather aggressively and looked back at the fire.

"Why are you guys so far from your palace?" Xio asked.

I welcomed the conversation change and reminded myself to return to the plan of escaping.

"We're on a mission to find something," Holt hesitated looking over at Cree. "Something important for our kingdom. It was located near the human border, which just happens to be as far from the Storm Palace as possible," he responded with sadness in his tone.

He seemed more than open to our questions about Maya yesterday, but this answer felt a little more reserved.

"Did you find what you were looking for?" Xio said gently.

"We did. Now we just need to make it back to the Storm Palace. Of course, we weren't expecting to pick up two freeloaders on our way, so hopefully, we can still make it back in good time," Cree said with annoyance rather than the sadness Holt spoke with.

"Again, you're choosing to lug us across the country. You could have let us go," I said.

Cree made a gesture that looked like a gag, and I rolled my eyes. He clearly wasn't serious about gagging us at this point. I'd brought up them letting us go multiple times since that threat.

"Not only did you steal from us, but we also need to know why you could make it across the barrier. If humans start pouring in, we could have more problems than we already have," Holt responded.

Cree looked at him like he had said just a little too much and I smiled internally. So there were problems we could exploit.

Noted.

"Where are our weapons?" I asked.

"Hidden, but those weapons were far too superior for two thieves. Did you steal them from some poor soul?" Cree responded quickly, looking at me with disgust.

"No, they were with us when we—" Xio started, and now it was my turn to look at her for saying just a little too much.

"They are ours. They have always been ours. We did not steal them," I said absolutely.

Cree looked at me like he hardly believed me, and I rolled my eyes.

My eyes would end up stuck behind my head at the rate this man had me rolling my eyes.

"You men are insufferable," I growled out, barely loud enough to hear, but they both looked at me like they were offended.

Which they should have been, but they looked like I just told them I wanted to chop their heads off.

"We are not human, so we are not men. We are Fae. We are referred to as males," Holt said firmly. Cree had been the rude one, but Holt seemed to have a bit of it in him too.

"You *males* are insufferable," Xio said mockingly, and Cree and Holt seemed less offended than when I said it. I laughed at my sister and silently thanked her for always having my back.

"It's about a half day's ride to the next town. Tomorrow, we will stop for supplies. After that, there isn't another village on the route we are taking for a few more days."

"Are villages that far apart?" I asked.

"Not all of them, but we are taking a route to try and avoid some of the bigger Serpent tribes since there are just two of us. They reside in the Grasslands. Scouts advised they were in the southern sections currently, so we're trying to stay mostly in the forests," Holt explained.

"What are Serpent tribes?" Xio asked.

"You would get along great with them. They're thieves just like you," Cree grumbled.

"They are also murderers, so maybe just a little worse than them?" Holt responded jokingly, and Cree laughed at the jest at our expense.

Little did they know we were murderers now too.

"If you're their Prince, why would they harm you?" Xio followed up.

"I am the Prince of Maya, but the Serpent tribes are nomads. They don't really abide by all the rules of the land. We don't see much of them since they live on land that isn't inhabited by our kingdom. There is something like a treaty between them and us. They don't mess with us, and we don't bother them. If a royal is found tracking through some of their lands, it could be seen as breaking the treaty. We don't tend to venture this far, so it's never been a problem before, but it is causing us to take a more indirect route back to the palace."

I had always been a risk-taker. But I was sure my human sister and I couldn't take on a tribe of deadly Fae, so I nodded my agreement with avoiding them as best as possible.

I'd make sure that when we escaped, we avoided them as well.

"That's not to say the route we are taking lacks any danger. These last two days, we have been in the part of the forest where no Fae live, but once we pass this village, we are venturing into places where there are still plenty who would like to rob us or harm us," Cree spat out.

"From that point on, we need you to listen to exactly what we say. You may think we are just two insufferable males, but if you want to stay alive, you'll follow orders. There has been some," he hesitated, "unrest due to recent events, and some people are angry. Anger leads to people making poor choices, and we don't want to be on the wrong end of one of those choices," Holt said firmly.

If two powerful Descendants of whatever Gods created this place were cautious about the dangers we were coming across, then I definitely wasn't going to argue, for once.

"Can you die? Being a God?" I asked.

I was referring to the situation but also...for my own purposes.

"Descendants, we are not Gods. But yes, we can die like any other Fae. We have great power, but our bodies are made with the same flesh as anyone else. Our hearts are just as fragile. Tougher to accomplish, sure, but not impossible," Holt responded.

"Got it," Xio said, and I nodded my agreement.

Good to know they did have vulnerabilities, even if they were harder to take advantage of.

"With that being said, let's call it a night. This may be one of the last nights we can all get completely peaceful rest," Holt said.

We all got up to head towards our tents and Holt flicked his hands, the fire ceasing to exist in a moment.

This was the first use of his elemental magic outside of his demonstration. I was too exhausted to question it, so we continued into our tent. Since they didn't bind us together, we were able to get much more comfortable.

"It sounds like the village may be the last place we can escape. After that, we will have to wait until we safely make it to the palace," I whispered as quietly as I could. I waited for Cree to yell out that he could hear us, but no comment came from their tent.

"You're right. If one of us sees a way to escape, scratch the left side of your nose, and the other will follow along," she suggested.

I wouldn't have thought to suggest that and probably would have ended up right back where we started.

"Genius girl," I whispered back, and she chuckled.

I rolled close to my sister, relishing the warmth of her body that always made me feel so safe.

I closed my eyes and quickly fell asleep.

I was back in the strange place I always was, but there was something very wrong. There was shouting and the sound of steel against steel. I looked at my sister, and she had a frightened look on her face. Everything faded to black.

Chapter 7

Xio

I woke up with my sister still curled up next to me.

She looked so peaceful when she was sleeping. Her face was fixed into a permanent scowl these last few days, and I couldn't help but relish her relaxed brow and calm closed eyes.

I shifted beside her and made to go outside. Stepping carefully over the soft bed roll and slipping my shoes back on. I pulled open the flap of the tent and poked my head out before I heard the sound of a struggle. My body stilled halfway out of the tent as I tried to find the source of the sound.

I found Cree and Holt engaged in a fight on the other side of the camp. I pulled my head back in to figure out what to do. If the two males holding us captive offed each other, that might make Camila and I's lives a little easier.

I slowly lifted the corner of the flap, and my eyes landed on Holt's muscular form. He disarmed Cree and was straddled over him with a knife to his throat.

Cree laughed. "I yield."

Holt held it there a second longer and chuckled back, jumping off of his friend and helping him up.

At some point during the struggle between the Fae, my sister woke up, and I looked down to see her head peeking out near my feet. She looked up at me with wide eyes. She must have thought they were engaged in a serious fight like I did when I first heard the signs of a struggle.

"Nice to see you overpowered!" she yelled at Cree, and both males looked over, surprised that we had just witnessed their brawl.

Holt laughed, and Cree scowled at my sister. She really knew how to start the day. She would be riding all day with Cree again, and her little outburst probably would lead to even more unpleasantness than she was already enduring.

"Get up and pack up your bedroll and tent. You two will start carrying your weight from here on forward!" Cree barked.

"Worth it," my sister murmured and started packing up our side of the camp.

The males made quick work of stowing away the rest of the site and strapping everything to Night and Thunder.

I found myself once again mere inches away from the Fae Prince on the big gray stallion.

"Sleep well, Prisoner?" Holt murmured in my ear as he wrapped his arms around me to grab Thunder's reins.

"As good as any prisoner can sleep," I responded sharply, and he chortled, always seeming to find my remarks humorous for some reason.

I lacked the venom my sister always had an endless supply of, even though I was just as quick-witted as Camila. I wrapped my wrist bindings around the saddle horn like I did the previous day and whirled around at the sound of my sister cursing.

"You could have warned me. I didn't need your help. I told you I could get onto the horse myself!" she yelled at Cree while he mounted Night.

"We both know that wasn't going to happen. You looked like some rabid animal jumping up and down trying to get a hold of the saddle," he responded.

He had a point there. Her already unruly curls were falling in front of her face while sweat gathered on her forehead, causing some of them to stick to her.

"Just warn her next time, Cree," Holt yelled out, and Cree gave him a look that yelled, *'are you serious, they're prisoners?!'*

Holt returned that look with one that said, '*Who just put you on your ass this morning'* and Cree rolled his eyes, huffing his defeat.

"Next time, I'll wait until you ask me nicely," Cree murmured in my sister's ear, and she made an incomprehensible sound that I'm sure was laced with curses.

Holt flicked his reins, and Thunder started into a gallop. I twisted as far as I could to see my sister and Cree in a stare-down before Cree broke the stare, and Night started moving to catch up to us.

I didn't know how much longer those two were going to be able to stand each other. Holt definitely had a contemptible side to him, but Cree appeared to live his day-to-day life like someone woke him up with a punch to his face.

We really needed to make it to the palace as fast as possible.

The path to the village was beautiful, even after being on it for hours, I still hadn't grown tired of it.

Everywhere I looked, there were plants and flowers I'd never seen, rivers and ponds that sparkled like they were made of precious gems, and trees that were plucked right out of a fairy tale.

We rounded the path, and the sight of a massive tree with purple-gray bark and deep blue blossoms caught my eye.

I gasped at the alluring ambiance of the tree. Small bursts of light sparkled near the blossoms, and Holt followed my line of sight.

"That is a ceiba tree. They are rumored to be the home of the Alux, magical little sprites that can guide your fate or ruin your day if they feel you can't be trusted. I've never seen them, but my mother swears she's had an encounter with them. She also believes in old prophecies and dragons, so I'm not sure this encounter ever actually occurred," he said warmly.

Even though he was poking fun at his mother, he still spoke with such love.

"I feel like I'm being pulled towards it," I murmured, and the sparkles grew brighter before disappearing, and the trance I was under broke.

I shook my head and looked forward. Holt peered at me with a befuddled look before pointing slightly to the right of my eye line.

"There's the village," he said.

I couldn't help noticing that the trees and flowers started to become more sporadic, not completely gone, but the plethora of foliage I'd grown to love on our path here thinned slightly.

Before I could ask about it, a blur of black crossed my vision to the left of us, and I saw Cree laughing at himself while my sister cursed him for going so fast. He looked over at Holt with taunting eyebrows, and Holt gave Thunder a cue that had him running at full speed.

The speed we were at caused me to jump up and down, and I tightened my grip to try and keep myself in the saddle. Holt's corded arms were around me, and I doubted he'd let me fall, but I didn't trust him enough to not try and save myself.

I slid back, and a line of pricks ran down my spine as I lined up with Holt's chest and inner thighs. Before I could assess that unwelcome feeling, I was tossed back forward as we came down a slight hill, and the horse came to a stop.

The speed we were running had my hair in front of my eyes, and I used my bound hands to slide it out of my face and looked up to find Cree already helping my sister off Night.

"I told you Night is the fastest horse in all of Maya, but you never believe me," he said proudly with that lop-sided smile stretching across his face.

Holt crossed his arms across his chest. "You had a head start."

These two were just as competitive as Camila and I, and a part of me respected that. This thought brought my gaze over to my sister, who did not have a look of respect on her face.

Her face painted the perfect picture of disdain as she scowled at Cree.

I walked over to her and bumped her shoulder to pull her out of whatever murderous plan she was concocting in her head, and her face relaxed as she looked me in the eyes.

I raised my eyebrows, hopefully reminding her that this was our last chance to get away. She nodded with a look of understanding and determination as she looked around.

Cree and Holt tied the horses to a post with a few other horses. The other horses were not in the royal shape of Thunder and Night. They were clearly working horses that had seen better days.

We followed them towards the village, but Holt stopped before we passed the first building and turned to my sister and me.

He grabbed us both by our arm, and I made to pull away before a warmth prickled all over my body. I looked up at him, confused as to what he did to us.

"It's called a glamour. The Fae have an excellent sense of smell and sight. They will know you're human immediately. The glamour hides your scent and makes you appear Fae," he explained.

"Everything looks the same to me," Camila said, rubbing her rounded ears.

"It only works on outside sources. It's not an actual physical change," he explained before turning back and leading us into the village. "They've never seen a human before. We don't want to cause any further problems than we already have," he finished.

Holt and Cree both pulled their hoods up to hide their identity as well.

This was the second time he mentioned that there were problems in Maya. We just needed to figure out how to leverage them to get back home.

Wherever home was.

Until now, Cree and Holt were the only Fae we'd seen, but the village was filled with these magical creatures. They all looked at us as we turned on the path past the first home.

It was alarming how similar the Fae village was to ours; ours was definitely much poorer, but the layout and housing seemed so similar. There were rows of small homes made of brick and stone, just as our little shack may have looked when it was initially built.

Small children were playing in the street, and a little girl who was maybe around six years old walked up to me and smiled. My heart warmed as I peered into her big green eyes. She had curly hair like mine and wore a pale green dress that made her eyes stand out even more. She waved quickly and returned to play with her friends as giggling filled the air.

"Let's keep moving," Cree said, and we followed behind them.

Cree seemed to always be on alert as he surveyed the area, moving his eyes back and forth.

I noticed that he was now adorned in lightweight black armor with silver finishings that gleamed in the sun. He nodded to Holt with his eyes on a small building to the left of the path, and they directed us to follow them into the building.

Cree eyed Camila with a look that told her not to get into trouble, and she threw a gesture back at him, telling him exactly how she felt about the look. Cree turned around quickly and opened the door to the building.

The shop was lined with shelves containing various foods, and my stomach growled as the different smells hit me. The smell of bread caught my attention, and I followed the scent to a counter in the far back corner where a short round male sat on a stool, stocking the display with flaky bread.

Cree and Holt removed their hoods as the male realized that we had walked in. He nearly fell out of his seat as his eyes locked with the males ahead of us.

"My prince!" he gasped and started to try and bow, but, in doing so, tripped over a broom that was left propped up on the end of the counter.

Holt rushed over to offer him a hand and helped him up with a slight smile on his face that looked as if it was meant to put his subjects at ease.

"Oh, my prince, I am so embarrassed. It's just that we don't usually see royalty in these parts, and I was not expecting you to wander into my shop!" the male breathed out while dusting himself off.

"We will have to rectify that, Mr..." Holt looked at him, asking for his name.

"Pan, Sir! My name is Pan, and I am at your service. How can I help you? Do you need bread? Dried fruits? Cake? Oats?"

Pan started to run around, grabbing various items off the shelves and placing them on the counter, huffing breaths and turning around quickly each time he placed something else on the counter.

He looked down at the bounds on my wrists and turned his head slightly but continued gathering items from his shelves.

"We're on the road back to the palace, and the path we are taking has this as the last stop for nearly a week," Cree said, offering him his version of the smile Holt gave Pan after he fell, which was not quite as warm.

THE SUN, THE STORM, & THE SHADOWS

"Oh, I've got just the things you'll need! I call it *'The Traveler's Sustenance.'* It will definitely last you a week!" Pan said proudly and scattered back over to the shelves.

I noticed Camila shuffling to the back of the building quietly, and she looked at me, pointing her lips slightly to the door in the back left corner of the building. She scratched the left side of her nose, and I nodded while I looked back at Holt and Cree. They'd fallen into a conversation with Pan about how he came up with *'The Traveler's Sustenance'* last year and how it's become so popular that he isn't sure how he'll keep it on the shelves much longer.

"I'm sure you're aware of the crops..." he started cautiously.

I focused on getting to the back of the shop and ignored their conversation.

Camila made it all the way to the door, and I focused on our escape plan. I tip-toed over to where my sister was while Holt and Cree's backs were turned to us.

Camila was trying to push the knife out of the sleeve of her leathers, the move difficult through the bounds on her wrists. We made it a few steps from the door and I looked up at Holt and Cree, who were now alone. Pan must have been grabbing something from the kitchen through the other door by the counter.

Neither of them was paying us any mind as they sorted through the food. Camila's step into the door frame caused a slight creak to sound from beneath her feet. We both shot looks up at the Fae males, who were now looking directly at us through narrowed eyes.

Before I could do anything, the knife Camila stole flew through the air directly at Cree. His Fae reflexes allowed him to dodge the blade by a hair as it grazed his arm and lodged into the wood behind him. His eyebrows drew together as he bared his teeth at the realization of what Camila had just attempted.

Shadows started to curl over his arms as he formed a weapon with his magic.

"And you lovely ladies, is there anything I can get for you to make your traveling more enjoyable?" Pan said with a smile as he walked back into the room.

All four of us were at a standstill as we stared at each other, wondering who would move first.

"Everything okay out here?" Pan asked as he watched us all warily.

Cree drew his shadows back into his body and moved towards us, crossing the space between us in long strides and put his arm around my sister forcefully.

"She will love what you've already supplied us with," he said with a mocking smile on his face.

He grabbed my arm and pulled the both of us over to where Holt stood.

"Very well! I'll get this wrapped and thrown into some satchels for you to be on your way!"

Holt pulled out a few large gold coins from a small pouch and placed them on the counter for Pan.

"Oh, your highness, I could never accept your money! This is on old Pan. Don't you worry about that!" Pan turned around to finish packing the items he was trying to gift us.

"I must insist, especially with the situation we're in," Holt responded as he picked up the coins and stretched his hand out to Pan to take the coins.

Pan grew red and had a look of worry flash across his face before replacing it with a smile. He reluctantly took the coins from Holt and slid them into a pouch resting on the counter.

"Well, it was a pleasure. If you're ever here in my village again, please be sure to stop by and say hello! No one will believe I supplied you today. When I tell Marcie about this..." Pan said with so much excitement that he seemed to be jumping up and down on his heels. Cree cut his thought short.

"It would be best if you kept our visit a secret for now. We have a long way back to the palace and don't want any interference if we can avoid it," Cree said, placing another gold coin down on the counter.

"Oh my, how terribly rude of me! I meant no harm, I would never place you in harm's way! I should have thought you wouldn't want anyone to know you're here!"

Tears started to well in his eyes, and he placed his hand on his forehead like he might pass out from the sheer thought of him causing the Fae prince harm.

"Pan, you have been a great help today. I am sure you meant no harm, but maybe tell Marcie in a few weeks when we're safely back at the palace," Holt said with that warm, reassuring smile while placing his hood back on his head.

Pan nodded as he wiped the sweat that gathered on his bald head with a rag he pulled from his pocket. Cree dragged my sister out of the building by her arm while I followed Holt towards the door.

I looked back at Pan. He seemed to be coming out of the shock of the whole encounter, a giddy smile across his face as he cleaned up the counter.

The door closed behind me, cutting off my view of the cheery male. I whirled around and ran smack into my sister, who was in a stare-down with Cree, again. My clumsiness knocked her into his chest, and she jumped to the side like he was made of something toxic.

"What in the nine hells is wrong with you? Did you really just attempt to stab me?" Cree yelled at her.

"I don't know what you're referring to," Camila said with her chin high.

The look might have been intimidating if Cree didn't stand two heads higher than us. He stepped to my sister, grabbing her by the arm again with his teeth bared, causing the Fae in the street to stop what they were doing and stare.

"You're raising attention, Cree," Holt said.

Cree made a noise and turned and looked at Holt. Holt just shook his head and started to make his way back to our horses, and they went to strap the items we bought to Night.

I walked up to Thunder and patted the side of his neck, and he looked at me with an all-knowing look a horse should not have been capable of.

"Oh, don't you give me that look. You have no idea what happened," I whispered, and he snorted like he really did know what Camila and I were up to.

I ran my hand through his mane before a shadow loomed behind me, and I turned around, locking eyes with Holt's storm-ridden eyes.

"He likes you," he said with a slight smile, and I looked back at Thunder right as he tried to tuck his head into the nook of my shoulder.

"He has good taste," I said in a voice that sounded a little too close to flirting.

I scowled at myself while Holt chuckled.

"What you and your sister were about to do was very, very dumb, Prisoner," Holt said, crossing his arms across his chest and looking down his nose at me.

"Can you blame us?"

I raised my wrists to remind him that I was, in fact, a prisoner, and he surveyed me for a moment. The look in his eye showed that he was choosing his following words carefully.

"You are our prisoners. Any attempt to escape will fail. Any attempt to kill us will fail. You are humans in a land where everything is designed to kill you. Whether you like it or not, your only chance to stay alive is with us."

I looked down at the dirt, not wanting to confront the truth in his statement.

He stepped forward with his hands raised towards me, asking permission to place me on the horse, and I nodded a faint nod and turned around.

His action so at odds with the comment he just made.

His hands gripped my waist, and I let out a breath as he placed me on the horse as if I weighed nothing, still in awe of the strength these Fae possessed.

I looked over at my sister and Cree, who were still going back and forth about our getaway attempt.

"Do you have a death wish?" he asked sharply.

"You have no idea what Xio and I are capable of! We have been training for years. We know how to take care of ourselves!" she said, trying to point her finger at him, though her hands were bound, so it didn't give the effect she was going for.

"Oh yes, I'm sure two *trained* humans would be able to take on any dangerous Fae that you came across! And where exactly were you going? Did you think this plan all the way through?"

He looked at her like a father might look down at a child as he scolded them, or at least what I assumed it would look like.

She opened her mouth to retort and closed it, opened it again, and huffed a sigh. He had a point there. We had no idea what our plan was to get back home, we just wanted to escape.

"Exactly, idiotic. If you ever try and stab me again, I'll relieve you of your fucking hand," Cree said far too calmly.

I almost didn't realize the threat in his statement.

He didn't allow her to respond as he grabbed her by her waist and plopped her on the horse.

She kept her gaze forward as she tried to tuck the curls that fell in front of her face behind her ear, but she miscalculated her balance and started to shift off the horse.

Cree jumped up behind her and stopped her from slipping off as they locked eyes for a second too long.

"See, you can't even stay on a horse. How were you going to make it to wherever you were going?"

Camila whirled back around and placed her bindings on the saddle horn just as I had.

I didn't realize how long I watched this exchange when Holt returned to where I was seated on the horse with two bundles of cloth.

One bundle was black, and one bundle was a deep navy blue. He must have gone to one of the shops while I was watching my sister.

He walked over to Cree, handed him the black bundle, and muttered something before coming back to Thunder.

"I got you and your sister cloaks. We need to make sure we can cover those odd human ears as much as possible. The glamour will help, but just as a backup. Some Fae have trained to see through glamours like the one I used on you. It also will get a little chilly once we get close to the mountains," he said, unraveling the bundle.

The stitching was silver, and the material was heavy as it fell. He jumped up on the horse and clasped the cloak around my shoulders. His fingers grazed my neck for a second, and I had to choke down a small breath of air.

"I think you have weird ears," I said quietly, unsure how to respond to this random act of kindness from the male who bound my wrists and just told me there would never be a chance for me to escape.

Holt chuckled and looked over to Cree, who finished wrapping the black cloak around my sister reluctantly.

"We'll make good time if we leave now. We should make it to the next campsite by nightfall," Holt said, and Cree nodded his agreement.

"Will Cree hurt my sister for what she did?" I asked quietly as we trailed their horse out of the village.

"No, he will not," he answered firmly.

My shoulders relaxed. I didn't realize how tight my body was after the events in this village.

Thunder and Night fell into a gallop, and we were back in a forest within a few minutes. I welcomed the greenery and the florals around me, feeling slightly defeated at the fact that we would now have to wait until we made it to the palace to escape.

It left Camila and I with plenty of time to devise a plan, so I tried to hold on to that little slice of hope as the trees became thicker and we made our way across the land.

Chapter 8

Xio

Holt mentioned that we had about an hour left until we reached the clearing we would be camping at. I was thankful for that because I still was not accustomed to all-day rides on a horse. I peered out down the path, and movement shifted ahead of us.

"Did you see that?" I whispered to no one in particular as Holt stopped the horse.

I should have known he'd seen it before I did. He seemed to always be one step ahead of me. Holt turned to Cree, and the look on his face showed he also saw what we saw.

"There was motion ahead of us, I didn't get a good look at them, but we should assume they are not the forest welcoming committee," Cree said sarcastically.

Holt let out a breath of laughter and nodded before fixing his face into concentration, calculating what we should do next.

"Let's keep ahead slowly. We'll react accordingly," Holt said, and Cree nodded.

We slowly crept forward. I looked side to side, expecting something to jump out at us at any moment when I heard a grunt from ahead of us.

Cree stopped his horse and jumped down swiftly, pulling out his two short swords from his pack on the side of Night. Holt brought our horse to where Night stood and waited as Cree yelled out a battle cry.

Two males charged at him with just as much ferocity. One was a few steps closer than the other, and Cree stepped to the first attacker. He was met with their sword swinging down towards his shoulder and he crossed his short swords blocking the attack, using their own momentum against them.

Shadows started to curl around his blades as he used the sword in his right hand to slice the Fae's leg, causing him to stumble and fall. Cree shifted to the other attacker, a slightly larger male than the last but not as tall as Cree and apparently not as skilled.

He seemed to think he could stop him with brute force, but Cree was too quick. He twisted around the attacker as the male put all of his power into trying to slash Cree in two. He cut into the male's left side and right leg simultaneously, causing the second attacker to fall right on top of the first.

I wondered why they didn't strike to kill immediately as Cree turned around to come back to us.

Suddenly, more shouts came from ahead and on either side of the path we were on. I looked over at my sister, whose gaze was fully fixed on Cree. She looked enamored with how he moved, and I laughed internally. This was the first time she wasn't scowling at him.

I quickly remembered what was happening when Holt looked over at us, stuck between fighting and ensuring we didn't run away.

"Cut us free. We can fight! Where are our weapons?" Camila shouted at him. Holt looked at her with his head turned slightly to the side, surely wondering if this was some sort of trick for us to escape.

"We know we won't last here now. Just cut us free so we can defend ourselves," I said firmly, looking over my shoulder at Holt.

He nodded and slashed between my wrists with a dagger I didn't see him grab before removing me from Thunder and doing the same for Camila. He went into a pack on the left side of Thunder and drew our weapons.

A breath caught in my throat as he handed me my sword. No other weapon felt as comfortable in my hand as my sword.

It was a great steel sword with a gold hilt and embellishments that ran up the entire length of the blade like vines, and there was a bright red stone set in the pommel that glittered in the sun.

I extended it out, gazing at this beautiful weapon of mine. My sister was doing the same with her daggers, which were miniature versions of my own sword but not small by any means.

Holt pulled his own weapon out, a vast obsidian battle ax that seemed to vibrate in his hand. He started walking towards the aggressors, stopping for one second to look over his shoulder.

"Stay here. Defend yourselves."

His gray eyes locked with mine for a second as he seemed to wonder if leaving us here with weapons was a good idea, but he turned around to help Cree.

Cree sliced through the assailants with a grace that could only be achieved through years of vigorous training. I tore my gaze away from Cree, and it fell on Holt, or a version of Holt I had not yet seen in my time with him.

Lightning glided across his skin and channeled into his ax as he took a great swing at the first person who dared step up to him. He, too, seemed to try and avoid killing the attackers as he threw the lightning into the aggressor's arm.

The male tensed for a second as if stuck in time before he fell to the ground, twitching. Holt whirled around to the next person and kicked them in the chest, knocking the breath from them. He opened a gash in their chest, and they clutched the wound screaming with such terror that bumps spread across my flesh.

Motion tore my eyes away from Cree and Holt, and I looked over to see someone running toward us from behind Camila.

I knocked her out of the way and raised my sword to meet the Fae's attack.

He was strong, but I managed to redirect his sword's path, and he stumbled a step.

That step cost him.

My sister whirled around him and slashed him across the back of his knees. We may just be humans, but we'd been fighting together for years and knew how to get ourselves out of a bind.

The attacker fell to his knees, and I drew my sword across his arm so deep that I saw bone as he fell the rest of the way to the ground. Camila took this opportunity to kick him in his head so hard that he was knocked unconscious.

"Bastard," she muttered, looking up at me, and I nodded my appreciation for her.

Another aggressor made their way to us while we took down his friend. By the time we noticed him, he was too close for us to defend ourselves successfully.

The male had pale skin and blonde hair soaked with blood, he already had his sword raised, prepared to kill me. I scrambled to bring my weapon up in defense, but within a second, his muscles tightened, and lightning covered his entire body. His flesh and bones turned to ash and blew right into my face.

I let out a cough trying to remove the male's ashed body from my throat before Holt appeared in front of me.

This was a male to be feared, to be worshiped. He told us he was a Descendant of a God, and right now, I had no questions about it.

None of the gray of his eyes showed, they now resembled the lightning that he took down the attackers with. Holt's body was covered in blood, his curls stuck together in clumps of dark red, and his entire body went rigid as he looked at me.

"Are you hurt?" he asked as his jaw ticked slightly.

I shook my head, unable to form words.

He looked at my sister and asked if she was okay as well.

She responded with a quick nod, followed by words I didn't hear her offer others too often.

"Thank you," she whispered.

Holt's shoulders relaxed slightly as he accepted that we were both okay and we looked over as Cree took down the last attacker and dragged him to the side of the road.

Somehow we made it over to where he was standing, I don't remember telling my body to walk or move, but I was thirty strides from where I was initially.

"Serpents?" Cree asked, directing his attention to Holt.

Holt looked down at the pile of unconscious men. They didn't fight the way I would assume a tribe would fight together. They seemed angry and willing to take down anyone who appeared on this road. Their clothing was similar in a way that people from a village had similar clothing, but they didn't wear armor or any type of uniform tribe warriors may wear.

"I don't think so. I think they were just thieves looking for gold," he said, shaking his head.

A groan came from behind us, and we all whirled around with our weapons raised. The sound came from one of the first attackers, who lay face down in the dirt, trying to right himself and reach for his weapon. Cree rolled him over and kicked away the sword he was going for in two quick moves.

"Why did you attack us?" Cree asked through tight teeth.

The male had tan skin and cropped brown hair, parts of his clothing hung off of him due to the fight he initiated. He had many scars across his hands, and the visible parts of his forearms showed he probably worked in manual labor.

"My farm is completely barren. It was our last resort to feed our families. We would do anything to protect the ones he loved," he said proudly and closed his eyes, coming to terms with the fact he was probably going to die in the next few moments.

Holt and Cree shared a look, and Holt stepped forward toward the male.

"Attacking innocents is not the way. I understand these are hard times. We won't kill you, but we won't allow you to follow us and attack again," he said.

The farmer seemed confused about the prince's decision and stared at him somewhere between devastation and appreciation.

I heard the sound of clinking steel and saw Cree piling their weapons together before moving to tie the males up on the side of the road. My sister and I made our way back over to the horses as we watched Cree and Holt clear the road so we could get through.

Holt turned around and sent a burst of lightning so hot and bright that the weapons the assailants used melted and turned to ash in seconds.

Most of them were still unconscious as they lay on the side of the road, tied to each other in a similar way Camila and I were on the first day we came across the Fae. The male that Holt spoke with had his eyes directed at the dirt.

He wore a look that may have been regretful at attacking us, or maybe it was regret that he didn't steal all our gold.

Part of me felt for this group, my sister and I had been so hungry or poor that we made substandard decisions like they did.

We hadn't tried to murder four innocents in cold blood, so my feelings were mixed.

Holt stepped up in front of the brown-haired male and mumbled, "find a better way."

He placed me on the Thunder without another word, while Cree did the same with Camila. We quickly made our way past the tied-up figures, and I looked back and sighed.

Holt saved my life. He killed someone who was striking to cut me in two, and I didn't know how to thank him.

"Pan mentioned something about the crops, and that male back there mentioned something about his farm being barren," I said, not really a question, but I didn't know if he'd answer me if I came right out and asked what's wrong with the land.

"There have been some problems with the magic in Maya lately. Crops are shriveling before we can gather them, cattle are growing sick and dying, and the people are hungry and angry. That's why we're out here. We were looking for something that would help, in a way," he said sorrowfully.

He truly loved his kingdom and the people in it. It's why he didn't kill the attackers. He knew they were just trying to survive, I realized.

"Why'd you kill the male who attacked me but not the others?" I asked without looking over my shoulder.

His entire body tensed.

"He was going to kill you," he snarled as if my life meant something to him, but before I could think of a response, he continued. "You may be my prisoner, but no harm will come to you while you are with me."

I wasn't sure whether I should feel relieved, but part of me found comfort in knowing he would defend Camila and me until we made it to the safety of the palace.

"Am I still a prisoner?" I asked as I looked over my shoulder and wiggled the fingers on my free hands.

"A little less than a prisoner now, I suppose," he laughed.

I looked over at my sister, and my chest filled with warmth. We could have both died today, but we survived.

Neither of us said anything else as we rode the rest of the way into the night.

I would ensure we continued to survive, even if that meant traveling with the males seated behind us for another fortnight.

Chapter 9

Camila

We seemed to fall into something like a routine, which was odd since we had only been *'traveling'* together for a few days.

Cree appeared to get over my stabbing attempt pretty quickly. Holt mentioned something about the Fae being inherently violent creatures and that it wasn't the worst thing I could have done.

In Zuma, if someone attempted to stab you, there would be no level of forgiveness given to the assailant. Any attempts to stab me would be met with violence, undoubtedly.

Just another one of the many reasons we needed to get out of this otherworldly land.

Murder attempts aside, there appeared to be a level of trust building between us all. They didn't bind our hands, and we made no further attempts at escape.

After Holt saved my sister's life, I reluctantly felt something close to safety around the two males. Once we left the area where we were attacked, Cree and I rode in silence.

A part of me knew he was protecting Holt when he took the attackers down, but another part of me knew he was protecting my sister and me as well.

I wondered whether that was because Holt wanted us to make it back alive to understand why we made it across the barrier, or because he cared for our well-being.

I was pretty sure it was the first option, though.

I finished with the last stake of our tent, and my sister went inside to set up our bedroll and blanket. I made my way to the fire where Holt and Cree were already sitting, discussing something they didn't want us to hear.

I plopped down on the area that looked like they set up for Xio and I and, then smiled.

"So, food?" I asked.

Holt laughed while Cree rolled his eyes at my interruption, and part of me took a little happiness in the fact I pissed Cree off even the slightest amount.

Holt handed me my portion of what they bought from Pan, a mixture of nuts, dried fruit, oat bars, and dried meat.

Great. More of what we've had the last few days. I really shouldn't complain, we had days of less appealing food over the years.

Still, I thought Pan's special concoction would have been different. Cree saw the look on my face and seemed to find my disappointment humorous.

"We need to eat food that will sustain us. This will keep our energy levels up so we can continue on," he said.

He probably ate like this out of choice.

I wasn't asking for a chocolate cake, but something more than this would have been great. A flaky portion of bread fell in my lap, and I looked up to see Holt smiling while Xio sat down beside me.

"We bought this prior to the flying knife," Holt said with a judging look.

"Oh, that bread looks delicious," Xio said.

She reached her hand out to grab it out of my lap, and I jerked away from her and stuffed the entire portion in my mouth.

"Don't lose your hand," Holt chuckled, handing my sister her portion of food for the evening. I looked over to see Cree with his lip pulled back, like I genuinely would have bitten my sister's hand.

"I am not some wild animal. I'm just starving since somebody refuses to let me have snacks throughout the day," I said as I stared right back at Cree.

"We have to make sure the food lasts us until our next stop," Holt said.

I tore my gaze from Cree to find Holt with his lips clamped as he tried to hold back a life and rolled my eyes.

"Can't you just magic up some food or something?" I asked.

"We can't conjure up food, no. There is magic pulsing through the ground, but we can't use it to create food that is not there," Holt responded.

"And the Descendant power?" Xio asked.

"That is why I was able to use the lightning to stop that male from killing you," he said tightly, "it's also how I started the fire. It doesn't help in regards to creating food, but I can create rain storms and a few other things."

A part of me didn't really believe him when he explained some of this the first night, but now it seemed like anything was possible.

"A few other things?" Xio asked again.

The look on her face said she was curious, but it also portrayed a hint of admiration I wasn't sure how I felt about.

Cree looked over and chuckled. "Humans truly know nothing about the Fae."

"We were told fairy tales about a land with magic and people with pointed ears, but no one actually believed it was true. We just thought they were bedtime stories for children," I responded.

Holt seemed to accept this answer while Cree still looked at me with a crease between his brow.

"Most Descendants of the main Gods can shift into an animal form," Holt said, answering Xio's inquiry about what other power he possesses.

"What does that mean?" Xio responded.

Holt lifted the bottom of his shirt, pulling it over his head and tossing it on the floor beside him. I looked over to my sister, wondering why the question warranted him removing his clothing. The reflection of the fire danced on his brown skin, sliding over his abs, somehow making them appear even more defined than they already were.

I found Xio practically drooling over the expanse of skin on show, and I nudged her to snap out of it. I looked back over to Holt just as enormous eagle wings were forming on his back, and I gasped.

I completely forgot that Cree showed us his wings of shadow the first day we met them. I wondered why they didn't just fly everywhere if they had wings. If I could fly, you wouldn't be able to pull me from the sky.

"This is a half shift, but I can fully shift into an eagle if I want. I don't do it often because I like to be able to fight with more than just talons and a beak," he said as if he was pointing out the obvious.

I thought back to when we were at their camp. Was there an eagle nearby watching us try and steal their food?

"Can you shift too?" I asked Cree.

"Unfortunately, I haven't been able to access that type of magic. No one knows who I descend from," he said with just a hint of desolation, "but for whatever reason, I have these shadows. So I can create wings for myself with them," he finished, allowing the shadowy wings to appear on his back.

"No need to get undressed like lightning boy over here?" I asked.

"I can if you ask nicely," he said with a smile that immediately turned to a frown when he realized it was me he was flirting with. I threw him my middle finger and continued eating my food.

Holt took the opportunity to shift the conversation. "I mentioned there were other Descendants. There was also a Sun Queen at one point. She was a Descendant of the God of the Sun, Kinich. She was able to shift into a jaguar and was able to form weapons of fire and light the way I can with lightning."

"That's badass," Xio said, and I laughed.

"She was, yes," Cree said, and the use of the word *'was'* stopped the rest of my laugh from forming, and I cleared my throat.

"We'll pass Sun Palace on our way back to Storm Palace, it's in a bit of ruin, but it's still a breathtaking sight," Holt said, and I nodded, sure that he was correct in this assessment.

"Will there be somewhere to bathe soon? Between riding all day and that fight, I'm in dire need," I asked.

"I noticed," Cree said under his breath.

It hit me how truly terrible we looked. Our curls were matted in some spots, our skin was caked in a mixture of dirt and blood.

A sudden flash of water fell over me, and Xio and I jumped up, nearly stumbling into the fire.

Xio's hair was plastered to her head and body, and I was sure I looked the same. The dirt and grime slid off our bodies and onto the ground, and I looked up to find a storm cloud just above our heads.

Cree fell off the log he was sitting on, laughing and clutching his side. Holt let his hands down, and the cloud dissipated. He also fell into laughter, not nearly as intense as Cree, but he seemed to find our appearance humorous.

"What the hell!" I yelled at him, trying to shake the water out of my hair which threw Cree back into his laughing fit.

"I was just trying to get you ladies clean, that's all," Holt said between laughs.

I was ready to fight this Descendant of the God of Rain until I heard what sounded like a laugh from my sister, and I whirled to face her.

"Drowned rat, yet again," she said, laughing harder at whatever face I was making.

If I looked anything like her, I did indeed look like a drowned rat.

I started laughing with my sister, and we all broke into intense laughter. We eventually composed ourselves but realized we were sitting in our drenched clothes.

"Do you still have our bags? We should have an extra set of clothing in there," Xio asked as she rang the water from her tight curls.

Cree got up to retrieve our bags and returned with Xio's bag and my satchel with a hole sliced through the bottom.

"Damn it, that was everything I had!" I yelled in frustration.

"It must have been cut earlier. I didn't even realize anything fell out in the carnage from the fight," Cree said.

His face almost looked apologetic as he tossed us the still intact bag, and Xio looked inside to inspect what we lost.

"Yeah, our clothes were in your bag. This is just a tent and a bedroll," she sighed.

"I have an extra blanket in my pack that one of you can use to cover up. You can lay your clothes near the fire to dry overnight," Holt said, handing Xio the blanket he mentioned.

"And I'll take that," Cree said as he took the extra tent from Xio's bag and walked away.

"If I have to wake up with Holt cuddled up next to me one more time, I'm going to lose my mind," he mumbled while setting up the stolen tent.

"You're just so warm and cuddly," Holt said jokingly, which had all but Cree laughing. He rolled his eyes and threw the bedroll into the tent.

Cree stepped into his tent, leaving me, Xio, and Holt around the fire.

"One of us will bring our clothes back out to hang by the fire," I said, and we made our way into the tent to peel the cold, wet clothing off our bodies.

Chapter 10

Xio

I was thankful for the lack of dirt and blood, but I wasn't grateful for the lack of, well, clothing. My sister and I stared at each other, trying to decide which of us would take the clothes out to dry.

"I almost died today. You should do it," I said to her.

She placed her hands on her chest in a mocking gesture. "And you don't think that affected me? Arguably, I would be the one who had to carry on without you, so really, it was my life that would have gotten worse because of it."

I couldn't help but laugh and roll my eyes at my sister. I should have known she would somehow turn this around and win the competition of who had the worst day.

"Fine, give me the thicker blanket," I said, pointing to the dark blue blanket that Holt had handed me earlier.

My sister helped wrap it around my body, so no unwanted skin was showing. I tucked the fabric around my arms, trying to create something like arm holes so I could carry our clothes out there to dry.

My sister laid down and closed her eyes when I was finally situated enough. I could have sworn I heard snoring when the tent flap closed behind me.

I didn't see Holt near the fire, so I laid out the clothes on the logs we were sitting on, ensuring that everything was flat so that neither of us had to wear damp clothes in the morning.

I turned to go back to my tent and caught Holt staring at the sky with a look of despair on his face.

The stars twinkled in his gray eyes, and he ran his hand through his curls.

Part of me felt like I should just leave him to stir in whatever feelings he was going through, but then I remembered that he saved my life.

Damn my stupid heart.

Camila would have left him out here, but unfortunately, I had a little more empathy than she did.

"Hey," I said quietly, not wanting to startle him though I was sure he already knew I was there with his heightened senses.

He looked at me like he didn't realize I was there at all, as he pulled himself out of whatever thoughts he was stuck in. His gray eyes locked in with mine, and he held the stare, looking relieved that it was me.

"Hey, Prisoner," he responded.

He made that nickname sound like a term of endearment. Which, unfortunately, I didn't hate.

He ran his eyes down his blanket wrapped around my naked body.

"What were you looking at?" I blurted out before his gaze got too heavy on me.

"The night sky always seems to bring me some resemblance of peace," he whispered.

He looked back at it while I stood beside him and raised my gaze to the sky. It was truly beautiful, deep blues and purples lit up by sparkling white and silver stars. The moon was so big here it felt like it took up a third of the sky.

The daytime sky had always brought me the peace he seemed to find in the night sky, but I stared out into the abyss following his gaze, and peace began to settle across me too.

Everything felt connected here: the sky, the stars, the forest, and even us, which was odd. I'd never felt any sort of connection to anything other than with my sister. Not having memories can do that to a girl.

"It really is beautiful, I've always loved looking out at the clouds during the day, but here the night sky feels just as peaceful," I said with a small smile starting to pull across my face.

I turned to find him now looking at me, not the night sky.

"You fought well today. I forgot to mention that earlier," he said with a hint of pride I was sure he didn't expect to use on a little human like myself.

"Me and my sister have always loved training together. Those weapons are our most prized possessions. We have a tendency to get into..." I trailed off, wondering why I was telling him anything. "Situations that we had to fight our way out of."

"I imagine the mouth on your sister can put you in some of those situations?" he said with a breath of laughter.

He definitely wasn't wrong, but I wasn't going to let him put all the blame on my sister like that.

"We both seem to have a knack for it," I said sharply, and he looked at me apologetically.

"That doesn't surprise me much, actually."

But before I could try and make an argument, he continued. "Me and Cree are the same way, Cree tends to lean more towards the asshole approach, but we both have found ourselves in situations we could have avoided over the years."

"You've known each other a long time?" I asked.

Curiosity was always getting the best of me, but he waited a moment, and I wondered if maybe I had asked the wrong question.

"All my life," he answered.

They appeared more like brothers than anything, with their wordless conversations and mid-morning tussles, so being life long friends made a lot of sense.

"You feel about him the way I feel about Camila," I stated.

"I do," he said, flashing me the sight of his straight white teeth as he smiled at the thought of the male we spoke of.

"I know he seems difficult at times, but he is the best Fae I know. I would not have trusted anyone else to come on this journey. I trust him with my life," he said proudly.

I wondered if I could finally figure out what their mission was. He hadn't been very open about it before, but it seemed like we were treading different water than we were before.

"What were you two looking for?" I asked gently.

He looked at me, assessing whether he should trust me, and if I were him, I'm not sure I would trust me either. I would have accepted it if he had told me to mind my business and go to bed. I looked into his eyes, displaying something like submissiveness to show him that I meant no harm.

He saved my life at this point, and my best bet at staying alive was definitely with him. So I wouldn't be planning on running away or attempting to murder him at any point soon. He seemed to accept my submissive gaze and took a deep breath looking back at the sky.

"My father, Arlan. He's referred to as the Storm King in Maya," he said, staring out into the sky. "He is sick, very sick, actually."

My heart hurt for him, I'd never known who my father is, but I could empathize with how difficult that would be for someone who had that in their life.

"The healers came to me in my chamber one day and said their magic can't stop whatever is taking him. They told me of a flower out near the human barrier that had medicinal qualities and could possibly save him. Its petals are shaped like a butterfly.

We found it just before you two came to steal our food," he said, looking back at me with a small smile. "They told me he has less than a year left to live, so I decided that Cree and I would come to find the flower before it got to that," he finished, looking back out into the expanse, seeming like he was looking for answers in the stars.

"Only my mother knows why we left. I told her what the healer whispered to me in confidence. I don't think he wanted to give my father false hope. I left the following morning with Cree."

He took a deep breath again, I wasn't sure how to console this type of devastation, so I nodded my head, encouraging him to continue. The moonlight shone silver streaks on his skin as he brought his gaze back to mine.

"I told you how the land is suffering? My father has been so sick that he can't fix it. If I can heal him, I hope he'll know what to do and how to fix it. I feel so helpless. Nothing I do seems to fix the issue. I've found the land still fruitful and brought more farmers out to help tend the land, but the areas that are not barren are becoming smaller and smaller. I fear there will only be a few years left until we aren't able to feed our kingdom."

I couldn't imagine having that weight on my shoulders. I began to understand why he was looking at the stars for answers. There wasn't much any one person could do.

"I'm sorry you're going through that, and I'm sorry for stealing the food you had," I said, feeling a little guilty about the thievery.

We didn't have any food, but it felt worse stealing from someone who was in a famine.

"Attempt at stealing, don't forget we caught you," he replied with a wink.

"Oh, how could I ever forget?" I said mockingly, and we both laughed and fell into something oddly like a comfortable silence.

"That's another reason I insisted we didn't let you go. We can't afford for humans to start to slip into our lands," he said, almost sounding sorry for taking us captive.

"I can assure you we didn't mean to end up here. We just stumbled across whatever barrier you mentioned without knowing," I said with more anger than I meant to.

"I know, but we can't let it happen again. I'll have the scholars take a look at you and see if there's some reason the barrier let you through. They can monitor the barrier and the readings that come near it. No human has ever made it through, so we must ensure the magic remains intact."

I understood he was trying to protect his lands, but my sister and I were unfortunate enough to be the humans who made it through. I shifted on my feet, unsure where to go from here.

I was about to tell him I was returning to my tent to get some rest, but before I could get that thought out, a shooting star shot across the sky, creating a sparkling arch that stretched as far as we could see.

My face lit with a genuine smile. I couldn't remember the last time I saw a shooting star, and I made a quiet wish that my sister and I would make it through whatever it was we would be facing. My chest filled with warmth, and my smile grew even wider.

I turned to Holt to let him know it was time for me to lay down, and I found his eyes already set on my face, the intensity of his gaze sent bumps racing across my skin.

We stared at each other in the soft moonlight. He truly was beautiful. While his eyes glowed with electricity in the fight earlier today, they now resembled the color of endless storm clouds before a downpour. He shifted his mouth like he was about to say something but stopped, the movement drew my attention to his supple bottom lip and the soft arch of his top lip.

A cloud shifted over the moon, and the light slipped away from his face. The wind began to blow gently, sending one of my tight curls over my eyes.

Holt reached over, moved it from my eyes, and tucked it behind my ear.

"You have beautiful eyes," he said gently.

Funny that I was thinking the same thing about him. I suddenly became very aware that I was naked under the navy blanket he lent me as my nipples hardened from the cool wind, and I wrapped it tighter around myself.

"Thank you," I whispered, unsure why this felt like a secret.

"Get some sleep," he said.

He turned his face back to the stars and I nodded my agreement and returned to the tent I shared with my sister. I walked past the tent Cree acquired from us, heard a deep snore from within, and smiled. He felt the need to call us out on our snoring but sounded like a hibernating bear himself.

I passed Holt's tent that was set between where Cree was sleeping and my own and looked over my shoulder at Holt's figure before entering my tent. His dark leathers almost blended in with the night. His brow was tight with confusion as the cloud moved back away from the moon, and he was once again covered in the moonlight, looking the very picture of a God. I dipped into the tent and let out a quiet laugh at the sight inside.

My sister took the opportunity of my absence to spread all of her limbs in different directions, her head tossed to the side and mouth open.

She let out a snore, and I laughed to myself. She and Cree had more in common than they thought.

I shifted her over slightly, and she mumbled something I couldn't make out before wiping a line of drool on her chin and falling back asleep.

I tucked the blanket around her to make sure all of her bare body was covered if one of the males came to wake us up. I laid beside her, ensuring I was also wholly covered, before closing my eyes and trying to decipher everything that happened today.

The attack and the conversation with Holt played over and over in my mind. Something about him pulled me closer and made me want to learn his secrets. He made me want to tell him my own, which felt more dangerous than anything.

I was stuck in a nightmare. The guard I killed in the Cursed Forest lay rotting on the ground, and his body began to twitch. The males who attacked us on the path here were charging at me. I lifted my sword to slice through them. I killed the first attacker that made it to me, and I watched his soul leave his body. I looked down at my hands as they began to shake. Everything went black.

Chapter 11

Camila

I felt a warm hand rubbing my forehead, I hurt myself in training today, and my cheeks were wet with tears. The hand I felt was comforting, even more than my sister's, which led me to believe it was my mother. I tried to turn my head to see what she looked like, but her figure was a brown blur. She hummed a tune, and I closed my eyes.

I squeezed my eyes as tight as possible, trying to will myself back to sleep, but no sleep came.

I was nearly twenty-five years old, but the hole left in my chest where my mother should have been still ached like it did when we woke up in that shack.

Xio seemed to accept our predicament and focused on our future, but I could never shake the empty feeling the lack of memories left me with. It was worse when I had these dreams.

They felt like memories but never gave me enough to know if they were real. This one seemed the closest to being an actual memory, and I huffed my frustration before hearing a loud yelp outside the tent that sounded a lot like Xio.

I leaped off the bedroll and ran to open the tent to investigate what was happening. I threw the flap open and surveyed the grounds but was met with a cool breeze that covered my skin.

All of my skin that was not covered by clothing, due to me removing them before bed.

Cree's back was turned to me, and I heard Xio laugh.

That was enough to complete my investigation on whether my sister was okay and return my naked body to our tent. I thanked the Gods that Cree didn't see anything and wrapped the black blanket around my body.

I removed any proof of sleep from my hair and eyes and stepped out of the tent again.

"I'd say good morning, but that would be a morning without having to look at you," I muttered to Cree while walking over to where my clothes lay on the log.

The way I woke up spiked adrenaline throughout me, making me feel like I could take on anything.

He looked at me with a smile that said he was evaluating how he wanted to respond to my warm morning message. His lopsided smile grew.

"You look warm, wouldn't want to catch a chill out here in the morning wind, would you?" he said with a smirk, as he raised his eyebrows in a knowing manner that caused the blood to somehow rush from my head to my toes and back up into my cheeks.

I thought my morning nudity went unnoticed, but it appeared I was incorrect. I opened my mouth to try and bite back, but no words came to my mind. I was sure I resembled something like a fish out of water and my fists tightened at my side.

"Where's my sister?" I said sharply, and he pointed out in the field beyond the trees that lined our campsite.

"I was going to spare you the embarrassment of knowing I saw, but you just had to wake up spitting venom, didn't you?"

I turned to grab my thankfully dry clothes off the log and stomped back to the tent. I pulled my brown pants up and tugged my head and arms into my leather top before I fixed my hair that got ruffled while I angrily dressed.

The laces on my boots kept getting tangled, and I tried to calm myself enough to finish getting them on. Eventually, I was successful and stepped back outside, the sun peeked through the trees, and I savored the warmth it brought. Fallen branches snapped beneath my feet as I trudged through the trees to where

Cree said my sister was, and stopped in my tracks when I saw my sister training with Holt.

My sister held her sword firmly and blocked a blow from Holt. It was evident he wasn't trying to hurt her and was pulling back some of his strength but she kept up with his pace.

She took a step to the right pulling her sword away from his and spun under his still-lifted arm. I never really got to see my sister in action, as she was always right next to me when we got into trouble.

The pub was often the place we got into our skirmishes after one too many ales, whether that be us or another party who welcomed the liquid courage into their veins after a hard day in our village.

A smile split my sister's face as she once again spun under Holt's arm taking advantage of the height difference between the two. Holt caught onto this and turned with such quickness my sister didn't register it. He lifted his elbow and knocked her to the ground, flat on her butt. She seemed to accept this defeat quickly, he threw his hand out to help her up, and she allowed it.

I wasn't sure when my sister got so cozy with our captor, but I supposed his saving her life yesterday had something to do with it.

A figure in black caught my attention, breaking through the trees. Cree walked up to me and handed me my daggers.

"We're training. Holt and I typically train together, but since you two are going to be with us for the next few weeks, we decided we should all train together," he demanded while pulling out his short swords and removing his shirt.

We'd all been pretty heavily clothed up until this point as the forest we came from was more chilly than the field we now stood in. Cree always had long sleeve leathers, armor, and sometimes a cloak on when we rode.

I took in the sight of all the tattoos that covered every bit of skin between his knuckles and his neck. His entire body seemed to be covered in smoke, shadows, and flames, with other figures nestled between them. A snake trailed up his corded forearm where an eagle sat on his bicep. Across his chest were a plethora of clouds with the sun and moon peeking through on either side. I trailed my eyes over to his other arm, where a jaguar let out a growl of defiance when I felt his black eyes on me.

"Enjoying the show?" he taunted.

I definitely was, but I wasn't going to admit it. He was attractive, there was no denying that, and I'm sure he knew it. Between the tattoos, the muscled form, and his choppy black hair that was always a little disheveled, he was a work of art. An asshole, but a work of art.

"I just don't understand why you removed your shirt," I said as if the sight didn't bring me any kind of pleasure.

"Didn't want to get any blood on it," he replied.

"Mine or yours?" I asked.

He smirked at me, advising exactly whose blood he was trying to save his shirt from.

"I'll train with my sister," I said absolutely and turned to walk to where she and Holt were still training. Cree materialized before me out of the shadows, and I jumped back with my breath stuck in my chest.

"You need to train with Fae. You don't have any power here. At the very least, you need to learn how we fight," he said.

My heart was still beating at top speed after the jump scare he had caused.

"How did you do that?" I yelled, forgetting about the topic of my training completely.

"Magic."

He pointed his swords towards my dual daggers, advising me to get ready. I wouldn't mind knocking him on his ass. I smirked and lifted my blades, twisting them in my hand.

"No magic, just steel," I said, and he agreed before darting towards me with less speed than he was capable of and slashing down his left sword towards me.

I blocked the hit and slid under his arm, taking a note from my sister. He whirled around, but not before I had already lifted my dagger and nicked him on the back of his arm.

"See, *your* blood," I said mockingly.

He looked at me with his eyes shifting between denial and anger, making my victory just that much better.

"I was just seeing what you're capable of, Viper, but I won't underestimate you again."

He lifted his left sword into a position to strike and I registered the fact that he favored his left side to memory, sure that I'd be able to use that later.

"That would be wise of you," I replied.

I was fast and strong in the human world, and more than talented with a blade, but I knew I was no match for a Descendant of a God. But confidence was a power in itself, especially when it came to males who consistently underestimated our clearly superior gender.

I barely moved fast enough to block his strike, I crossed both of my blades and took a jump back, allowing him to lose some momentum.

I loved the quickness and flexibility my daggers allowed, my sister was gifted with her sword, but I always preferred my weapons.

Cree didn't know that they connected into one double-sided weapon. I twirled, allowing my back to face him just for a second as I clicked them together with such ease that only came from me doing this maneuver every time my sister and I trained. Cree took my back turning to him as an opportunity, and charged towards me.

By the time I again faced him, my weapon was transformed. He looked down at me with confusion as he stopped in front of me, hesitating for half a second.

That gave me enough of a window to swipe his foot and bring him down. I twisted the dual daggers in my hand and pointed one end toward him with a smile.

"Yield," I whispered as I leaned close, looking down my nose at him.

His eyes were on my dagger and trailed up my arm to my face. My brows scrunched with confusion while I took in the look on his face. His eyes were wide with surprise, but they softened for a moment, making him almost seem in awe of me.

"Take that asshole!" I heard my sister yell while clapping from the other side of the field.

That snapped the shadow bastard and me out of our stare down. I looked up at her with a smile of victory and felt Cree knock my daggers out of his face while he rolled over and got back on his feet.

"You had the element of surprise there. It won't happen again," he growled.

I shrugged and readied for another attack. Clearly, he was holding back. He could split me down the middle in half a thought.

But, it still felt good.

He was right.

I didn't win a single round after the first one where I put him on his ass.

Even though the fact I was able to accomplish that filled me with joy, it would have been nice to do it at least one more time.

I looked down at my tired body, I ended up rolling my sleeves after I began to sweat with the sun beating down on us. Our movements warmed me more than I was expecting as I was trying harder than I liked to admit, and I had bruises to show for it.

I even had a gash on my right arm.

That wasn't Cree's fault. I was on my back, and rather than taking his hand to help me up, I slammed my arms into the dirt in defiance and came down on a sharp rock at the wrong angle. After that, Cree told me to return to camp since we needed to move as soon as possible.

I didn't argue and returned to the camp to pack our things and felt my sister running up behind me. This was the first time I was able to talk to her since she was caught in her own intense training with Holt.

I told her about my little incident this morning, and she just about fell out onto the floor laughing. I didn't find it nearly as funny when it happened, but something about my sister's laugh had me wheezing right next to her.

"How did you forget you were naked? Did you not look down at all when you woke up?" she barely got out through her laughter.

"I thought you were hurt! I just ran to save you. I didn't have time to look down!"

We fell into laughter again and finished packing up our tent. Xio filled me in on her conversation with Holt from the night before, and even I felt an ache in my chest at the predicament Maya was in.

"What do you think the scholars need to do to us? Sounds like we're going to be poked and prodded," I said grimly.

"I'm not sure. He said they can read signatures or something like that from the barrier. I think the magic near our house just needs to be reinforced. There really isn't any other explanation for it."

I agreed with her, and we made our way over to where Cree and Holt were talking.

"You two ready?" Holt asked with his gaze on Xio.

She nodded and walked over to Thunder, and the air seemed to shift between them. Their little heart-to-heart appeared to change the general disdain I thought my sister and I felt for our captors.

Maybe I should pour my heart out to Cree so he's nicer to me.

I looked away from my sister, and my eyes landed on Cree, his face already set in a glower. He still hadn't let go of the fact I was able to draw blood and knock him on his ass this morning.

So, no to the heart-to-heart for today. Probably ever.

Definitely worth it.

"You're going to get permanent wrinkles if you maintain that look on your face for too much longer," I said with a smirk.

"You are aware that you scowl just as much as I do?" he asked, not relaxing a single muscle in his face.

I shrugged. "Got me there."

I was fully aware of my typical attitude.

I turned, giving him my back, my way of asking him to lift me onto Night.

He lifted me up and jumped up behind me quickly. He placed his arms on either side of me to grab the reins and paused for a second.

He brushed his finger to my cut, and I felt warm tingles spread from his finger to the gash on my arm and the other green and yellow bruises covering my skin. The incision knit itself together, and my bruises faded from sight. I opened my mouth to ask how he managed that, but he answered before I could get it out.

"Magic."

"Clearly," I muttered, debating what I should say next. "Thanks," I whispered as low as possible.

"What was that, Viper?" he purred in my ear.

"I didn't say anything."

I stared straight ahead and Cree chuckled in that knowing way he always did, and we set out to cover as much land as possible.

Chapter 12

Xio

We were back in the thick of the forest. While the land seemed less alive near the village, it was once again booming with life and color.

I looked ahead to see a faint line of mountains peeking over the tree line. I'd always been infatuated with the mountains. We didn't live close enough to visit them in Zuma, but on a really clear day, I could see a faint outline in the distance and always wondered what they would be like.

The sky was painted orange and pink while the sun began to set behind the clouds. If I had any artistic ability, this would be a scene I would want to paint. I was reminded that I still sat on a horse with Holt when he started to pull Thunder's reins to slow down.

"We'll be in the mountains tomorrow, maybe the day after," he said before trailing off the path behind a line of trees.

There was a small area big enough for us to camp in, but there was not the ample open space we had for the last couple of nights.

Our tents would have to be directly next to each other, with the fire a few strides from them, but it would work. Holt jumped down and helped me to the ground, I grabbed my bag strapped on Thunder's side and went over to set up me and Camila's tent.

Holt grabbed my arm, and I whirled around to see him holding his other arm parallel to the ground while lightning gathered around his fingers. He cleared out some of the plants around us, widening the area in just a few seconds.

"For training in the morning, and so Cree doesn't complain about your sister's snoring," he explained.

I chuckled while walking into the now wider space to set up our tent. My sister and Cree were arguing, per usual.

I heard her say something about the fact that she can't help touching him when they are riding for such long hours. He responded with something about the fact she just needs a stronger core to keep her sitting straight as they made it closer to where I stood.

"My core is plenty strong!" she said, stomping her foot and coming to meet me.

"Another enjoyable trip, I take it?" I asked her.

I couldn't help laughing while digging the stakes into the ground and she huffed and crossed her arms.

"I don't know how he has any friends. He's such an asshole," she responded before I felt another body approaching us.

"He doesn't have any friends other than me."

Holt's voice came from behind us and he placed the bag Camila forgot to grab off Night while she and Cree were arguing.

"Well, I can certainly see why," she mumbled, grabbing the bag and the other stakes for our tent.

"Most people are scared of him. He's not used to people having the guts to argue with him about anything," Holt murmured.

His large form loomed over me while I was crouched down, finishing with the stake I pushed into the ground. The setting sun was lit behind him, casting his face in shadows and a halo of gold around him. He offered his hand to help me up, and I accepted.

"Scared?" I asked.

Yes, he was intimidating, but I don't see why any other Fae would be scared of him.

"They don't understand his power. Nobody knows what God it comes from though some people guess it's from some demon of the underworld due to its darkness. My mother disagreed but couldn't help him figure out who he was."

"His parents don't know?" I asked.

I suddenly realized Holt had discussed his mother and father, but I hadn't heard Cree reference his.

"He doesn't..." he trailed off when Cree came striding over with the rest of the supplies for their tent.

I looked to Holt to see if he would finish his thought, but he just turned around and went to help Cree with their tent.

We both found a comfort with each other that I couldn't describe over the last few days. I found myself telling him stories of the things my sister and I got up to in Zuma, and he shared some of the stories of him and Cree while we rode throughout the day.

My personal favorite was one of them as children practicing their magic. They were in the throne room alone, and Cree had just figured out how to manifest his shadows into wings. Holt knew he should have the ability to shift into an eagle like his father and told Cree that if he was high up enough, his magic should save him, and the shift should happen without him having to think about it.

Cree took the opportunity to test the strength of his wings, as he'd never tried to carry anyone with him. He managed to get up high into the vaulted ceilings with Holt in his arms and dropped him. Holt was not correct about his magic saving him and crashed into his mother's favorite vase, breaking his arm in the process.

He said his mother came running the moment he fell. She pulled both of them by their pointed ears into the kitchens and made them scrub the floors until the morning. I asked about his arm, and he said she put him in a sling and didn't heal it until she returned for them in the morning, and he never broke another one of her vases again.

Imagining these two warrior Fae as small children being scolded had me laughing so hard that I almost fell off the horse.

I told him about the man I had killed when we escaped Zuma.

The shock of the situation we found ourselves in after it happened dampened some of the dread I felt around it, but it was still there.

He listened to my concerns about taking a life, and he told me about the first Fae he killed.

He explained that no matter the situation, my feelings around it weren't wrong.

That if there comes a time when killing didn't take at least some emotional toll on me, then I should be worried. I protected myself, and he agreed it had to be done.

He was right, and that did make me feel better. I couldn't change what happened, but I could be sure it didn't make me a monster.

Neither of us understood why we felt comfortable enough to share these stories, but I had to admit it felt nice to find comfort in someone other than just my sister. I had a feeling he felt the same about me.

I imagined being royalty came with a certain amount of isolation. I may not have been royalty, but my sister and I had always felt isolated in our village.

To be fair, it was every man for themselves, so I was sure most people felt like that. But with us lacking the memories of the first half of our lives, we didn't really feel like we belonged anywhere. I tried to keep positive, but the thought that I honestly didn't know who I was made my chest ache every now and then.

"Let's go get some wood for the fire," I told Camila as she stepped out of the tent, and we tracked deeper into the dense woods.

The forest was stunning this time of day. The warm colors of the sky peeked through the tree limbs creating a beauty beyond what the trees themselves held.

I picked up some fallen branches, but the ones small enough to use for the fire wouldn't be sufficient for the night.

"There looks to be some more over there," Camila said as she pointed towards a broad tree to our left.

We rounded the tree, and I noticed a series of dark stone structures ahead of me.

There hadn't been much other than trees, plants, and flowers on the journey so far, so the stone stuck out significantly.

The closer we got, the harder the ground beneath me became. The stones weren't rough-hewn but smooth as I ran my fingers across them. I felt a dip and realized there were symbols etched into the first structure.

These were ancient monoliths, and they appeared to be as old as the land itself.

I brushed my hand across it, releasing the dirt caked in some of the etchings. Camila saw what I was doing and followed suit on the second and third pillars.

THE SUN, THE STORM, & THE SHADOWS

It looked like some sort of story, with small symbols illustrating each line. We got the last of the dirt off, and I read it aloud, trailing my finger from one side of the stone to the other.

"The quiet was loud, and the waters ran deep, but still, there were no creatures to keep.

The Heart of Sky separated the sky from the earth, and here is where Maya was birthed.

The Heart of Sky now had the Heart of Earth, and the two were separated by the Great Ceiba's girth.

Its roots gaped the earth, and its branches shot high, then plants and animals began to cover the ground.

Next, the humans were made, but weak, they were found.

The sky took pity on the small human men and decided to create something stronger.

The Fae were made with great power and the ability to live longer.

The Gods were now pleased but thought the world seemed too dark, so the twins were made to cast out light.

One lit the day, and one lit the night."

"That's beautiful," Camila whispered as we stood stunned by the magnificence in the rock.

The images that accompanied each line of the story were astonishing, such simple use of lines, but the pictures they created were unlike anything I'd ever seen.

The Great Ceiba tree's roots ran deep, and the branches spread wide. Nine twisting roots and thirteen strong branches.

We heard footsteps approaching and whirled around with the tree limbs we gathered raised.

"What are you two doing out here?" Cree asked with his arms crossed across his chest.

"We were getting firewood and came across this," I explained, pointing towards the stones.

"Origin of Maya," he explained shortly, "get back to the site. We need that fire."

Camila rolled her eyes and brushed past him quickly. He waited for us to pass before he trailed behind us back to the site.

As much as I was ready to get away, I couldn't deny this land was beautiful. When we did escape, maybe we could find somewhere here to stay.

Training this morning was highly intense. The clearing Holt created was just big enough for two of us to train at a time, so Camila and Cree sat quietly near the diffused fire while Holt and I battled.

Like before, I knew he was holding back, but I tried not to think about that too much while giving the fight every ounce of strength I had. Sweat dripped down my nose and caught in the curve of my lip, and the salty taste seeped between the seam of my lips.

I used the back of my hand to wipe it off and charged at Holt with the last of my strength, he quickly sidestepped, and I found myself falling face-first into a deep hole in the ground covered in mud.

I jumped up from the ground and found my entire face and arms covered in the sticky substance. Thankfully I still held onto my sword as I fell, so one of my hands was a little less muddy.

I used it to rub the mess out of my eyes and found Holt, Cree, and Camila dying of laughter.

"This is not funny!" I shouted.

This was not how I planned on ending the training, but I started storming off toward our tent. Holt lifted his hands, making to bring another storm cloud over my head to wash away the muck, but I quickly caught on.

"Don't you dare!"

He brought his hands back down, and we stared at each other, trying to figure out my other option for getting clean. I remembered hearing the sound of water not too far away yesterday.

"There was a river a little ways back. I'll go use that. This is going to take more than a little rain to clean," I said, grabbing the blanket out of the tent to dry off after I bathed.

"You're not going alone," Holt stated.

I turned to find him pulling out his ax and strapping it to his back. The sound of Cree and Camila starting to engage in their training came from beyond the tents.

"Absolutely not. There is no world where you're going to see me naked," I said before storming off.

The sounds of footsteps followed me, and I spun around to find Holt directly behind me.

"Did I not speak clearly?"

I really needed to calm down, but the mixture of embarrassment and rage still flowed through my veins.

"It's not safe out here to be alone. I'll turn my back until you're clothed again."

He stepped around me to lead the way, but I darted in front of him. I certainly didn't need to be following him. I was perfectly capable of making my way to the river.

I followed the sound of the water until I found the sparkling liquid. What I thought was a river was yet another waterfall and pond.

This actually made it easier for a bath without worrying about the current sweeping me away and sighed in relief.

I made it to the water's edge and dipped my fingers in, glad to feel the water was warm. I used a leather strap to tie my hair out of my face and turned to find Holt with his arms crossed, staring down at me.

"Can you turn around, please?" I said, the anger in my body waning a little bit at the thought of being able to take a nice warm bath.

Holt turned around, and I found a boulder to sit on while I removed my shoes.

"Sorry about that," Holt said, still facing away from me, "I didn't realize all that mud was behind me."

"I was too caught up in trying to beat you that I didn't see it either," I laughed.

Now that I was here, the situation was a little humorous.

"You did charge me like an angry animal," Holt responded, chuckling as well.

I was glad that we fell back into comfort so quickly. Having to be angry with him all day on our ride wasn't how I would have chosen to spend the day.

I finished taking off my pants and shirt until I was just in my underwear. I laid my clothes on the rock next to my shoes and bent down to slide myself out of my underwear.

I didn't see the vine wrapped around the bottom of the rock and stumbled and fell once again. I let out a small screech, and by the time I hit the ground, Holt was already at my side, trying to help me up.

He picked me up by my shoulders and set me on my feet, the places his skin met mine tingled like a thousand tiny fires.

My right shoulder stung slightly more than the other, which was odd. I turned my head to look at Holt, whose eyes assessed my body for injury. Once he found no injuries, the gaze became something else.

He slowly ran his eyes over my stomach and down the curve of my hips. I'd never been self-conscious about my body, but right now, his stare was so intense it made me want to cover and hide all the skin that was exposed.

Somehow I also relished the pleasure he seemed to find in it. His eyes trailed over to my right shoulder, where I felt the odd tingling, and he blinked a couple times. He traced the scar under his hand with his finger, and the prickling sensation increased.

"What is this?" he asked.

I wasn't sure how to explain it without getting into me and my sister's odd lack of memory.

"I've had it for a long time," I responded, "why?"

"There's magic within it. I recognize the signature it's giving off as another Descendant. You really don't know how you ended up with this?"

"No, me and Camila both have one. It's always just seemed like an odd scar to me. It never gave any impression that it was magical," I whispered while the warmth intensified as he placed his entire palm on it and closed his eyes.

"It's a binding spell. I think I can break it. I have no idea why a human would have a binding, but there has to be some explanation."

I turned over his suggestion in my head. A binding spell? To bind what? Would this finally give me the answers I've always hoped I'd find?

"Do it," I said quickly before I had the chance to change my mind.

He nodded as he placed both his hands over the scar, and his face tightened with concentration.

It started to burn with the force of the sun, and as fast as that feeling came, it was replaced with what I could only explain as pure energy extending from my shoulder down into my toes and up into my head.

The mud on my face fizzled and disappeared, and the leather strap in my hair snapped, causing the curls to fall back down around my face. The energy gathered in my eyes, and everything became dark.

I doubled over, and Holt caught me before I hit the ground for the third time today. I opened my eyes with my face pointed towards the earth, and light poured out, casting two bright spots in front of me.

I brought my hands close to my face while a mixture of fire and light twisted around my fingers and down my arms. I stood up quickly, worried that I would burn Holt. But he just continued staring at me, trying to decipher what was happening.

The little clothing I had on shriveled and fell to a pile of ash around me. His mouth dropped open, and his eyes widened as he seemed to realize what the binding was holding in.

The energy began dissipating and soaking into my skin while my eyes dimmed, and I appeared as I did before he removed the binding. I looked down to realize I was completely naked and grabbed the blanket to wrap around my chest and body.

"It's not possible," he said.

I was at a loss for words, still unsure of what I had just experienced.

"It's not possible," he repeated while he walked to the edge of the water, gathered a bit into his hands, and splashed his face.

"What's not possible?" I asked.

He just looked at me with wide gray eyes and splashed more water into his face. Anxiety started to spread through every crevice of my body.

What did he do to me? What about Camila, would removing her binding have the same effect on her?

"Holt," I said, and he finally stood and looked into my golden eyes.

His wings tore through his shirt, splitting it in half as he shot us into the sky. My heart fell into my stomach as he soared over the trees. The wind blew in my face, and I looked up at him, hoping for some answers, but none came.

We were only in the air for a few moments when he glided into our camp.

Cree saw the urgency on his face, quickly pushed Camila behind him, and got his weapons ready for the fight he thought was coming for us.

Holt set me down, and Camila and Cree were both yelling at us, asking what was happening. But we both continued staring at each other, still at a loss for words.

Holt broke the stare and looked at Camila, who was still screaming at the two of us. He let out a deep breath and opened his mouth to say six words that would change the course of my life forever.

"They are the Sun Queen's daughters."

His eyes were still wide as he looked between my sister and me waiting for us to say something.

"Bullshit," Camila said, coming to hold my hand.

She must have thought Holt was losing his mind, but when her eyes met mine, she seemed to see some difference in my face.

"Your eyes are glowing," she whispered.

I gulped and nodded, wrapping the blanket tightly around my chest like a dress.

I tried to replicate the feeling of the power I felt by the pond, but all I could manage was small flames extending from each of my fingertips. Camila jumped back, her eyes lit with trepidation. She looked over to Holt, expecting an explanation, but he was just as shocked as I was.

Cree stepped up to me, and shadow unfurled from his fingers, his power linking with mine. The shadows wrapped themselves around the flames before extinguishing them completely.

"It's true. The power is as strong as Holt's and mine. I can feel the signature all around you now," Cree said.

"That's how you made it through the barrier. You were never human," Holt responded, staring blankly. That comment had me moving my hair from beside my face and trailing my fingers up to my ears.

I let out a gasp as my ears felt longer and placed my middle finger on their pointed tips. I looked over to my sister, whose face lacked all blood as she touched her own round ears.

"Someone needs to explain what the fuck happened at that river," she demanded.

"It was actually a pond," I said as if that was the most crucial fact right now.

"Take your shirt off," Holt said to Camila, stepping towards her.

She stepped back away from him, confused by the suggestion he was making. Cree took a step between her and Holt with a look of jealousy, which was something I didn't quite understand.

"Do it," I told her, and she tilted her head to the side in confusion but started to remove her top.

She sat in front of us in her undershirt, the fabric sticking to her with the sweat she obtained in her training with Cree. Holt went to stand behind her, and Cree stood to his side, looking at the scar I told Holt she had.

"Holy shit," Cree muttered.

"Um..." Camila murmured with confusion.

Holt placed his hand over the scar, and I could see Camila's eyes widen as it began to tingle. Without warning, Holt went to break the binding, and I grabbed my sister's hand.

She threw her head back as the power ran through her. The streaks of gold in her hair lit up bright as she doubled over, just as I did.

Still holding her hand, I didn't move fast enough to catch her, but Cree quickly shifted and fell to the ground breaking her fall.

He twisted her in his arms while she lay her head on his chest, working through the feeling of the magic pushing through her body. Her fingers started to produce flame and light, and she pulled them away from Cree, not before burning his shirt.

I noticed what was about to happen and grabbed the blanket resting on the log near the campfire. Her clothes began to wither from her slender form, and the energy calmed.

I threw the blanket onto her while she blinked quickly and jumped out of Cree's arms.

We faced each other taking in the differences in each other. Camila was beautiful before, but somehow all of her features seemed brighter. She swiped the hair from her face showing her newly pointed ears.

Our breaths came heavy, and we turned back to the males. Cree still sat in the dirt while Holt looked at me like he was seeing me for the first time. Cree got himself off the ground, and they both came to stand before us.

"How do you know the Sun Queen is our mother?" I asked.

"Your power, it's identical to hers. Only Descendants have the kind of power you do. The fire and light are from Kinich," Cree explained.

"The Sun Queen was very protective of her family. My parents knew she had children, but no one else knew who they were or their names. When we got word that everyone in the Sun Palace was murdered, we assumed her children died as well," Holt said, his eyes softening as he realized he was telling us that our entire family was dead.

"We were wrong," Cree whispered.

Chapter 13

Camila

The shock of what happened hadn't fully set in yet.

The part of me that always wanted to know where I came from was relieved, but our memories still were missing.

All the information I had currently was that we were Faerie princesses, we had power, and...our family was dead. We sat silently around the fire, no one really knowing where to go from here.

I would be lying if I didn't have a fantasy of a lavish life. The social hierarchy in Zuma made it so that there were very few who lived comfortably.

Most of the population were poor or close to it. I'd stay up thinking of what I would do in the Lord's position. The changes I'd make, the clothes and jewelry I'd buy.

THE SUN, THE STORM, & THE SHADOWS

It appeared like part of that fantasy was coming true. Now, we were powerful royalty.

Sure, our kingdom was gone. Still, we weren't helpless humans any longer.

"So, I've been thinking," I started, "does this mean we're no longer prisoners?"

Cree and Holt still stared us with blank looks on their faces and I raised my eyebrows when neither of them responded.

"She has a point. We're royalty now," Xio said before she burst out laughing.

Never in my years had I ever thought there was a possibility we were princesses, let alone magical Faerie princesses. The ridiculousness in this thought made me chuckle, and my sister's laughter grew louder, causing me to follow suit.

We gripped each other's shoulders, barely able to get our breath down, and looked over to find the males still staring at us expressionless. That had us honestly in tears as we doubled over and fell out of the spots we were sitting in.

"We're princesses," Xio said.

"Yes, yes, we are, your majesty," I said, sitting up and mocking a bow at her as I held the blanket around my still-naked body.

We wiped the tears from our eyes, and I found my sister's face starting to turn into something far different than humor.

She began to sniffle as more tears tracked down her cheeks, her eyes turned sad, and she stared down into her lap.

I moved from where I was and wrapped my arms around my sister. The hurt of not having a mother had always been there for us, but to know that we would never know her hurt more.

That we would never be comforted by her, share a meal with her, or receive any wisdom from her had my chest tightening. I knew my sister was feeling the same way I was, and I rubbed her forehead, just as my mother had in the dream.

The onslaught of emotions took its toll on me, and I sighed deeply.

"How did you two not know who you were?" Holt asked.

We had never told them about how we lacked fifteen years' worth of memories or how we found ourselves in the home we ran from.

My sister shifted out of my arms and sat up, her eyes swollen with grief. I caught her gaze, asking permission to explain what had happened silently.

She nodded, and I held her hand tight, anchoring her, so she knew I was still there for her.

"Almost ten years ago, when I was fifteen and Xio was sixteen, we woke up in the human lands with no memory of how we got there or anything from before that day. When we woke up, we only knew that we were sisters and how old we were. We were laying in a bed in..." I started to feel embarrassment but swallowed it down. "A shack. It had one bedroom, a kitchen, and a living room with a fireplace. Once we got our bearings, we found the weapons wrapped in dark orange cloth on a table in the kitchen. Some part of us knew that we would need to learn to wield them. I guess our mother left that to protect us."

Cree got up when I mentioned the weapons and brought them over to us. He handed Xio's sword to Holt and started inspecting my daggers.

"We should have known. They're obviously from the Sun Court," Cree muttered, turning over my dagger in his hand. "I didn't look that hard at them when we took them off of them."

Cree reached for Xio's sword, and handed my daggers to Holt. Holt clicked them together, creating the double-sided weapon I loved so much. He ran his fingers down the vine design on the blade and looked over to Xio.

"These weapons are made to channel your magic, just as my ax channels my lightning," he said, grabbing Xio's sword and walking over to where she still sat, looking defeated.

He wiped a tear about to fall from her eye and tucked her hair behind her pointed ears. Holt offered his hand to help her up, and she gently placed her small hand in his.

Holt guided both her hands onto the hilt of her sword, and she gripped it firmly.

"The magic you felt earlier, try and push that from your fingers into your sword," he said gently.

Xio squeezed and pulled her face into concentration. She let out a breath of frustration, and Holt placed his hand on the small of her back.

"Remember how it made you feel. For me, it feels like raw static energy. I feel it just under my skin, and I just have to encourage it to rise."

He lifted his hand, and lightning started to dip between his fingers before he closed his hand into a fist and extinguished the sparks.

My sister looked up at him and nodded. She once again closed her eyes and concentrated.

This time her expression was more relaxed, and the corners of her mouth lifted slightly as she opened her now glowing eyes.

She looked down at her fingers as pure light seeped into the hilt of her sword. The golden embellishments on the blade lit, and her sword hummed. Holt placed one hand over the both of hers and guided the sword toward the fire.

"The sword should feel like an extension of you. Push the energy into the fire."

She stared down the tip of her sword, and the light shot out before falling in front of the fire.

Her shoulders sank, and she looked over at Holt, expecting more guidance.

"You won't master your magic in one day, but now that we know you have it, this definitely changes things," he mumbled.

He always looked at her with more warmth than you'd think a prisoner would receive.

Xio had always attracted male attention with her luscious curves, beautiful brown skin, and golden eyes, but the way he looked at her didn't feel lustful.

He looked at her like he was afraid she would run away at any moment, and he would do anything to stop that.

I turned to find Cree walking towards me with my daggers outstretched. He handed them to me, and I silently thanked him.

"I'm going to take a nap," Xio said.

The day's events had certainly drained us, and I didn't blame her one bit.

She moved to make her way to the tent, and she stumbled slightly. Holt offered his arm and helped walk her over to the tent to lie down.

I watched as he opened the flap to the tent and ensured she was comfortable before retiring to his own tent.

He, too, seemed a little drained. His forehead puckered as he appeared to turn over what happened in his mind. I looked down at my hands, savoring the familiar feeling of my daggers.

I eagerly tried to push the magic into them like my sister did but had no such luck. I stomped my foot in frustration, and Cree walked over to me.

His face wasn't fixed in the permanent scowl it usually was, and I took this opportunity to take in the softened features of his face.

While Holt could be described as classically beautiful, Cree could be described as ruggedly devastating.

His dark angular eyes were framed in thick black lashes. When he blinked, they nearly brushed the top of his high cheekbones. His tan skin was covered in those black tattoos, and he had his sleeves rolled up, showing his muscular forearms.

I hadn't noticed when we trained that he was also covered in scars, proof of a life full of danger and courage.

My eyes caught on a faint scar that ran from his temple down the front of his ear and stopped at his shoulder, the most extensive scar I could see on the exposed skin.

I wondered what might have caused that before he made it to me.

"You have to relax. If you get too frustrated, your magic won't cooperate," he said before walking away from me.

I looked over my shoulder, expecting him to be a few feet away by now, but he was directly behind me. His eyes were still soft as he wrapped his arms around mine and placed each of his large hands over top of mine.

"Take a deep breath," he said.

That suddenly felt impossible while caged in his hard body. I swallowed, tried to will my hormones into cooperating, and managed a jagged but deep breath as he brought his head down near mine.

"Now, just like Holt said, imagine how the magic felt earlier. While he feels electricity under his skin, I feel mine in my gut. It feels like a cool presence I can access at any time. Close your eyes and see where you feel your magic pooling."

I closed my eyes and tried to focus on my magic. His thumb idly rubbed mine, and I felt something in my gut, but I wasn't sure it was my magic.

I centered myself again and felt a warmth in my chest. It moved and flowed like a never-ending liquid.

"I feel it in my chest," I said quietly.

"Good. Now imagine that you're moving it from your chest into your fingers," he responded.

I imagined my body was a great body of water. I let down the dam around my chest and let the warm liquid run into my arms and down into my fingers.

I felt a tingling in my hands, and I opened my eyes to see flames beginning to gather in my palm. I jumped up with a smile as the flames shot into each blade on either side of my hands.

Cree let me go as I stepped forward to the fire and directed the magic straight into the existing flames.

They shot up high into the sky before settling back down, and I couldn't help but feel accomplished as my face was split by a smile.

I looked to Cree, who had his arms crossed, assessing me. His gaze didn't feel judgmental, but my smile softened, as my eyes were locked on his.

"This might be the longest period of time that you have been nice to me," I said jokingly to break the tight air around us.

He chuckled. "Let's just say I have a soft spot for broken things. Orphans and those going through an identity crisis invoke a little kindness in me."

I hadn't had time yet to process that Xio and I were officially orphans. Yes, we were adults who hadn't known any kind of parental love but putting a label on it had me plopping down onto the log behind me.

I watched the fire between Cree and me. The flames seemed so free and confident, like I always tried to be.

Right now, I felt neither free nor confident.

I had some idea of where I came from, but somehow having part of the story felt worse than not knowing anything.

Cree slowly walked over to where I sat.

His face said he was trying to decide whether to sit with me or let me stew in my emotions alone. He chose to sit with me, and we both stared at the flames in silence for what felt like forever until he spoke so quietly I almost didn't hear him.

"I'm an orphan, too."

I tried to read the expression on his face, but he was looking away from me, and I was again struck by his beauty.

"Well, at least I think I am. I don't know who I am either," he said, returning his gaze to the fire.

"Holt told Xio you've known each other your whole life. I assumed you grew up in the palace with him," I said.

His statement had starting to understand his general demeanor a little better, a demeanor so much like mine. Even if i wouldn't admit it.

"I did. When I was a baby, Holt's mother found me outside the throne room after a day they held court. She said I was holding a silver rattle and she heard the sound and followed it to find me wrapped in a black blanket by the door. Holt and I were about the same age. At least, that's what they assumed since they weren't sure when I was born. She took me in, and they treated me like I was their own son."

"You two do act as brothers would. It sometimes reminds me of Xio and I's relationship," I said.

He smiled his slightly unbalanced smile, one of the most genuine smiles I'd seen him make, and it had me returning his with one of my own.

"So I understand how you feel to a certain extent, the feeling out of place, having power you don't quite understand. Chara, Holt's mother, tried to help me the best she could by searching in all of our texts for something that mentioned any power similar to mine, but she could never find anything. Some people started to whisper that I must be the child of a demon and told the King I shouldn't be allowed in the castle. He didn't listen, but part of me always felt a little more out of place after that. I know they love me, but sometimes I wonder if they're scared of what I might be, too," he said as looked back into the forest surrounding us.

"I have these dreams," I said quietly, "they feel like memories, but everything is slightly out of focus. Just out of reach for me to piece together. I don't know what's real and what I'm making up. I sometimes drive myself mad trying to decipher any clue out of them, but I always just get a headache."

"That feels worse than knowing nothing," he responded, and I nodded because it was.

We seemed to understand each other better, and I wondered if maybe he wasn't as intolerable as I initially thought. I grabbed his hand and handed him the cup he was drinking from earlier. I went to grab mine from where I sat before and lifted it from across the fire.

"To being broken," I said.

The corner of his mouth lifted. "To being broken," he repeated, "but damn powerful."

I tossed the remaining liquid in my mouth, broken but powerful, an oxymoron if I ever heard one.

However that might be, it resonated with me deep in my soul.

We sat in comfortable silence until I quietly went to join my sister in sleep.

Chapter 14

Xio

I was determined for today to be better than yesterday.

While we finally knew where we came from, we still didn't know why our mother wiped our memories and abandoned us in Zuma with the humans.

I was grateful to be alive when the rest of my family didn't have that luxury, but I still wished I had some answers.

All I ever wanted was a quiet, safe, comfortable life for my sister and me. I didn't need riches or power.

Now, I had an abundance of both.

Holt mentioned that the Sun Palace treasury was sealed when they came to investigate the tragedy that came to my home.

That everything, including the palace, was mine and Camila's.

I didn't want it, but where was I supposed to go?

We were no longer human. Never really were. We wouldn't return to Zuma. It wouldn't seem right to try and run and hide in some corner of Maya while the lands are dying.

No matter how I sliced it, I was royalty, and the palace was mine. Begrudgingly.

I fixed my face into a mask of determination while Holt came to sit next to me. We were about to start our traveling for the day. With everything that happened, one small joy I could take was seeing the mountains today.

I always wanted to see them. Something about them seemed to call to me.

Now I knew why.

"I think we should stop at the Sun Palace. We may be able to find some answers about what happened," Holt said, "it's in the direction we're riding. We'll make it there before sundown today. We can camp near there for the night."

The thought of going to the place where I was born and spent the first half of my life terrified me, but also sent excitement running through me. Being there could spark some of our memories.

"If it doesn't set us back," I said, still feeling a little guilty for already adding time to his trip.

"It won't. It's on our way. We would have had to camp near it. We will still make it to Storm palace in a little over a week," he insisted.

He wasn't the type to say something and not mean it, so I knew he wasn't lying. I still wanted the reassurance, remembering the reason our paths even crossed. I smiled and went to join my sister and let her know what Holt said.

"Are you serious? That could be enough to jog our memories!" she said with a little more hope than she usually showed.

I started to worry that Camila would be crushed if we made it to the palace and nothing happened. She really didn't deserve to have any more bad luck.

Neither of us did.

"Just, don't get your hopes up too high. We really don't know what we're walking into," I reasoned.

"Oh, come on, I'm the glass-half-empty sister. Don't you go switching up on me now," she said, knocking my shoulder and chuckling.

I typically tried to see the shinier side of things, but something this big had things looking a little less...shiny.

"I know, I know. I think I was partly trying to convince myself. I don't really know how to feel about all of this. This isn't the life I imagined for myself," I said as I pulled my hands down over my face and rested them on my temples.

"Hey," Camila said, grabbing my hands from my face and looking me in the eyes. "I know it's not. But we will do this together, just like everything else," she finished and rested her forehead against mine.

"Together. Always." I whispered back to her.

A cough sounded beside us, pulling us out of our sisterly moment. Cree shifted on his feet, and Holt looked away from us quickly.

Camila tilted her head to the side. "Did you two need something?"

"Oh, no. We were just waiting..." Holt said, giving off more awkwardness than I'd ever seen him display.

"Moments over. We're ready to go," I stated and moved to join them near the horses.

"If you say so, Prisoner," Holt responded.

"It's Princess to you," I said, lifting my chin in a way I imagine royalty would. I felt the ground move away from my feet as I landed on top of Thunder. Holt sat behind me, cradling me in his arms as he took control of Thunder.

I felt the heat of his face next to mine, and his breath against my ear. "Are you ready, Princess?"

My lips parted, a moan almost escaping me as warmth spread from the point of contact down into my core. I tilted towards him, and my eyes found his mouth closer to mine than it should have been. I slowly tracked my eyes up from his lips, past his perfectly straight nose, and into the storm brewing in his eyes.

Our gaze held, neither of us wanting to look away when I heard a scream of victory coming from beside us. I blinked out of his trance to see my sister in Night's saddle while Cree stared at her with wide eyes.

"I told you I could do it! In your smug little face!" she hollered, throwing her hands in the air as flames shot from her fingers, scorching the branches above her, and causing Night to toss her from his back while he was startled.

"Oh shit," she yelped before falling backward.

Cree caught her before she hit the ground, and she peered up at him bashfully.

"That was an accident. Sorry Night!" she yelled to the inky stallion.

He grunted at her and stomped his hoof to the ground. He may need more than an apology from her.

Cree used his shadows to extinguish the flames in the tree above them, leaving the branches dark and leafless.

"But I did it! I'm so freaking strong now," she said, jumping out of Cree's arms and back onto Night.

Camila rubbed the side of his neck and placed a kiss on his head, and he whinnied his forgiveness. Cree laughed at my sister and mounted behind her.

Seems like those two might be crossing over from disdain into something less—

My thought was cut off when Cree pushed Night into a gallop catching my sister off guard. She nearly fell off the horse, and Cree smirked as they shot out of sight.

We were doing this. We were on our way to the place that held half of my story, where my mother and father lived until their death, where my sister and I learned to walk and talk.

I let out a deep breath as we followed behind Cree and Camila.

While just a few hours' ride in reality, the journey to the Sun Palace felt like it took forever. Also, somehow simultaneously too fast.

All of my emotions felt at odds with each other, which was a theme since we found our way into Maya.

I was terrified but excited.

Hopeful, yet discouraged.

My heart was both full of love and empty with grief.

We started to slow down and veer off the path we were following and onto a path that could have been missed if you didn't know where to look.

The trees and foliage were growing into the trail, and it felt darker than where we were previously as I looked up to find no blue sky. The trees were all connected here, creating the illusion of one big tree. We stopped suddenly, and Holt hopped down, standing in front of two fallen trees crossing the path.

They were huge, and I wondered what could have taken them down. Unease set in as I realized we might have to find another way. Holt reached his hand out and shot hot bolts of lightning at them, and they turned to ash.

Ah, yes, magic.

I still hadn't grown used to the ability. The smoke and ash cleared, and the light poured in through the exit the trees were blocking.

Holt jumped back onto Thunder, and we slowly started to trot out of the trees. We found ourselves on top of a hill, the sun shining on us as Night came up beside us out of the trees. I gasped at the sight in front of us.

This was the Sun Palace.

Our home.

A tear escaped my eye as I took in my surroundings. I soon realized we weren't on a hill but on the side of a mountain.

A bridge of stone stretched across to the mountain adjacent to us. The palace looked like it was abandoned for the last decade, but that didn't change the majestic quality of the structure.

It was made of white stone, built directly into the side of the mountain, with long grass surrounding its base. The grass swayed in the wind as I tracked my eyes from one end of the palace to the other.

Nestled in the middle was a triangular formation. The base was broad, and the steps grew increasingly narrow until they reached the golden door. The illusion of steps continued until they came to a gold-tipped point far above the door.

The rest of the palace extended off the formation, though the rest didn't mirror the same shape. The tower-like extensions were made of the same white stone, each one shooting higher than the one in front of it.

Windows carved into the stone allowed anyone inside to look out and see the beauty of the mountains around it.

There were homes on the surrounding mountains and down in the valley where the subjects of Sun Court must have lived before moving over to Storm Court.

I forgot I wasn't alone for a moment and found my sister with the same look of wonder I was sure mirrored my face.

"This is our home," she said gently, as she reached for my hand.

I smiled and looked back across the mountain. "Home."

While still reluctant about our new situation, I found myself really liking the sound of that.

Holt brought us to the edge of the bridge and left us to inspect its integrity.

"It looks safe enough to cross, but maybe we should do it one at a time," he suggested, and I nodded a little too excitedly.

Cree went to cross first, and Holt stopped him.

"I'm going to do a perimeter check. It doesn't look like anyone has been here since…" he stopped, unsure if he should bring up the last known event here before entering. "Just to make sure it's safe."

Cree agreed, but before Camila and I could respond, a flash of light came from where Holt stood, and a great eagle burst from it.

He took to the sky, and I was taken back by his eagle form's sheer size and power.

He didn't mention that his wingspan stretched double the length of my body when he told us that he could shift into an eagle.

He let out a screech as he glided around the palace, flying lower to the structure. His surveying took a few minutes before he came and swooped down in front of us. Another big flash of white burst from him, and he stood in front of us again in his Fae form.

"Well damn," Camila muttered, staring at Holt with her eyebrows nearly touching her hair.

I felt the same.

"How'd your clothes stay on?" I asked.

He looked me up and down like he wanted to make a suggestive comment, but just shrugged. "Magic."

Something about the power Holt held made me feel things I didn't want to put a name to.

"It looks safe enough to me," he said confidently, mounting Thunder behind me.

"The four of us are Descendants from Gods. We're definitely safe," Camila said smugly.

She seemed to accept our newfound identity pretty quickly, and I let a nervous chuckle escape me. Holt placed his hand on my knee that I didn't realize I was shaking until the sudden contact stopped my movement.

"Ready?" he said gently, and I nodded.

I was as ready as I'd ever be.

The sound of my heart beating and hooves hitting the stone bridge was the last thing I heard before my life changed forever once again.

Chapter 15

Camila

We made it to the base of the steps and tied Thunder and Night to a post nearby.

It was hard for me to understand, but this place truly did feel like home.

Everything about it felt right.

The sun was beaming down where we stood, making the golden door glitter in the light.

Xio was fidgeting with her cloak, she always claimed to be worried about our future and not our past, but I knew it ate at her the same way it did me.

Seeing her anxious like this had me stepping into that hopeful position for her. We'd always been each other's other half, filling the areas the other lacked. I grabbed her hand and gave her a reassuring smile.

"Let's do this," I said with my chin raised to the palace.

She squeezed my hand tight before we stepped onto the first step. Tingles ran from my feet all the way up my body as I made contact with the hard white stone.

I looked over my shoulder to see Cree and Holt still standing at the base, unsure if they should follow us.

"Don't feel the need to protect us in the abandoned palace anymore?" I said with a smile.

"We just weren't sure..." Cree trailed off.

"Oh, come on, you know you're just as curious as we are," Xio said.

I was glad that some of her anxiety seemed to be slipping away as she joked with them.

The sound of their soft footsteps followed us as we made it to the tremendous golden entrance.

I placed my hand on the metal, and felt warmth under my skin. The door opened immediately at my touch, and I jumped back a step.

"Looks like the Sun Queen sealed it," Holt said while he stepped into the foyer.

"What do you mean seal?" I asked.

"With a warding spell, only allowing her kin or Fae she trusted to enter. She was known to be a powerful spell caster. Not everyone has a knack for it. It's how she bound you," he responded while we made our way into the room in front of us.

There was a great mural on the wall. It depicted a winged jaguar and eagle flying together between the sun and the moon. At first glance, it looked like they were locked in battle, but the longer you gazed, you realized there was no malice written in their features. The paint was beginning to chip at the edges, but it didn't make the image any less beautiful. It gave it a ruggedness that I thought really complimented the art.

A memory of something Holt said previously dawned on me.

"You said our mother could shift into a jaguar?" I asked, looking over to my sister, the signs of realization also shifting over her features.

"Yes, I think this is a depiction of her and my father. The eagle, my father. The jaguar, your mother. The two sides of royalty that ruled Maya before the palace fell," Holt responded.

"She had wings?!" Xio shrieked.

"Yes, I said she could shift into a jaguar?" Holt said with confusion, "do jaguars not have wings in Zuma?"

"No, they're just big cats! I've never even seen one. I've just heard stories," Xio responded.

She turned back to run her fingers across the depiction of our mother. Her feathered wings were spotted just like her fur, they looked extremely powerful.

Her beast form was something of beauty. Terrifying, malicious, savage beauty.

My sister's focus shifted to the great eagle flying with our mother. I was led to believe that maybe she was thinking about this particular eagle's son as her face softened.

I noticed more than once now that something seemed to be going on with them. They were far more comfortable with each other than I was with Cree.

We had that moment after Holt removed our bindings, but we didn't speak at all on the way to the palace. I felt a little exposed and suspected he felt the same.

Neither of us were people that wore our hearts on our sleeves.

A flash of light caught my attention as something whirled around the corner of the mural and down the hallway to its left. Holt and Cree had their weapons out in seconds as they went to find out what the source of the light was.

We followed behind them. I gathered some fire in my hands without realizing I was doing it and turned the corner to find Holt and Cree staring up at something with shock drawn across their features.

"What are you guys looking at?" I asked as I followed their eye line.

My mouth, too, dropped open as I looked at the sizable tree nestled in the middle of an expansive courtyard. The tree had purple-gray bark, and blue blossoms sprouted out from every branch. It was tall and wide, taking up most of the courtyard that was settled in the prism-like formation we entered. But the thing that took my breath away was the sparkling figures dancing around the blossoms.

"Alux," Xio whispered as she came to stand beside me.

I looked at her with a crease between my brows.

"Holt said that they were magical sprites that guide fate. They live in ceiba trees. I saw some before we made it to the village, but I thought I was hallucinating."

I thought back to when we were in the Cursed Forest. I swore the clearing we exited out of sparkled when I spotted it, and again when we were officially in Maya. I assumed I was just dehydrated and hungry.

"I saw them, too," I whispered to her.

"They've been guiding you since you got into Maya," Holt said, a line of confusion running between his brow as well.

Cree continued staring at the tree. He didn't seem to believe what he was seeing either.

The sparkles began to grow, they almost appeared to be little people with wings, but they were so bright it was hard to see any defining lines. They began to float towards us, and I gasped a breath.

I had to stop myself from swatting them away from me on reflex. Holt said they guide fate, but I wasn't sure about them yet.

They swirled around Xio and me so fast that our hair lifted. I heard faint whispers, "they're here," "they've finally returned," and "they look just like her," before floating away from us and down a covered walkway that led to a door I assumed went into the palace.

They floated at the door, beckoning us to follow them, and I looked to my sister to see if she wanted to follow. She took a step forward, and the rest of us followed suit.

We made it to the door, and Xio placed her hand on it as I had. The door opened, and we walked through.

The Alux seemed a little too excited and kept flying off too fast for us to follow, but they came back to us giggling each time.

We wound down hallways, passing doors both open and closed. I thought I saw the throne room a few doors before, but the Alux were still moving too fast for us to do any kind of exploring. I followed until we made it to another pair of golden doors. I felt Xio grab my hand as we walked up to the doors the Alux led us to.

"Together," I whispered, and we pushed through the doors. They slammed behind us, not allowing Holt or Cree to follow.

"Are you okay?" Holt yelled through the door.

"We're fine. It's just an office. I'm not sure why they led us here," Xio responded quickly.

We started to walk around when something on a table near the window began to glisten. My sister and I both felt drawn to it as we walked over to the source of the light.

It was a beautiful crystal orb with flames swirling within it.

I reached to touch my finger to it while Xio's finger found its way next to mine. We both touched the orb before the breath was knocked from us, and everything went black.

I heard the sounds of mayhem before I peeled my eyes open to find my sister on the ground next to me.

I shook her shoulder, and she shot up.

We both took in our surroundings. The Alux were zooming around the room while the sound of a battle came from beyond the doors.

I turned to find a female holding two girls in her arms while the sound of crying escaped them. The two girls had their heads buried in the female's chest, and her head sat on top of the girl to the left.

She lifted her chin, and all of the blood left my head.

It was our mother.

Those two crying little girls were us.

How did I not realize? They looked just like us, just ten years younger.

This was the memory of the last time we were in this room. It was an odd sensation being in this memory. I could feel the feelings the younger me felt at the time. I fell to my knees, inspecting the female I now knew was my mother.

I knew she couldn't see us, but I reached out my hand to touch her face, and my hand slipped right through her. I found Xio on her knees beside me, staring at her.

Her skin was closer to the shade of mine, a few shades lighter than Xio's. Her brown hair, streaked in gold, fell in waves down past her shoulders—my hair. She wore a dark orange dress that brought out the golden color of her eyes—Xio's eyes.

She rubbed the top of our heads. "I will never leave you. I will always be right here," tapping on both of our chests above our hearts.

"Right now, I need to get you out of here. You don't understand, but you are the key to defeating a great evil that is coming for our land. The prophecy spoke of it. She's too powerful, the wards will only last but so long against her," she murmured, placing a kiss on each of our foreheads.

"Mamá, no, we will fight with you!" I shrieked at her.

Even then, I was a risk taker, it seemed.

"My dear Mila, not even I can defeat the evil coming. But one day, you two will," she said, looking at Xio and me. "Today is not that day," she finished with a small smile.

A crash sounded nearby. Whoever was coming for us was getting closer. She looked over to a bookcase on the back wall and shook her head.

"I'm going to bind your magic and place you in the human lands," our mother muttered.

"No, we won't survive without you!" Xio cried, tears sliding down her already wet cheeks.

"You will. You two are far stronger than you know. She won't come for you there," she said while she turned the both of us around and placed her hands on our shoulders.

"Who, Mamá?" I questioned.

She took a deep breath and brought us into another hug.

"I thought I had more time. I could never see when she would come. Just what would happen after she did," she took a deep breath. "In ten years, you will have to fulfill the prophecy. You and your sister are the keys," she hesitated, looking off into the distance again.

"I'm going to have to take your memories. You'll just find your way back here too soon. Your father's stubbornness runs true in both of you," she huffed a laugh at the memory of our stubborn father.

"I don't want to forget you," I whispered.

She wiped the tears from our cheeks and smiled warmly. "I wish it was avoidable, but Maya's fate depends on it."

She placed one hand on the side of each of our faces.

"No star shines as bright as you. My love for you two has no bounds, whether I'm with you or not. Whether I am still in this world or not."

I gulped down a sob that tried to escape my throat.

"I love you, Mamá," Xio and I whispered simultaneously.

"I love you too, my little warriors. *Inhala exhala*," she whispered to the both of us.

We both listened to her directions and loosed a deep breath. I placed my hand in my sister's. I was terrified, but at least I would have her with me.

We would defeat whatever evil was coming for Maya if it was the last thing we did. She once again turned us around and placed her hands on our shoulders, I looked over to see her eyes bright and the streaks in her hair glowing.

I had never seen my mother cry before, but her eyes were puffy, and her cheeks were glistening.

Heat gathered where her hand sat on my shoulder before a burning sensation set in, and Xio and I passed out.

The Alux were still floating around the room, and she asked if they would guide our fates, now and when we returned. They buzzed around her, and all worked to lift us up in the air and out of the window.

My mother jumped out of the window behind us, shooting a blast of fire back into the office. Bright yellow light burst from her, and her jaguar let loose.

She let out a mighty roar before swooping back to the front of the palace.

She fought dark figures tooth and claw with such ferocity I was sure she would come out victorious until a figure in smoke appeared, and everything went dark.

We hit the floor hard, the magic that kept Cree and Holt out dissipated, and the doors opened. The memory now shared with us, the magic no longer needed to seal them out.

They stormed into the room with weapons raised and their powers sliding over their skin as they surveyed the room for any signs of an attacker. Once they were sure everyone was safe, they ran over and helped us up. I couldn't stop the tears from rolling down my face.

We finally had some of the answers we'd been looking for. I fell into my sister's arms, and we held each other for a long moment.

My heart was broken by the loss of my mother, but there was also warmth in my chest.

"She loved us," I whispered to Xio.

"She did," she answered, squeezing me tighter.

The puzzle in my mind still wasn't clear, but the edges of the pieces started to fit together. For the first time in ten years, I truly had hope that one day the parts would become one.

Chapter 16

Xio

We were still sitting in the office around the table staring at the orb.

The fire no longer moved, the flames stood frozen within the glass. I tried to touch it again to get another look at my mother, but the magic within it was gone.

I turned over every feature of my mother in my mind, memorizing the details that were her beautiful face.

My sister and I were staring at each other, recognizing how much we looked like her. Camila had her golden-streaked hair, and I had her bright golden eyes.

It felt so good to finally put a face to her, though I would never see it again.

We filled Cree and Holt in on what we saw, and they questioned every minor detail until I was sure the memory was just as much theirs as ours.

"You can't remember any detail of the figure that came for your mother?" Cree asked.

"No, it was just dark and smoke. We couldn't see anything. Our mother did say 'she,' so I'm guessing it was a female, but that's all we know," I responded.

"I don't know who it could be. Our people have been living in peace for so long now. Who would do something like this?" Holt said, rubbing his temple the same way I did when calculating.

"Let's look around. Maybe we'll find something helpful," Camila suggested.

Even though the look in her eyes told me she wanted to see if anything else jogged our memory.

We left the office, and the Alux reappeared in the hallway, directing us to follow them again. We followed them in the opposite direction we came in.

The palace was breathtaking.

The white stone felt like it stretched on forever in every direction. Our mother definitely had an affinity for gold. Everything seemed to be embellished in it.

There were more murals throughout, small ones of the forest and the animals. We passed one that displayed the Gods near what looked like a banquet hall.

Kinich, the God of the Sun, was pictured in orange cloth. It wrapped around his strong shoulder and waist, held together by a gold chain. He had dark tan skin and golden eyes, and his wavy golden hair fell past his shoulders. He held light in one hand and flame in the other with a look of determination on his face.

Chaac, the God of Rain, of which Holt was a Descendant, stood next to him. He had ebony skin and cropped silver hair that seemed to move in waves extending from the center of his head. He, too, wore a cloth garment that was a deep navy blue with silver embellishments.

His body much resembled Holt's, and I wondered what he might look like in that type of garment.

Moving on from that thought.

On the other side of him stood a female with pale skin and long dark hair that hung like a curtain down to her waist. She was looking over at Kinich with admiration in her eyes. She wore what looked like a black dress, but when I shifted to get a better view, it was a very deep purple. Two panels of fabric covered her chest, and connected into one panel below her hips where a thin black rope hung across. She was slender, but it was evident that she was also in excellent shape judging from the lines of muscles on her arms and legs.

"Who is that?" I asked Holt.

"That's Ixchel, the Goddess of the Moon. She was said to be the most beautiful and kind of all the Gods," he explained.

She certainly looked it.

Something about her made me want to sit next to her and listen to anything she might have to say.

"Why is she looking at Kinich like that?" Camila asked.

"Some of our histories say that they loved each other. Others say the sun and the moon couldn't exist in the same space," Cree explained, "no one really knows if they were together before Itzamna murdered them."

I looked up above the three figures to see a much larger man who seemed to be a combination of all the other Gods' features.

He had brown skin, but his hair was a combination of silver, gold, and black. With eyes that seemed to be every color but also absent of color. He wore a crisp white garment as he looked down on the other Gods. He didn't look malicious, but he looked damn powerful.

"Why did he murder them?" I asked.

They looked like they lived in such harmony in this picture that it was hard to understand how he could grow to act in such a way.

"The histories aren't clear on that either," Holt started, "some say that he grew jealous of the other Gods taking over his own creation. He was here when our world was just water and lacked people or sound. He created the land and the other Gods to help him rule and bring balance to Maya. They each had powers and roles to play to ensure we thrived. But the other Gods started to be worshiped more than him. He didn't have any direct Descendants as he technically created us all."

I listened intently. Something in the back of my head told me I knew this already, but I couldn't access the knowledge, so I nodded my encouragement to continue.

"The humans were separated once the Fae were created because their consciences weren't strong enough to wrap their minds around the Gods and their power. They were given the human lands, Zuma, as you know them. The Gods still watched over them, but from afar, not wanting to interfere and cause the humans to go mad."

"What does that mean?" Camila asked.

"The humans were created first, from the wood of the ground. They didn't have any power and died easily. The Gods came to visit them, and some of the human's sanity slipped away. They were unable to understand what the Gods were. They took pity on them and moved them away. The Fae were their second creation, made of corn. They made us stronger and faster and gave us power and magic. Each of them put their blood in a Fae, and that is where the line of Descendants started," he paused, looking back at the mural. "These were the main Gods, but there were other smaller ones that did some of their bidding, which we don't know much about as they too seem to be gone. However, these are the ones who started it all."

I tried to soak up all that information, but maybe spending ten years as a human had made my brain soft because I was still in slight disbelief.

A flash of light drew my attention away from the mural, and I followed the Alux to another room. Beside me, Camila stood at the door directly next to mine, where the Alux led her. We pushed open the doors to find what must be our bedchambers.

I stepped into mine with Holt, and she stepped into hers with Cree at her heels. Holt stepped around me and assessed the room. He found no danger and continued into the room, allowing me space to enter as well.

My bed was wide and covered in bright yellow and orange blankets. Like everything else in the palace, the bedposts were adorned with gold. A large window behind the bed let the sunlight in, and the rays fell directly onto the bed.

A faint memory of waking up to the sun's warmth every morning flashed across my mind but was gone before I could grab onto it.

I turned to find Holt inspecting what looked like a vanity. He had a comb in his hand and pulled a strand of hair from it. It was my hair, shorter, but there was no denying the curl pattern matched mine.

I met him where he stood and ran my finger across the vanity, creating a long line in the dust. The mirror was old, and the edges were starting to turn dark, but its reflection stunned me.

Holt and I stood close to each other. He looked at me like I was a Goddess, and some part of me was.

His eyes were tracking up and down my body as I took in the place where my mother used to do my hair.

Another piece of a memory flashed in my mind, a much smaller me smiling up at her while she pinned my hair back with golden butterfly pins.

I loved butterflies as a child. That part of the memory stuck with me.

I turned, the movement somehow putting me even closer to him. I could feel his chest moving up and down in deep breaths, matching the pace of mine.

His eyes burrowed into my soul, he turned his head slightly to the left in that assessing look he loved so much. He ran his tongue across his bottom lip. Something I'd come to know meant he was about to say something but wasn't sure if he should.

Someone entered the room, and I jumped back from him like we were engaged in some sort of behavior I didn't want anyone to see.

I didn't even want to think about what he was about to say.

All of the events of the last few days didn't leave me much room to ponder on the looks he gave me.

Or how my stomach dropped a little when he looked at me.

Or the static sensation I felt when his skin grazed mine.

"Freaking princesses!" Camila shouted while coming over to me, jumping up and down. "That room is a princess room if I ever saw one, and it's mine! Your room is so bright and cheery," she finished, looking around and inspecting it.

"Is your room not?" I asked her.

Everything in the palace was bright and cheery.

"No," she laughed. "Mine is much darker than yours. Come see," she said while running out of the room, not even looking to see if we were following.

I knew, unlike me, she always fantasized about having great wealth. So she was truly living her wildest dream right now.

I looked back at Holt, and he had a slight smile on his face as he walked behind me. I walked down the hall to where my sister's room was located, right next to mine.

Our rooms had the same exact setup, but her room was darker. My room was covered in bright yellows and oranges, but hers was covered in deep wines and auburns.

I looked around for the window above her bed, everything seemed the same as mine, so I was sure there should be one. I realized it was covered with heavy dark red curtains. The sister I knew now was not a morning person. It appears the child my mother knew wasn't either.

Cree stood at the door, waiting for us to finish up the inspection of our rooms. Camila stood at a trunk that rested against the wall to the right. She opened it up to find lots of small wooden trinkets inside. She pulled out a jaguar figurine, it was painted, but the paint was starting to deteriorate at the spots her fingers touched. It looked just like our mother did in the memory she saved for us.

"I remember this. I used to play outside near the ceiba tree and pretend it was her when she was busy," she said, running her fingers over the jaguar's wings.

A realization dawned on me.

"Camila," I said, the smile still on her face as she remembered the time in her childhood.

"Do you remember our father?" I asked quietly, and her smile slowly slipped away.

THE SUN, THE STORM, & THE SHADOWS   167

This whole time I was so excited that we knew who our mother was. I didn't realize our father wasn't in the memory from earlier.

She placed the jaguar on the bed as her mouth turned down. "No."

Cree walked back into the room. I didn't realize he had left while we looked at Camila's old toys.

"We do," Holt said, almost too quiet for us to hear.

We both spun around to look at him. His face told me that whatever he was about to say wouldn't be a memory I wanted to hear.

"Come with me," Cree said as he directed us out of the room and down another hallway.

"I took a look around while you guys were looking at your rooms," he said as he guided us over to double doors more prominent than the ones that marked our rooms.

The designs on the doors looked like the forest we'd been traveling through. Half of a ceiba tree sat on each door. There was no doubt this was our parents' bedchamber. I took a deep breath and pushed through the door.

I stepped through but realized my sister was still in the hallway with Cree.

"I don't know if I want to know," she said, biting her lip with anxiety.

I turned back to grab her hand. "Together."

She eyed me like she was still unsure whether that was enough to make her want to enter the room. She battled her thoughts and eventually stepped through with me.

Our rooms were made for princesses. This was fit for a Queen and King.

The bed was double the size of ours, and sheer fabrics were hung over the bed posts. They, too, had a window behind their bed, and the sun highlighted the dust that moved around the air.

I turned to the right and was met with another mural, but this one of my family.

My father. This is what my father looked like.

While my Camila had our mother's complexion, I had my father's. His brown skin seemed so warm and lifelike that I reached to touch his hand, which rested on the shoulder of the younger version of me. He had endless brown eyes, reminding me so much of Camila's.

I looked over at her to find tears welling in her eyes. My mother stood next to him with a smile stretched across her face, her hand resting on Camila's shoulder where they stood behind us.

"What was he like?" I asked, not taking my eyes off my father.

"I only met him a few times," Holt started, "the first time was when Cree and I were young. We went with my parents to the meeting between our kingdoms. We met every few years to address any issues that might have arisen in the lands. They usually made it a tournament that lasted a few days, we brought some of our best warriors, and they brought theirs. They would battle each other, and one of our courts would come out the victor. It was all for sport, but this time the Sun Court had won the last two tournaments, and my father was determined to win. He was so certain we'd win that he wanted Cree and I to come along with him to witness it. When we got there, our parents greeted each other warmly and discussed who they thought would win. They were great friends. That's why our kingdoms were able to coexist so easily. The next day the tournaments started, and Cree and I were so excited we stood on the side practicing with our own swords. Your father was a great warrior himself. He was legendary. He was said to be integral in the war against the Serpent tribes. He saw us practicing and came to watch us, he gave us some advice, and we were enamored with him. He was so warm and kind. You wouldn't expect someone so intimidating to be as kind as he was. You," he hesitated, looking at me gently. "You both have his smile. He ruffled our hair before standing with my father to watch the tournament. Storm Court took the victory that year, and we all celebrated together."

I felt the warmth of my tears running over my cheeks, and a faint memory of Camila and I chasing him through the courtyard surfaced. He pretended to trip and fall and allowed us to jump on him.

After we caught him, he ruffled our curls and told us we'd be great warriors one day. I let out a breath and looked over at my sister.

She seemed to remember something about him as well that had her looking at the image of our father with warmth.

"What happened to him?" I asked, not wanting to know the answer but also needing the resolution,

"He grew sick, a sickness similar to Holt's father. By the time they realized he was sick, nothing could be done. The Fae are strong, but some illnesses even we can't beat. He lived a long life, nearly 600 years. He died when you were young. Your mother was devastated," Cree stated.

"600 years?!" I asked.

Though I was Fae, I still didn't have the memory of our history outside of what Cree and Holt had already shared with us.

"Yes," Holt said, realizing that we weren't aware of how long the Fae lived. "The Fae live much longer than the humans."

"How old are you?" Camila asked.

"I'm only 203," Holt responded.

This whole time we thought they were the same age as us, but we were clearly wrong.

"And you?" Camila asked Cree.

"Same, I don't know when my birthday is, but when I was found, I appeared to be about the same age as Holt."

Once again, my brain felt like liquid.

Were we going to live for centuries? It didn't seem possible, but here they stood, 203 years old, looking no older than a 30-year-old human.

"I need some fresh air. I don't know how much more shocking news I can take," I said, leaving the room to find the courtyard with the ceiba tree.

The memory of us playing with my father ran through my mind. It was evident they both loved us greatly. I tried to hold onto that rather than sink into the jaws of the grief that would consume me if I thought too much about the fact he was gone.

Him and my mother.

Everything they said about our parents made me wish they were still here. I yearned for a warm embrace from my mother and for my father to ruffle my curls the way he did in my memory.

Before I knew it, I was sitting under the ceiba tree.

The Alux watched me from above. They were fascinating little creatures. The fact they were around when my mother was alive had me inspecting them further.

"Can I ask you questions?" I whispered to none of them in particular, and one came to float near me.

"We can't interfere with your fate, only guide you," they whispered in a child-like voice. I couldn't tell if they were male or female. They all sounded the same.

"What should I do next?" I asked them.

"The path you are on is the right one," they whispered back.

"How will I know if I make a wrong decision?"

"You must lead with your heart and soul. That is all I can say."

The sprite zipped around my head, casting light all around me and lifting my hair in the wind they created again.

Once the light they spread around me cleared up, I saw Holt standing across the courtyard, watching me warily. I offered him a smile letting him know it was okay to approach me. He walked over and sat on the grass next to me.

The Alux started to swarm the both of us before heading back up to their spots on the ceiba tree.

The tree roots had spread to all sides of the courtyard, and parts of the stone were cracking from the impact they created.

Some of these cracks seemed older than others, leading me to believe that the tree had been close to this size for a very long time. The backside of the prism was open, allowing a view of the sky in the courtyard. The sun peeked through the branches, the blue blossoms appearing translucent, showing the purple veins that ran through them.

The purple-gray bark of the tree was smoother than I thought it would be as I rubbed my hand over it. I could feel the magic pulsing through it, bringing mine to the surface.

I allowed myself to fully feel the extent of my power. I reached down into what felt like my reserves, and my magic felt bottomless.

My grief made me want to light the world on fire, but the words my mother spoke in the memory returned to me. I turned to Holt, finding him studying my face as I went through these emotions.

"Do you know the prophecy my mother spoke of?" I asked.

"I have a faint memory of one she might be referencing, but I can't remember the specifics. My mother would know. Once we make it to my palace, she'll be the first person we find."

I nodded. My mother said we would be the key to saving the world.

The heaviness of this was almost too much to bear. Knowing that his mother would be able to help us calmed some of my worries. I wasn't sure what we would do after that, but the Alux told me to follow my heart.

My heart told me I should stay with Holt.

"Where's Camila and Cree?" I asked.

"They went to do some more exploring. They're hoping to find something that will pinpoint who attacked. My father could never figure it out, but maybe we'll see something he didn't."

Determination burned through me.

My mother believed in us.

So I decided I would too.

Chapter 17

Camila

Cree and I swept through every inch of the palace we could, but found nothing that could help us find who attacked.

He told me that the Storm King had investigated after word of what happened made it to his kingdom. I wasn't going to be able to rest until I also did my own investigation, but we came up fruitless.

My sister and Holt found us towards the end of our search, it took most of the day, and we were running out of daylight. We did all we could, so I accepted that we would have to leave.

Getting to the Storm Palace seemed even more critical than before.

The fact that Holt's mother would be able to decipher the prophecy my mother referenced made me eager to get to her.

Also getting back to the Storm King to help his sickness before it took him like it took my father.

We found ourselves once again in the courtyard. It brought both Xio and I a sense of peace we desperately needed before we'd have to leave.

"I think we can stay here for the night," Holt said, walking through the covered walkway. "We won't make it very far before night falls anyways. We'll make up for it tomorrow. Night and Thunder will be plenty rested. Well," he hesitated, "that's if you still want to stay with us? We can't really claim you as prisoners anymore," he finished.

A few days ago, I would have jumped at the idea of being rid of them.

But now...

"We will help you defeat whoever came for our mother, whatever is plaguing Maya. We'll stay with you," now it was my turn to hesitate, "if that's okay."

A smile spread across Holt's face as he looked over at Xio to confirm what I said.

She nodded, showing that she felt the same way I did.

"Yes, that is okay," he replied.

My heart jumped at the idea that we could spend more time in the palace. I may have searched every corner I could in the hours we had, but maybe I would be able to find something else.

There were some places in the back of the palace I couldn't make it to, so that would be the first thing I did when I had the chance.

Cree was walking towards us with our bags. He must have gone to make sure Thunder and Night would be okay for the evening and retrieved our things.

He sat the bags by the tree for us and plopped down on the soft grass.

"Chara has told us so many stories about the Alux, and I never believed them. She spoke of one encounter, saying they guided her to meet the King. We all thought she was just lovestruck," he spoke around mouthfuls of food.

The Alux did not seem to like the denial of their existence, and they began to shake the tree until a small branch fell and whacked Cree in the head.

"Hey! I'm not saying you don't exist now, just that I didn't believe in you before!" he yelled at them, and Xio and I doubled over in laughter.

The Alux seemed to realize this was the closest thing to an apology Cree was capable of and went back to humming around the tree.

Cree and I still didn't speak much throughout the day, I was waiting for him to make some sharp remark or to make fun of me, and he hadn't yet. Not since our time around the campfire.

He threw my daggers down by my feet, and I jumped back.

Did he know I was just thinking about the fact he wasn't being an asshole? He must have.

"What the hell, Cree!" I said, grabbing my daggers from the earth.

"We've missed training. Now's as good a time as any."

He pulled out his own sword and stalking towards me. It looked like he decided to just fight with one today rather than the two swords he usually preferred.

I saw my sister run away before she could get dragged into the training session with the shadow bastard. She shot me an apologetic look before darting back around the corner.

I hoped Holt found her and made her train too.

"You could have warned me. I could have lost a toe," I said before blocking the first swipe of his sword and moving out of the way.

"I never miss."

He turned toward me, lifting his sword again. I ducked under his arm and dug my elbow into his back before he could turn around, and he stumbled a few steps from the power in my move.

My newfound speed and strength surprising him and me. I jumped up excitedly, thinking I got the best of him, but he whirled around quickly.

I linked my daggers together and let my power fill the weapon, flames licked up both ends, and I twisted it in my hand, creating a circle of fire. He, too, allowed his shadows to consume his own weapon, and he started to smirk.

"Don't hold back," he said, shooting a line of shadow toward me.

I spun my weapon again and willed the fire into a shield as I had done earlier. I removed one hand from my weapon and shot a burst of hot light out of my fingers down at his foot, and his shadows blocked it a second too late.

He looked down at his foot and back up at me with something like pride. I smugly lifted my eyebrows because, damn, I was proud of myself for that maneuver.

"Good girl," he said with a smirk before the courtyard was suddenly black.

The Alux lit up the space like stars in the night sky. I couldn't see where Cree was; all I felt was his magic surrounding me. Before I knew it, he was behind me, and I felt cold steel against my neck.

The shadows cleared around me, and he brought his lips to my ear. "Yield."

"That's hardly fair," I said before stomping my foot down on his and sliding out of his hold. Cree found my thought about fairness funny and let out a dark chuckle.

"First rule of fighting like the Fae, use every weapon in your arsenal," he said with a shrug.

Once I figured out all the power I had within me, I certainly would, and he would be sorry.

We continued fighting until we were both covered in sweat. I found Cree using more of his strength with me now that I could handle it. He still had two centuries worth more training than I did, so I could tell he was just keeping pace with me.

He lifted his shirt to wipe the sweat from his brow and graced me with the view of his muscular stomach. I ran my eyes over the tattoos dipping down his stomach below his pants before he put his shirt down, and I suddenly found a blade of grass very interesting.

He smirked like he knew exactly what I was up to but didn't call me out.

Holt and Xio's laughter reached us before they did as they sauntered into the courtyard holding bottles of a dark liquid.

"We found some wine in the kitchens, it's a decade old, but that should only make it better," Xio said, stumbling slightly.

It looked like she may have already tested that theory out.

I desperately needed a drink, so I ran over, grabbed one of the bottles from her hand, and brought it to my mouth. I gulped down as much as I could in one breath.

I took a look at the bottle, and less than a quarter of it remained. Holt and Cree looked at me with horror-stricken faces.

"That was a terrible idea," Cree said, "that is not the wine you know in the human lands. It's much more potent. One or two glasses would have you stumbling, and you just drank the equivalent of five."

"Oops," I said through a belch.

The world already began to spin slightly, and Xio's laughter filled my ears. She was wheezing now, unable to catch a breath.

"You are so fucked," she got out between breaths.

There was no going back now. I shrugged and downed the last bit of wine and tossed the bottle onto the ground at my feet.

"Idiotic," Cree mumbled, which may have been the funniest thing I'd ever heard.

At least right now, it seemed like it.

He wasn't kidding about the potency of this wine. It all hit me at once. I laughed, and he stared down at me with judgment in his eyes.

The humming from the Alux sounded like music in my ears, and I began to dance around the courtyard. I grabbed my sister and spun her around. A smile split her face, and it warmed my heart more than I could put into words.

We both had been through too much, and the fact we could dance around and smile right now instead of cracking under the pressure filled me with even more joy.

I tossed my head back to look into the exposed sky. The sun was all the way set.

I shot my hands in the air and danced until I couldn't dance anymore.

Chapter 18

Xio

Dancing with my sister in the courtyard of our home was an unexplainable feeling. She lasted much longer than we thought she would after downing as much of the wine as she did.

She eventually stopped dancing and advised that she wanted to lay beneath the ceiba tree and watch the Alux. Before we knew it, she was knocked out.

Cree announced he would take her to her room and ensure she was okay.

The wine was still running through my veins, I wasn't nearly as intoxicated as her, but my face was still warm, and the happiness it brought me remained.

I trusted Cree and Holt.

Other than tying our wrists, even as prisoners, they treated us pretty well.

They made sure we were fed, offered us their tent, and protected us throughout our journey. Cree was less pleasant than Holt, but even so, I now knew he would never hurt my sister.

I watched him pick her up gracefully and exit the courtyard.

My eyes fell on Holt, who sat under the tree watching us while we danced, laughed, and made fools of ourselves. I was sticky with sweat and looked down at myself to find I was quite dirty as well.

"Come with me," Holt said, standing up and walking away.

He didn't turn to see if I was following, but he knew I would.

We walked down near our bedchambers, and I peeked into Camila's room to ensure she was okay. She was laid in her bed looking peaceful while Cree shook the dust from her blanket and laid it over her.

I ran to catch up with Holt, and instead of turning right toward my parents' chambers, he turned left. We walked down a long hallway, and I felt moisture on my skin as the air became warmer and we walked down steep steps.

I heard rushing water before I saw it. Holt's prominent figure moved into the room at the bottom of the steps, and once he shifted out of the way, I saw where he was taking me.

This had to be the very back of the palace because the back walls were raw mountain, not the smooth white stone the rest of the building was made of.

There were multiple pools of water separated by walls of stone, I dipped my finger into it and found it was warm, and

I nearly jumped with excitement. Holt still stood by the door. He, too, was covered in dirt and needed a bath.

"There's more than one pool here. We can both take a bath, just turn around until I'm in, and then you can get into the one on the other side of the wall," I told him.

The water running down the mountainside and into the spring created enough bubbles to make my body less visible to him.

"You sure? I think you might be drunk," he said as he stepped forward.

He would have turned around if I had changed my mind. But I didn't want to change my mind.

We both needed to get clean, and it's not like I was expecting anything to happen—I think.

The effects of the wine had finally started to dwindle away, not affecting my decision-making skills. Once I saw my sister down the wine, I didn't drink anymore, just in case she started to get sick.

"I'm sure," I said, removing my clothing, and he turned around. I laid my leathers on one of the more dry areas of the space and dipped myself into the water.

The water lapped over my skin and pure bliss spread throughout me, the closest thing to a proper bath I'd had since we made it into Maya. I wasn't going to waste a second of it.

I dipped my hair into the liquid. My curls stretched from the weight of the water, falling down to the middle of my back. I made it far enough into the spring, where the water was just below my neck, covering enough to allow him to turn around.

"You can turn around," I said, the rushing water loud behind me.

I thought he didn't hear me over it for a second, but he slowly turned around and stared at me.

A faint spark of lightning ran over his skin. I would have missed it if I had blinked too fast, and we stared at each other for a few moments.

"I have to turn around, but you don't?" he smirked while starting to remove his shirt.

He pulled it off his body, and I quickly turned around, embarrassed that I didn't think to remain turned around until he was in.

I heard his clothes hit the floor, and his footsteps made it to the edge of the pool next to me. The sloshing of water filled the space until only the sound of the rushing water behind me remained.

"I'm in," he said.

I turned to find him propping himself up on the stone wall between our pools. His arms glistened, and he rested his chin on them, smiling wide.

"I see," I said, ignoring the holes his eyes felt like they were burning into me.

I dipped under the water, submerging my entire body in the glorious liquid. I swam over to the stone wall separating us and propped myself up the way he did.

When I got there, he was no longer at the wall. He also decided to submerge himself when I did. The waterfall that created the bubbles in my pool did not reach his side.

I realized this pool was slightly lower than mine, and the water poured over the side of the wall where it joined mine at the mountain. I saw some movement before me and looked down into the water to see him coming up for air.

The realization that his pool was missing bubbles was evident as I caught the sight of a lot of glistening brown skin.

The wall separating us was about one of my arms wide, so we were both able to prop ourselves up across from each other.

He ran his hand through his wet curls and wiped the water from his long curling lashes. There was that feeling again, the warmth in my gut that he always invoked.

I was no stranger to sex.

I had plenty back in the village we came from. There wasn't a lot that could take away the dreariness of where we lived.

I was confident in my body and never balked from its form. But here, right now, I was glad that the stone separated us before I did something I probably shouldn't do.

I barely knew him, but it felt like I'd known him my entire life. That had my body wanting to do...something with him.

Whatever was between us felt like it would be more than casual sex. I wouldn't be making any rash decisions, for right now.

Although it would probably be amazing, hot, steamy—

"Hi," he said, pulling me out of the thought before the imagery got too vivid in my head.

"Hi," I tried to reply, but my voice cracked slightly, and blood rushed to my cheeks.

"This is amazing," I followed up with, trying desperately to move my thoughts from where they were heading.

I looked around at the pools of water surrounding me, wondering if I ever swam here with my family.

"It is. I can't remember the last time I had something so close to a proper bath," he said with a smile.

As a prince, I'm sure that was a little out of the norm for him.

"Of course, some soap, salts, and oils would be nice," Holt said, pushing a wet curl away from his face that fell while he spoke. "But, this will do."

Was I still drunk? Every part of my body seemed to be on fire right now, and not just my magic that I knew lived there.

I dipped into the water, not responding to him, and swam over to the waterfall. I placed my hand on the wall and let it separate the water.

Suddenly the waterfall stopped and began to vibrate. It peeled from the wall, and I looked over to see Holt's hand raised with a look on his face that said I wasn't going to like what was about to happen. He swiped his hand to the left, and water poured over my head.

I dipped back under the water, quickly avoiding the worst of it, and swam back to the wall. Holt roared with laughter before dropping back under the water to avoid the fire I shot at him.

I, too, fell into laughter and splashed my arms down onto the water's surface in defeat.

"I don't know why you love doing that so much!"

"You're cute when you're wet," he replied with a grin.

Blood rushed to my cheeks, and I once again ignored him and dipped into the water. I was sure the water sizzled as I plunged as deep as possible.

I pushed off the stone floor of the pool and swam to a more shallow area. I stood and started to work the dirt and knots out of my hair. Holt was doing the same in his pool with his back turned to me.

I took in the curve of his biceps as he brought his hands to his head and ran his fingers through his hair.

The surface of his back had deep ridges, a certain quality of someone who spent time swinging a weapon and training. I didn't notice before, but he also had tattoos, not nearly as many as Cree but more than I would have thought.

I couldn't determine precisely what they were, but I also found that he had plenty of scars. If Fae could heal themselves, I wondered why he was still scarred. He turned around, and I didn't avoid his sight fast enough.

He could undoubtedly tell I was staring at him. He pushed through the water to stand near the wall again, throwing his elbow up on it casually.

"How's it feel to be back here? I'm sure a lot is going through your head right now?" he asked.

He had no idea how much was going through my head about him, but I'll keep that secret for now.

"I'm so happy that we were able to find out who we are, where we came from, that we weren't abandoned out of something we did…"

Part of me always thought that we could have been the reason for what happened to us. It was a relief to know that it was an act of love.

"But another part of me is filled with grief for my parents, for what my life could have been with them. They seemed to be full of such love. It would be nice to experience that now, I don't know, it's hard to explain," I finished looking down at my fingers that held so much power now.

"Your parents were soul-bound," he said softly, with his eyes looking up into the waterfall he used to drench me earlier.

"What's that mean?" I asked.

"Also hard to explain," he chuckled. "Basically, it means they were destined for each other. Their love was inevitable. To find your soul-bound is to find your other half, the one to help fulfill your purpose for life," he said, his eyes locked in on mine now.

I wanted to look away. Still, I couldn't get myself to pull away from him.

"My parents are too. Remember how we told you that she believed the Alux guided her to my father?" he asked, and I nodded.

"It's fate. Not everyone gets to experience it, but the ones who do never separate. Never in all our years have soul-bound

Fae chosen to leave one another outside of death. My father told me that your mother grieved for years when your father died. She did her best to pull herself together for her kingdom, but losing your soul-bound is said to be excruciatingly painful, almost physically painful."

My heart hurt for my mother. *Did we help bring her out of that grief? Did we understand what was happening?*

"I worry for my mother if my father doesn't get better," he said sadly, breaking our locked gaze. "Some say it feels like electricity between them. Like they're drawn to each other and don't understand why. They feel comfortable the moment they meet and can sit in silence for hours without feeling the need to fill it. My mother said the moment she locked eyes with my father, there was nothing that could stop her from being with him," he said, moving closer and closer to me.

This all sounded a little too familiar, and my lip quivered.

"Ever feel anything like that?" he muttered.

I opened my mouth to answer, but nothing came out. Was he telling me that he feels that with me? Did he know that I felt that way about him? He's a Descendant of a God. I'm sure all the ladies felt that way about him.

I gulped, and he smiled like he knew my answer without me having to say it.

He turned and walked over to the stairs in his pool as the water poured off his body. Flashing me a view of his formed backside and strong legs before going to grab a towel I didn't know was there. He must have found this space earlier and brought them down because three more towels lay next to the one he grabbed. He wrapped it around his waist and held out another one in front of him for me. I squeezed the excess water from my hair again and ascended the steps to accept the towel.

He locked his eyes in mine with what looked like a lot of willpower and wrapped the towel around me. He was so large that my head only reached the bottom of his chest.

I looked up at him to find his face hovering inches from mine, and a scent I didn't recognize hit me.

My heart was beating loud enough that he had to hear it, he brought his lips to my forehead, and sparks flew at the contact. He removed his lips from my skin and peered down at me. I couldn't breathe, couldn't speak. He turned and placed his hand on the small of my back.

"Let's go find you something to wear," he said, and I followed him out of the room of springs into the hallway.

I didn't catch my breath until the moisture in the air disappeared, and a coolness ran over my still-damp skin.

Chapter 19

Camila

My mouth was dry, and my head was pounding. I didn't want to open my eyes to see where I ended up.

My back was laid on some soft material, and I was covered with a warm blanket. This realization caused me to open my eyes, and I found the room around me dimly lit.

I looked around and recognized it as my bedchamber we found the day before. I was expecting to still be in the courtyard, the last thing I remembered was downing the last bit of wine, and the rest was a blur.

I rubbed the sleep out of my eye and saw a cup of water on the table next to my bed. I reached for it and heard a faint snore.

I peered around the room and found Cree on the ground next to my bed. His arm was draped across his forehead, and his mouth was slightly open. He was still fully dressed and had some sort of small blanket over his body. He snored again, and I couldn't help but chuckle.

That caused a dart of pain to shoot through my head, and I grunted in pain.

He opened one eye to look at me and sat up slowly as he rubbed the back of his head. Waking up after a night on the hard floor probably didn't feel great.

"Good morning," I rasped.

My throat felt like it lacked any sort of moisture. I took a sip of the water left out by my table, hoping it hadn't been sitting there for the last ten years.

The water slid down my throat, and I felt some relief. It tasted fresh and crisp.

"Hello, Viper," he said smoothly.

It lacked the usual undertones of annoyance he used when he called me that.

"I don't remember anything," I said, rubbing my head.

I tried to sit up, and my face pulled tight with pain. My head was not going to allow me to move that quickly yet. He stood up and sat on the edge of the bed.

Cree reached for me and placed his hand on my head, a warmth seeped from his fingers, and the pain began to dwindle away. I took a deep breath and sat up again without pain.

"I didn't think you would. I was actually surprised you lasted as long as you did," he responded.

He smirked and I closed my eyes so I didn't have to look at him.

"Did I do anything particularly embarrassing?"

He laughed.

Fuck.

"I guess that depends on what you find embarrassing?" I could hear the smile in his voice, and that told me I, indeed, would find it embarrassing. "You danced around the courtyard with your sister. She eventually got tired, and you danced by yourself for a while. Eventually, you tried to get me to dance with you...fairly aggressively."

Oh no.

"How aggressive?" I asked, pulling my face into a wince.

"You mentioned something about me being a shadow bastard with a stick up my ass and that I didn't know how to have fun. That was before you plopped down in my lap. Your sister removed you pretty quickly, though, so not as embarrassing as it could have been."

Looks like drunk Camila didn't care that he's a shadow bastard with a stick up his ass.

Thank the Gods that my sister saved me from dry humping said shadow bastard.

I lifted the blanket, scared to see what I might find underneath after finding out I threw myself at him. All my clothes were still on, and I sighed in relief.

"I may be a bastard, but I would never take advantage of you," he scoffed.

"Was more so worried about the possibility of me removing my own clothing after you said I plopped down into your lap," I murmured, and he let out a chuckle of relief.

"I'm flattered," he said, the one side of his mouth turned up. "You fell asleep under the ceiba tree, and I carried you in here. I was—" he stopped abruptly. "I just wanted to make sure you didn't hurt yourself."

He stood up quickly and walked toward the door looking frazzled, and I cocked my head to the side.

"Holt came in while you were sleeping and said that he found some hot springs to bathe in. I'm going to go clean up before we have to head out," he looked back at me. "I'll let your sister know you're up and ask her to show you where they are."

He exited before I could respond. I'd never seen Cree exude anything but pure smug confidence.

He seemed a little thrown off when he almost admitted that he was worried about me. I closed my eyes and laid back down, but flashes of my dancing came back to me, and I cringed and hid under the blanket.

The sound of footsteps entering my room had me peeking one eye out of the cover. Thankfully it was just my sister. She had some fabric draped over her arms and wore a new riding outfit.

"Good morning!" she sang. "I found some of mother's old clothing in her room. Some of it was ruined, but there were a few things we could take with us," she said, laying them on the bed beside me.

They were two beautiful gowns, one bright yellow and one a deep wine red. They were similar styles with long billowing sleeves and a neckline that plunged low. They looked like they would be tight through the hips, well, my sister's hips, and flow down to the floor, leaving some fabric flowing behind.

"They're beautiful," I whispered, running my fingers down the silky smooth fabric.

"I know! They look like they'll fit us, so I figured we could try and pack them in our bags. We can't take everything, but I thought one dress each wouldn't be too much," she said with a smile splitting her face.

She set down some more clothes that looked similar to what she was wearing.

"I also found some new riding leathers, so you can switch out of what you have on," she finished.

"Cree mentioned somewhere to bathe?" I asked.

"Oh yeah...I need to fill you in on some things," she said, placing her finger on her temple. "Follow me. I'll tell you while we walk down."

She led me down the hallway and explained what happened last night with Holt, and I was only partly surprised. They've been making eyes at each other since the first day they met.

I knew it was only a matter of time until she realized it too. She told me how our parents were soul-bound and sounded like she had more to say, but we made it into the hot spring, and I smacked into a half-naked Cree.

"I'm sorry I wasn't paying attention," I said.

He stared at me with a flat face and walked around me.

"Well, that was awkward," I muttered after he was out of our line of sight.

Xio laughed at me and handed me a towel. "Yes, it was. Here's a towel you can dry off with when you're done. I'm going to go get some last-minute exploring in before we need to leave."

She twirled out of the space and I removed my clothes and let the warm water consume me.

We packed up all of our things and were ready to leave. I wished we could have stayed longer, but the literal fate of the world depended on us, so we really needed to get going.

I pulled the entry doors closed and felt the magic seal back up. Whatever magic my mother placed on the palace, so people didn't enter, still stood firm.

I savored the feel of her for a moment and turned to follow the others down the steps. Xio stood at the bottom, looking up at the castle, a tear slipping down her cheek.

"We'll be back," I promised, which every part of me knew was true.

If we survived long enough to make it back here, we would come and reclaim our home.

I walked over to Night and rubbed his neck. He got a day of rest, but I knew we would be pushing them hard for the rest of the journey. I successfully mounted the horse without slipping or spooking him and smiled victoriously.

My sister also mounted Thunder without assistance, and I could see how proud she was. Cree jumped up behind me and grabbed the reins.

He still hadn't said anything to me since us waking up in my room.

Every time we had some sort of genuine moment, he went back to being an asshole. Not that I cared, but it would be nice to have a pleasant riding partner since we still had a week to go.

"You didn't give me a chance to say thank you for last night, so...thank you," I said, trying to break the tension.

He grunted his acceptance and turned Night to cross the bridge.

I looked over my shoulder at our home and felt at peace.

My body relaxed, and I accidentally leaned back into Cree. His body tightened, but he didn't tell me to remove myself from him like before, so maybe there was some progress.

I shifted back forward and heard him let loose a breath.

We traveled through the overgrown path and back onto the one we used to get here.

The wind started to blow in my face, and we officially were on our way to save the world.

We rode almost the entire day after leaving the palace. We had only a few more hours until there wouldn't be enough light left to continue.

Cree was still being stubborn about his almost-admittal. I had too much on my mind to think too much about it.

Being in the palace made me feel like an actual princess. Just existing in the same space my mother and father once did was surreal.

Something I didn't think I'd ever experience.

I wished we could have watched the memory more than once. I would have stuck it into my bag and watched it every day.

"Camila," Cree muttered, slowing down Night.

"Yes?"

"Grab your weapon from the saddlebag," he said firmly. "Hand me mine, too."

He pulled us to a complete stop and I located them both quickly and handed his over.

Holt and Xio were further back than us, but I heard Thunder's hooves trotting closer to us.

Cree held up a fist, which appeared to be a signal that Holt would know meant to slow down and stop.

They slowly made their way to us and stopped directly next to us. Cree's gaze shifted back and forth between the trees on either side of the path.

"What is it?" Holt asked.

"Something is wrong. I feel it. I just can't find the source," he whispered.

We all surveyed the area for a few more moments, but nothing looked out of place.

"I don't see—" Holt started to answer but was cut off when a dark figure started walking towards us down the path.

They were completely black, like they were made from obsidian stone. Their eyes, their hair, everything was the deepest of blacks. It carried a black sword, dragging it across the dirt path.

We all jumped off the horses and left them on the side of the path, walking towards the figure.

Suddenly, the figure vanished in a puff of smoke.

Smoke.

Just like in the memory our mother left us.

We hadn't trained on how to fight as a unit, but we instinctively formed a circle with our backs to each other.

Magic danced across all of our weapons, ready for the coming fight.

A puff of smoke appeared to my left and another to my right. Cree moved first, shooting shadows from his weapon at the strange figure.

There was no holding back here, only strikes to kill. These weren't angry village folk. I couldn't even tell what they were, but one thing was for certain.

These weren't Fae. They were something evil.

Holt moved to the other one, leaving Xio and I where we stood. We shifted to fight back to back, ready if another one of these creatures appeared.

Neither of them puffed into smoke again, leading me to believe this ability wasn't something they could do back to back.

Holt struck the figure with a deadly blast of lightning, but the figure didn't die. It was slowed down, but it continued moving.

"What the actual fuck," Xio muttered behind my back.

Cree was locked in battle with the first figure, lunging and slicing, but the creature was fast. It dodged every deadly blow. Cree used his ability to shift in the shadows to vanish and materialize behind them. He had his sword ready as soon as he appeared and separated the creature's head from its shoulders in one swift move.

"Cut off his head! It killed the other one!" I yelled to Holt, who was still battling with the second creature.

Before I could see if Holt had taken the advice, a third puff of smoke appeared in front of Xio, and she instinctively pushed more magic into her weapon.

We'd seen a lot of oddities since we'd been in Maya, but whatever these creatures were took the cake. So close to it now they looked like they lacked a soul, nothing in their eyes.

The creature lifted its heavy sword and began swinging at Xio. She blocked the first hit with her sword across her body and used her new Fae strength to push it back.

My daggers were light in my hands as I charged behind the creature and stabbed it between its shoulder blade. Its arm went limp, and its sword fell to the ground.

Xio took this opportunity to yell a battle cry and bring her flaming sword clean across its neck, just as Cree did.

Its head stayed on its shoulders for a few seconds before sliding from its dark body and hitting the floor. I took no chances and quickly lit the creature on fire. It didn't burn like a normal body would, but my fire didn't hold back.

When I was certain it was no longer a threat, I whirled around again to find Holt with lightning skidding across all of his limbs, he moved and rallied and blocked. The obsidian creature was fighting like a rabid animal.

Like it didn't mind if it lived or died.

Holt lifted his left hand and used his elemental magic to form a tornado around the creature, caging him in.

The creature was trying everything it could to get out of the current, but it kept throwing him back into the center. Holt walked up to where the tornado raged and dropped his hand while simultaneously bringing down his great battle ax.

I heard the sound of hard flesh hitting the ground before I saw what Holt did.

The top half of the creature's body was lying ten feet from the bottom half. Cree made it to where Holt was fighting and chopped the creature's head off for good measure.

"What the fuck was that?" Holt asked.

We moved to join them to inspect the attackers. Up close, they were even more odd looking.

They genuinely looked like they were made of stone, all of their features looking to be chiseled out of a block of obsidian.

I tried to get closer to touch one of them, but they went up in another puff of smoke, leaving no trace behind but the odd black blood that leaked from them.

"Is that what the smoke looked like in the memory?" Cree asked.

Xio and I looked at each other, horrified.

"It was," I whispered, like saying too loud would make it more true.

"Fuck," Holt muttered, dragging his hand across his face.

"They're coming for us. Our mother was just the beginning," Xio gulped.

She looked back in the direction of the palace, and I followed her gaze.

"Let's get the fuck out of here," Cree exclaimed.

We mounted our horses and ran as fast as they could take us.

Chapter 20

Xio

We rode for two more days after the attack and finally made it to the next village to get some more supplies and food.

We weren't prisoners this time and wouldn't be trying to escape.

Funny how a few days can change things.

We trained early every morning, and I was getting a grasp on my powers. I leaned more towards my light power while Camila tended to choose the flames.

They both were scorching hot and had similar effects when we used them, but I found the light to be more manageable than the flames.

My sister liked the wildness of the flames. The way she managed to control them in such little time was impressive.

She always reminded me of wildfire, free and passionate, so it fit pretty well. Camila has mentioned every day that she was picking the food on this round and reminded them since we were also technically royalty, they shouldn't deny us our wishes.

Cree didn't want to bend to her will, but she finally put him on his ass in training this morning, so he reluctantly agreed.

Wildfire.

We didn't make it into the village until almost nightfall, so Holt advised we'd stay in the inn for the night and leave first thing again in the morning.

We were only few days from the palace, and the looming intensity of what that meant for us sat heavily on our shoulders. Everything would change from that point. As of now, we had no idea what our fate holds. Just that we needed to decipher the prophecy and act accordingly.

Holt strapped Thunder to a post outside the village and helped me down.

We both knew I didn't need the help anymore, but neither of us said anything about it.

"Food first," Camila said, trotting into the village.

We didn't need to hide our identity now since we no longer appeared human. Holt and Cree still wore the hoods of their cloaks to avoid being seen, but no one knew who we were. I followed my sister while she looked around to find a shop to purchase some food. This village was similar to the other, but whatever was plaguing the country seemed to hit harder here.

The streets were bare, not as many children playing in them. There wasn't a lot of greenery, and most of the earth was dry and brittle.

A male crossed the street with what looked like his young son. While the land may be less alive here, the people were no less happy. The boy skipped next to his father, holding his hand tight. I smiled, hoping that we could help them keep that sense of happiness.

My sister found a shop and sauntered in, and I followed behind her.

I felt Holt and Cree's presence somewhere behind us, but I knew they wouldn't let us out of their sight now that they really knew how important we were.

This shop seemed identical to Pan's, but the shelves held slightly less. We found what could have been Pan in female form entering from where I assumed the kitchen was. She was short and stout, and her smile was just as cheery.

"Hi, welcome in!" she shouted, setting down some buns that must have just finished baking, the heavenly smell floated over to us making my stomach growl.

I heard the front door shut behind us, and Cree and Holt came to stand on either side of us, they took down their hoods, and the female immediately recognized who they were.

"Oh, my Princes!" she started.

"Yes, yes, they're very important and handsome," Camila said, cutting her off before she started to act the same way Pan did. "But the smell of those buns is doing things to my brain I can't explain. I need one as soon as possible," she said, coming to stand in front of the baker.

The female laughed, and her belly shook. "My name is Loren, and these are my famous buns. Everyone around here loves them. I have to make a new batch every hour if you can believe it!"

Loren handed my sister one on a small square cloth, and Camila shoved it into her mouth, immediately moaning.

"Well, make another batch because we're taking all of these off your hands," she muttered around bites.

Loren laughed again and went to grab a satchel to store the items.

"We will need more than just buns, Camila," Holt reminded her.

Putting her in charge of the food may not have been the best idea.

"Fine, yes, we'll need some food for our journey too," she rolled her eyes and licked the butter from her fingers the bun left behind.

Loren nodded and went to gather things from the shelves. She brought everything back up to the counter, and Holt handed her a bag of gold coins that was certainly more than necessary.

"Oh, thank you so much, my Prince! I can't tell you how this will help my family," tears started to well in her eyes. "I won't tell anyone you're here. I know how things are right now. People are hungry and angry, which makes them particularly stupid. Especially the males," she said, rolling her eyes at the thought of them.

I liked her.

"Thank you, Loren," Cree said, offering her his crooked smile. "Where is the inn located?"

She provided us directions on how to get there from her shop, and we all thanked her. I saw Camila slip another half of a bun into her mouth and snatched the satchels from her hands.

If we left all the food with her, it would be gone before we made it out of there.

"There will be food at the inn, you pig," I murmured, bumping into her shoulder.

"You'll understand when you taste these buns," she responded with a shrug.

Judging from the smell, I was sure she was right.

We found the inn a few streets down and entered to the smell of stew. Downstairs was a dining area and bar, and it looked like the rooms were up a stairway to the right of the front counter.

Cree walked up to the female sitting on a stool. She didn't smile or welcome us in like Loren.

"We've only got one room left," she said without looking up, "you want it?"

"Umm..." Cree murmured, looking back at us.

The crotchety old lady raised her eyes and saw how many of us there were.

"There are two beds," she handed the key to Cree without hearing what his answer was.

"Food downstairs, sleeping upstairs," she stated, holding her hand out. "Two silver."

She used her other hand to pick something out of her tooth, waiting for Cree to drop something in her hand.

We all were a little confused by the interaction, but Holt stepped forward and dropped four silver coins into her hand.

She put it in her apron pocket and went back to ignoring us. I looked over at Camila, and she just shrugged as she followed the smell of the stew.

Our odd welcome had me worried about what we might find within the inn but everything was clean and in decent condition.

We found a table big enough for the four of us, and a young boy with bouncing curly hair came over with four steaming hot bowls, setting them down carefully.

"I'm Mario. Food comes with your room. Let me know if you want more. We have enough for you to have two bowls," he said before placing four cups of water down next to the bowls.

"Stronger stuff is over there. Let me know if you want any," he finished before running off to help another table with their food and drink.

I dipped my spoon into the bowl, mixing it around. They didn't tell us what it was, and I couldn't figure it out by looking at it.

"What do you think is in it?" I asked, looking up to find the three of them already digging into the stew.

"Good. It's good," Camila answered between spoonfuls.

I trusted her opinion so I spooned some into my mouth and immediately dipped my spoon back into my bowl for more.

The flavors were unlike anything in the human world, this was the first real Fae food we'd had, and I couldn't get enough of it.

Camila was already flagging down the boy for seconds by the time I was nearly finished, and I was happy to have another bowl waiting for me when I slurped the last of it up.

Cree looked at us with disgust. "When's the last time you two ate a real meal?"

"Um...I'm not sure, actually. We didn't have much in the way of food, and what we did have doesn't compare to whatever this is," I answered and brought the bowl to my mouth to drink the last of the broth, not caring about his judgment.

Holt eyed me with an amused look on his face.

"What?" I asked, and he reached up to remove a piece of carrot from my chin.

"Oops," I muttered.

I wiped it with a cloth napkin the boy left and four mugs of ale were dropped off by the time I was finished. I could see Camila deciding if she should indulge and smirked.

"Is this like the wine?" she asked, her mouth turned slightly down as she remembered the events of the prior evening.

Cree raised a brow, seemingly remembering the events of last night. "No, this won't have the same effects."

Camila looked over to Holt to ensure she could trust what Cree said, and he nodded before taking a gulp of his own mug. We both raised our cups simultaneously and took a sip.

Yeah, this was regular old pub ale. She seemed relieved by this and took another drink of it.

"So, we're going to have to share a room tonight," I said, avoiding eye contact with all of them.

"Don't worry, we'll let you two have a bed," Cree said, cracking a smile.

"Well, actually, I was thinking we would take one bed each, and you two could sleep on the floor next to us like good little males," Camila replied as she scrunched her nose at Cree.

"Did that last night. I think I'll pass," he responded, knowing this would embarrass my sister enough to get her to stop any more nasty comments.

She rolled her eyes and took another sip of her ale.

"I'm not sure how the two of you are going to fit into one bed. I doubt they're fit for royalty," I said.

I had to stop the laugh trying to escape me at the image of them spooning in my head.

"We'll make it work, or someone really will have to sleep on the floor," Holt chuckled.

"Someone, being you," Cree responded, and I could see the challenge rising between the two of them.

Cree lifted his mug to his mouth, and Holt did too. They eyed each other as they tried to swallow down the liquid as quickly as possible.

Holt won by a hair and slammed it back down onto the table. We all fell into laughter, well, everyone but Cree.

I'd found that he was a sore loser, much like my sister.

We sat around the table until Camila and I finished, and the males went to grab our bags off the horses.

Mario came to clean up our dishes, and I watched as he ran around collecting everyone else's dirty dishes. It looked like they would be shutting down soon, so we would have to make our way to the room.

We'd spent a lot of time together but being confined in a room instead of having an open space was going to be different.

Although, I was excited to sleep in a bed after a few days in the forest. We waited for Cree to return with the key and followed them upstairs.

Our room was the furthest in the narrow hall, and the sound of our footsteps bounced around the slender space. Cree turned the key and opened the door. As expected, the room was pretty small, and the two beds were a little bigger than a bedroll.

There was enough space on the floor for one of them to sleep if they decided they didn't want to try and make it work. Judging from the size of the bed, it looked like it wasn't going to be physically possible.

We sat our bags down, and all stood staring at the beds, wondering who was going to fold first.

"Well, Xio and I will take this one. You two can fight over that one," Camila pointed to the bed near the door while she plopped down onto the mattress.

"I grabbed us some nightgowns after my bath," she said, pulling them out of her bag and handing me one.

"I didn't even think about that," I responded.

We'd been sleeping in whatever dirty clothes we had on all day, so this was a luxury. I ran my fingers over the smooth fabric and looked over at Cree and Holt, who were still fighting about who would sleep on the floor.

Holt won the fight, and Cree huffed as he pulled out a bed roll and laid it on the floor between the bed and the door. At least he had the bedroll this time. Camila said he slept on the stone floor in the palace last night.

Camila started to remove her shoes and looked over at them. "Can you two stand in the hall for a minute?"

"Oh, yeah. Just knock when you're done," Cree said, turning quickly to the door while Holt followed behind.

Cree had been so awkward since we left the palace, like he thought we would all think he was a softy after taking care of my sister. Holt tossed a look over his shoulder before leaving the room and closing the door. I was still smiling when I turned around to change my clothes and Camila was looking at me with her eyebrows raised and her mouth pursed.

"Shut up," I said before she could spit out whatever comment she had.

She slipped the black nightgown over her body and tugged the edges until it fell to her mid-thigh.

"I'm just saying be careful, you barely know him, that's all."

I never finished telling her about his soul-bound comment, but I decided I would keep it to myself for now. I didn't know what it meant for me or if it was even a real possibility.

I loved Camila, but she would want to pick every part of it apart, and I wasn't ready for that. I tried my hardest not to acknowledge my feelings for Holt, even though I mostly failed at it.

I slid my arms into the arm holes and rested the straps on my shoulders.

The nightgown was a warm champagne color, a light and silky fabric that made it felt cool on my skin. I stepped over Cree's bedroll and knocked on the door, letting them know they could come back in.

Camila was already tucked into the covers by the time I turned around, and I heard the sound of the door clicking open.

My nightgown wasn't exactly scandalous, but it hugged my curves in a way that my riding clothes didn't. I felt eyes on my back as I flipped up the covers and slipped myself in, facing the direction Holt and Cree were in.

Holt had a slight smile on his face while he took off his shirt and shoes and got into the bed across from me. We were still facing each other when Cree blew the lamp out, and the room went dark.

I couldn't see anything, but I knew Holt was still looking in my direction. I could feel his gaze in any room, in any light, an awareness tingling in the back of my mind. I tried to close my eyes and go to sleep but had no such luck.

My sister let out a noise displaying that she was deep in sleep, and Cree returned the noise with one of his own.

I rolled back over to the side of Holt's bed, and once again, I felt his eyes. I also saw them this time as he let some lightning gather around his fingers, enough to illuminate his face. He lifted his eyebrows slightly, a dare and a beckoning.

I bit my lip, unsure of what I should do.

My sister, and his brother, by all intents and purposes, both slept on either side of us.

Before I made my mind up, I was already moving over to meet him where he was.

The floor creaked, and I stilled.

I waited for one of the sleeping to wake up, but they both were still breathing heavily. I sighed and took the last step into Holt's bed.

The electricity was no longer visible, but I felt it in every part of me as I laid next to him, and he covered me with the blanket. I felt his hand hover over me, asking permission to do what he wished.

I grabbed his wrist and placed his hand on my hip. He let out a low growl as his hands met the fabric of my nightgown.

He slid his hand up my side and dipped down into my waist and up my shoulder until he caressed my face. I let my eyes glow dimly so I could see his face and he could see mine. His face was full of hunger, his mouth hanging slightly open and his eyes studying my lightly lit face.

I don't know who moved first, but suddenly his mouth was on mine, or mine was on his I couldn't be sure. I parted my lips, allowing him access, and he took the opportunity without hesitating. His lips were soft and warm, and nothing had ever felt more perfect.

I took in his scent; he was a Descendant of Chaac and damn sure smelled like it. Like the calm before the storm, but also the thick of it when the rain was coming down heaviest, the lightning bursting through, creating a pungent burning aroma.

I moaned softly as he continued to explore my mouth, and I felt his hand slip down to explore the rest of me too. My eyes were closed, so he couldn't see my face any longer, and he stilled as his thumb grazed my nipple.

I opened my eyes, allowing him to see I still wanted this. The moment he read it in my eyes, he rolled it in his thumb before dipping down and taking it in his mouth.

I had to place a hand over my mouth to stop the gasp from leaving my lips, I felt him chuckle quietly against my skin, and I slapped him lightly on his shoulder.

He lifted up my nightgown and traced kisses down my stomach. Every spot his skin touched was burning hot and static like my magic and his mingled together, creating something more powerful.

He was so close to exactly where my body screamed for him to go, and he paused before he kissed his way back up to my face and turned me on my side.

He held me in his arms before dipping his finger right inside me and bringing it back to his mouth.

He growled his approval at what he found there and let out a deep breath. I could feel his length against my back and *needed* him to continue, but he didn't. He just pulled me in tight to his arms and placed his head in the crook of my neck.

"The next time I get the chance to explore you properly, I'm going to make you scream my name, Prisoner," he purred as quietly as he could, "I can't do that with an audience."

He laid his head back down behind me and twisted me in his arms to kiss me once again. We stayed wrapped around each other for hours, and he woke me up before the sun rose.

I tiptoed back over to the bed I was supposed to be sharing with my sister, and sleep had never come easier than it had in his arms.

The safety I felt was overwhelming.

I laid back down next to my sister and closed my eyes.

What did I just get myself into?

Chapter 21

Holt

Waking back up to the lack of warmth Xio provided me was jolting, which was odd because I didn't think I'd ever allowed myself to actually sleep with someone.

Sex, sure, but never truly sleep.

I never felt moved to allow it, and with my status, I always worried my partners were just trying to secure themselves a prince.

Deep down, I knew I was just waiting for her.

She was my soul-bound. I knew it in every intrinsic part of my body.

She made me feel sparks beyond the electricity I could create, and I couldn't believe how perfectly she fit molded against my body last night. Like she was made for me, and she was. I knew she wasn't ready to confront that, and I wasn't even sure if I was.

A soul-bound was a commitment for life, and she was still trying to figure out who she was. Not to mention the fact her mother said she'd be the key to saving everyone.

No, we weren't ready to face it, but that didn't mean I wasn't going to spend every second I was with her showing that I was the right choice when it came time.

Marriages in Maya lasted for days, and I found myself fantasizing about the feeling of our souls becoming one when she accepted it. The gold and silver tattoo that would adorn the space above our hearts would be my new favorite accessory.

I watched my soul-bound stretch awake, and her eyes found mine immediately like they always did.

Ever since the first time I laid eyes on her, I knew I wasn't going to be able to let her go. The way she looked at me with defiance but also curiosity had my heart jumping like she was the first female I'd ever seen.

Thankfully, I had the excuse of her stealing from me and being a human to take her with me, but I would have found a way.

But I found myself realizing that if she had told me she never wanted to see me again once we got to the palace safely, I would have listened too.

It would have been nearly unbearable, but I would have tried for her.

She held a power over me she didn't even know. I would bring the underworld and upper world all crashing down for her.

I always thought my mother was being dramatic about the way she felt when she first saw my father.

I definitely owed her an apology.

I really hoped this plant would be able to save him. I didn't know what I would do without him. He was my rock. I couldn't imagine a world where I didn't have him to imbue wisdom into me, to stop me from doing something without thinking about it, showing me how to be a fair king.

There had been times over my last two hundred years when I behaved less than royalty should. I didn't understand at first why we couldn't just use our power to end anyone who might disagree with us.

My father explained what a privilege this power was and that the Gods gave it to us to protect and care for the Mayan folk. There were Fae out there that might not agree with us, but they didn't deserve to die for it without a chance for an explanation.

That's not to say he was weak. He earned his position as King of Maya. He was ferocious when he needed to be, but he was fair and just.

We could respect that others wanted a different way of life without wiping them all off the face of Maya.

It took me a long time to understand, especially regarding the Serpent tribes. They never came near the palace, but there were whispers about them attacking villages they passed through, and some even blamed them for the famine.

That I was sure wasn't them, but they just seemed so feral. Which was a lot to say about Fae, who were inherently a little wild.

I hadn't seen much of them, but I always worried they would break the treaty at some point and attack. They didn't outnumber us, but they've been said to be great warriors. The decimation on both sides from the war between us was so bad the treaty was agreed to quickly to save us from extinction.

If it ever came to war again, I'd be ready. I hoped everything my father taught me would stop me from clearing them out completely.

Champagne-colored movement from the other bed caught my attention, pulling me out of my spiraling thoughts.

Gods, I loved that nightgown.

I could still feel the silkiness of it on my fingers, along with the taste of her smooth sweet skin in my mouth. I didn't know when we were going to be able to be alone again, but it needed to happen soon or I might just explode from the anticipation.

A few swishes of her hips had her grabbing the folded riding clothes on the floor, her head turned slightly like she just became aware I might be watching her.

I didn't even try to look away when she looked over her shoulder at me.

I had no shame in it.

She'd be the only thing I saw for the rest of my life if she wished it.

I flashed her a cocky smile. "Good morning, Prisoner."

I couldn't help but continue to call her that. Her attempt to steal from me is what brought her to me. I had no doubts that I would have found her eventually, but I wouldn't wish our meeting to be prolonged a second longer than it was.

Two hundred years isn't a very long time in Maya, but it felt like an eternity without knowing her.

Although, at this point, maybe I was the prisoner because she definitely held the key to my very being.

She looked over to see her sister and Cree still sleeping. She tip-toed her way over to me, and I propped myself up on my arm as she sat on the edge of the bed.

"Hi," she whispered.

Over the last couple of days, we'd talked a lot about our pasts. She seemed to have lived her life in a similar way to mine concerning sex.

Hearing that she had casual sex at all had a beast in me roaring to break free, but I knew that wasn't fair to her.

We were both in new waters, and I knew it was only a matter of time before we drowned in each other.

"Sleep well?" I asked smugly.

I knew she slept well because I was the one who held her for hours while she breathed gently against my chest. She dipped her head down to mine and laid a gentle kiss on my lips.

She lingered there for a moment before whispering, "I've had better."

She tried to jump away before I caught her in my arms and pulled her tight to me again. Our laughing stirred the others, and I placed one more kiss on her lips before letting her go.

I knew she didn't want to talk to Camila about this yet, so I wouldn't force her.

Even though my soul was screaming to claim her and not let anyone else even think they had a chance.

I'd bend to her every wish. Damn that power.

Camila sat up and looked around the room to find me lying in bed, staring at the ceiling, and her sister humming to herself and buttoning the last button on her pants. She groaned and laid back down, pulling the covers over her head.

"It's too early for that, Xio," she grumbled.

Camila eventually pulled the blankets back off her head, and started getting herself ready to leave.

I rolled off the bed and on top of Cree, immediately throwing us into a battle of who could overpower which.

Since I'd been awake for a while with pent-up energy thinking about Xio, I won quickly. I jumped off of him, laughing at his expense, which just made him angrier.

"You really should be ready for an attack at any time, brother," I said mockingly, and he tossed me a flash of his middle finger.

He may not be my brother in blood, but he was the closest thing to it. We grew up together in every way possible.

We learned everything together, how to fight together, practiced our magic together, even the most basic things like how to hold a spoon.

My parents were as much his as they were mine, even though I knew deep down he wished he knew who his biological parents were.

The fact the princesses were getting answers so quickly had to be eating at him. Even my mother couldn't figure out where he came from, and that was saying a lot because my mother solved every puzzle ever presented to her.

I'd have to make sure I checked on him later.

We made it over to our horses, readying to make our way home.

We only had a few days left now until we made it. I was both anxious and excited to get there. Everything felt like it was balancing on the edge of a blade, one wrong move from toppling over.

I couldn't wait to introduce Xio to my parents, though. That was one thing I had no anxiety about.

I watched her and her sister laugh about something while Camila flailed her hands around, telling a very passionate story about something I couldn't hear.

"Holt...Holt!" I heard Cree trying to get my attention. I turned back to him and lifted my brow in response.

"I asked if you're ready to go? What was that? Why are you smiling so big?" he asked, inspecting me.

I hadn't told Cree about my suspicions about Xio yet. I was pretty confident in what I felt but didn't want to bring it up with him until I told Xio.

Now that I did that in a way...

"She's my soul-bound," I said confidently.

Gods, that felt good to say out loud.

Maybe I should start telling everyone? Maybe not.

"Are you serious?" he asked, staring at me wide-eyed.

The more he inspected my facial expression, he realized I was very much serious.

"Holy shit," he muttered.

He looked back over to where the sisters stood still, engaged in conversation and we both watched them until they realized we were looking at them.

"It's rude to stare," Camila said, squinting her eyes at us.

Xio didn't seem to mind and just smiled, walking over to me.

"We're ready if you are?" she said sweetly, offering me her backside so I could help mount her on the horse.

I knew she could do it herself, but any reason to get my hands on her was enough for me. Camila and Cree were still giving each other the silent treatment.

He told me about how he almost admitted he cared about her. For him, that may as well have been a proposal for marriage.

He did emotional attachment even less than I did, so I knew he was battling his thoughts about her.

My advice was to ride out whatever feelings bubbled up, but he thought that was a terrible idea. He didn't want to have to care about anyone other than our family and the kingdom, but something about these females was magnetic.

I had a feeling he'd have to face it soon enough too. Though they covered whatever it was between them with layers of disdain and unpleasantness.

Cree wasn't used to anyone challenging him other than me, and Camila challenged him more than any other Fae he'd met.

I saw the assessing looks he cast her way when she wasn't looking.

Hate and love were two sides of the same coin, and I could take a guess which side their coin would fall on.

CHAPTER 22

CAMILA

We were about a day away from the palace, we'd been riding fast and true the last few days, and we all were starting to get antsy with the anticipation of being so close.

We stopped at a river for some water. We'd been discussing riding through the night since we weren't that far, but we hadn't decided yet. We knew the horses would get tired soon, so we let them drink from the river as well.

I was lying next to the riverbed, trying to relish the feeling of my muscles relaxing if we decided to keep going.

Xio and Holt were *'off training'* on the other side of the trees that lined the river, but I didn't hear the sound of any steel, just giggling and whispers.

I warned her about moving too fast, but it seemed like she had made her decision.

I'd support her no matter what, but it was my duty to protect her as her sister. We both always guarded our hearts closely, but Holt broke through her walls quicker than I would have liked.

It looked like he cared for her, so I hoped she would never end up brokenhearted. I'd need to have the old '*if you hurt her, I kill you*' talk with him soon.

I watched as the clouds moved across the sky and soaked up the sweet sun rays that covered my entire body.

I always took pleasure in the feel of the sun, but now that we knew we were Descendants of Kinich, it felt like it recharged my soul. I never felt more connected.

I looked over to find Cree bending over with cupped hands bringing water to his mouth to drink beside me.

Then all of a sudden, I heard a grunt, and he fell back. I sat up and saw a figure in smoke through the trees disappear. Before I could think about it, I was standing over Cree.

He had an obsidian arrow piercing his chest, and blood was starting to seep from the wound.

I grabbed my dagger and stood over his body, waiting for another to attack, but they were already gone.

"Fuck," he grunted, trying to sit up, and fell back to the ground.

"Tell me what to do. What do I need to do?" I asked frantically.

"Holt! Help!" I shouted.

My heart was beating so fast that it felt like it would burst. Cree's eyes started to close, and I slapped him across the face with every ounce of my Godly strength.

"Don't you dare close your eyes!"

He blinked a couple times but kept his gaze on me.

"Tell me what to do," I whispered, trying to calm myself enough to help him.

"Just pull it out," Cree grunted. "We can heal it. It didn't reach my heart," he finished before resting his arm across his forehead.

Holt and Xio came running through the trees as I tore his shirt and yanked the arrow out of him.

Blood started to spurt from the hole, and Cree passed out from the sudden blood loss. I pressed my hand to his wound and tried to figure out how to heal it.

"How do I heal him?!" I yelled at Holt as he finally made it to my side.

Xio grabbed me and tried to hold me still while Holt placed his hands on Cree's wound.

I need to see.

I couldn't stand back and watch him die. He irritated me to no end, but I found myself enjoying our back-and-forth banter.

I always found him attractive, who wouldn't, but I started to feel more than just a sexual pull towards him. I ripped myself from Xio's arms and crawled over to hold his head in my lap.

Holt's fingers glowed faint red light, and the blood started to get thicker and stopped dripping off his body. The flesh began to knit itself together, and he let out a grunt in pain.

Holt left his hands on his body a little longer, and Cree sighed in relief. His eyes flicked open and fell on me.

Hair fell in front my face, my eyes were filled with tears, and his blood covered my skin. He lifted his hand to tuck a strand of hair behind my ear and rubbed his thumb down the line of my jaw. His eyes were soft with the realization that I was worried he wouldn't make it.

"It'll take more than that to kill me, Mila," he muttered.

He never called me by my name, let alone the nickname my mother used in the memory she left us.

I didn't tell him that she called me Mila, and my heart skipped a beat. I chuckled through tears before he closed his eyes, and his head fell back into my lap.

"What happened? What's wrong with him?" I panicked.

"We can heal the pain and the wound, but he'll need to rest for a bit," he responded.

I nodded and I wiped the tears from my face before realizing it only smeared more of his blood onto my skin. I looked down at the blood on my shaking hands, and my sister helped me up and moved me to the water's edge.

She rinsed my hands and cleaned the blood from my face as she eyed me warily. It seemed like the worry I had for her with Holt, she now held for me.

I wasn't expecting to have such a reaction. If you had asked me a few days ago what I'd do if he was shot with an arrow, I might have just shrugged and said the bastard deserved it.

But not anymore, and that was made abundantly clear.

She opened her mouth, but before she could get a word out, I looked back to find Cree's body missing from the spot he was lying in previously.

"Where did he go?" I asked Xio, surveying the area around me.

Her brow pinched slightly as she waited a few moments to respond. "Holt took him to where we were training. We'll set up camp over there. You didn't hear him say that before he left?"

I didn't. I was still in a state of shock. I took a deep breath and followed my sister to where our tents were already set up.

Holt walked out of the tent that used to be ours, but Cree now used. I looked at him, eager to hear what his assessment was.

"He's resting. He'll be good as new in the morning," he said, placing a hand on my shoulder.

He looked at me just as a brother would to console their younger sister, and I smiled gently and nodded before sitting down to start setting up a fire for us.

"What happened?" Xio asked quietly, like she was scared I would break at any moment.

I didn't even remember to tell them what I saw on the other side of the river. Once I saw Cree bleeding out on the ground, everything else ceased to exist. My mouth dropped open as the pieces of the puzzle started to fit together.

"Smoke," I muttered, "there was smoke."

"Like from the attack and what we saw in the memory our mother left us?" Xio asked, coming to sit next to me by the fire that was now roaring.

My fire magic came so easily to me now I didn't even realize I sent a spark into the pile of wood.

"Yes, just like that. They were in the woods across the river one moment and then gone the next in a puff of smoke. After they—"

I stopped and looked over to Holt, hoping he held answers, but he just put his finger to his temple and rubbed it.

"Your mother was right. Whatever came for her is coming for us now. They're trying to stop us before we stop them," he muttered.

His eyes fell on the tent Cree was sleeping in, and I wondered if he was as scared as I was when he saw him lying near the river so still. We both looked away from the tent simultaneously, and he noticed where my thoughts were going.

"He's survived worse," he started, trying to reassure me, "you won't believe the shit we've gotten ourselves into in the last two centuries."

He gave me that warm brotherly smile, and I wished that made me feel better, but it only eased some of my worries. He patted me on my shoulder again and went to sit on the other side of the fire.

"I'm...I'm just going to sit with him," I stuttered, "he stayed with me when I was too drunk, not that it's the same thing, I just...I feel like I owe him so...."

"We understand," Xio said, stopping me from my nervous rambling.

I left the fire and opened the flap of his tent. He sat so still, but his face was no longer pinched with pain.

He looked so calm as his bare chest rose and fell evenly. Holt wiped some of the blood from him, but he didn't get it all.

There was a small bowl of water next to him, with a bloodied rag I assumed Holt used earlier. I sat next to him and gently cleaned the remaining blood from him, making sure to get every last drop.

I rarely got to look at him this long without one of us making a comment that got our blood boiling.

I thought I liked him sitting here quietly and pretty, but that wasn't true.

I loved how he challenged me and pushed me in training and how he could see I was nervous and redirect the feeling to anger with him.

I just didn't feel I was ready to commit myself to anyone.

I was just figuring out who I was. There were still gaps in my memory, and we had no idea what saving Maya would entail. I didn't think I had room for someone right now, but if I made room for anyone, it would be him.

One day. Maybe.

I took the opportunity to study his tattoos as I rubbed the last bits of blood from his chest with the rag. The area above his heart on his chest had shading of flames and shadow, but it was barer than the rest of his body.

I dragged the rag down where the blood dripped onto his abdomen to the top of his pants. More tattoos dipped beneath it, and I wondered if his legs were covered too.

There were so many lines and patterns of shapes wrapped around his body, they looked badass.

It made me want to get a few of my own.

He moaned slightly and shifted in his sleep. I set the rag down back in the bowl and continued watching him.

As if I dared to take my eyes off him for one second, the wound would open back up, and he would bleed out.

The tent's flap opened, and my sister peaked her head in. She was carrying my blanket, and she set it next to where I sat beside him.

"You okay?" she asked.

No, I really wasn't, but I nodded and looked back at Cree.

She left the tent, and I got comfortable next to him for the night.

I laid my hand on his arm so I could feel if he started to stir and closed my eyes.

My cheek was warm, and my head rose and fell gently.

I felt fingers running through my hair, and I opened my eyes to a heavily tattooed chest and a scarred wound.

At some point throughout the night, I shifted over to lay my head on him, and he hadn't pushed me away yet. I tipped up my chin to see him staring down at me with a small crooked smile.

"I knew it was you who snored," he said, laughing gently with his eyes on his fingers running through my hair. "You stayed in here all night?"

"Yeah. I figured I owed you one," I responded.

I suddenly felt a little embarrassed, but neither of us made any effort to move.

Cree raised his eyebrows suggestively, directing his look at his chest where my face still rested. "Funny, you look much more comfortable than I was when I did this for you."

"Shut up. It was cold," I replied as I sat up and checked his wound.

I pushed my fingers on it, expecting the injury to be soft from the hole the arrow made, but it was just as hard as the side I woke up on.

The healing magic really was handy, but he still had so many scars, and I remembered seeing a long scar on his face before.

I traced my finger where the scar lay in front of his ear all the way down to his shoulder and back up to his temple. "How'd you get this?"

"This was one of my first missions with the Warriors. We've lived in peace for a long time, but even in peace, there will always be unhappy Fae. Out on the outskirts of the kingdom, a group of Fae were trying to steal from the homes around them. The commander before me directed my unit to go and handle it, there were about six of us in total. The King always told us we shouldn't aim to kill our subjects immediately. Defend ourselves, of course, but with the people of our kingdom, we should try and disarm and understand them. These Fae...they were too angry, believing if they had the power to take from others, they should be allowed to. Believing in the old rules we lived by when we were nothing more than primal beasts. But there were mothers and children in some of those homes. They weren't even able to fight. There were more of them than we originally thought, so we had to fight more than one at a time. After getting one of them onto the ground and disarmed, another one came at me faster than I expected. I didn't have time to stop him. His dagger already ran across my skin from my ear to my shoulder. I stabbed him in the chest, and he died. He was my first kill. I knew it was justified, he was trying to hurt others in the kingdom, and my duty was to the kingdom. Not to mention if I didn't do it, I might have died had he gotten to my heart. But, the first time is difficult to decipher no matter the situation."

I let that sink in. Xio and I had always lived by similar rules. Up until we escaped Zuma, we hadn't killed a single soul.

But he was right. In this case, he had no choice.

I was sure we'd have to add more to that list soon.

Whatever evil was coming for Maya wouldn't get to give an explanation. They would need to be destroyed.

"Yeah. I know what you mean," I responded.

He watched me carefully, like he wanted to ask how I could relate, but I didn't want to open that dam right now.

If he knew how little I felt when I sliced that blade across the guard's neck, he might not look at me the same again so I quickly diverted the conversation.

"Why do you keep the scars if you can heal them?"

I wondered this before but never asked him about it, but after that explanation, the question felt even more important.

"Scars are a map of where we've been, what we've survived. We don't shy away from them in Maya. We celebrate them. In the case of this one, I wanted to remember," he said confidently while running his finger over the mark.

I wished that's how I felt about mine.

Back in our village in Zuma, I had an unfortunate run-in with Lord Wayward on a day he was feeling particularly evil.

He used to visit the market solely to find people to torture, and that day it was my turn. We didn't have any power then, we knew how to fight, but I wasn't a match for the four guards he stuck on me.

He said I needed to be put in my place when I wouldn't bow to him and kiss his feet. He wasn't royalty, just a rich asshole with too much power that he never really earned. I refused, and he had his men whip me in the street right across the back of my thighs.

He said my back was too pretty to damage.

It took three guards to hold my sister back. I didn't want his attention to turn to her, so I made her stop trying to get to me and held in every scream that tried to escape me.

But the guard who held the whip, I memorized his face. I promised him death over and over until they left me in the street, bleeding.

It took weeks to heal, and my sister had to work double time to make sure we were fed while I couldn't help.

That was the real reason I wanted to steal from him, even though I told my sister it was just because it would help us leave the village. I knew she was fully aware of why I wanted to do it, but she didn't call me out.

She wanted revenge just as bad as I did, and was willing to help me get it. In a weird roundabout way, his actions set me on the path of finding out who I was, to meeting Cree and Holt.

Maybe I should be proud of them.

Would I still have stolen from Lord Wayward and had to flee into Maya if I wasn't trying to enact revenge?

"Something to think about," I said, quickly switching subjects again, "why do you have a serpent tattoo if it's associated with the tribes?"

He brought his forearm up to look at the tattoo I asked about.

"Full of questions today, aren't you?" he chuckled. "Serpents aren't meant to be a symbol of evil. The tribes use it as a symbol of predatorial ferocity, but that's not what the Gods meant it to be a symbol of. They symbolize great change, rebirth, and renewal. They can shed their skin and become new," he finished as he traced the serpent with his finger.

I could see how such a thing would resonate with him. It resonated with me, too, for similar reasons.

"Not to mention it looks badass," he said jokingly, always trying to deflect from his feelings.

Which I didn't blame him for. I would have done the same thing.

Oh my Gods, are Cree and I the same person?

That shook me enough to force myself to stand up, and I grabbed my blanket to exit the tent.

"I should go check on Xio," I said.

"Hey," Cree said.

I turned around to find him sitting up as he ran his hand through his hair, creating that messiness that was his signature look.

Who looked this good after being shot in the chest with an arrow?

"Thank you...For helping heal me and staying with me...You didn't have to do it...And I just wanted to say...Thank you," he stumbled over his words, and I swear I saw some blush rising into his rugged face.

I nodded my response and walked out of the tent into the fresh cool air.

It hit me like a stone wall, and I took a deep breath, stuffing down all of the sappy emotions that were trying to escape me.

Chapter 23

Xio

We were so close to the castle I could see its outline in the distance.

It was a massive formation, maybe even bigger than the Sun Palace, but it was hard to tell from this far.

A village full of thousands of Fae surrounded it. Once we made it through the gates, Holt and Cree removed their hoods.

This was the first time they allowed everyone to see who they were in our journey, and now I could see why. The kingdom burst to life the moment they were spotted by two young boys pretending to spar with wooden swords near the gate; they both dropped their swords and started running through the streets.

"The Princes are here! The Princes are here!" one boy shouted while the other knocked on all the doors of their friends until the streets started to fill.

"Maybe we should let you two greet your kingdom first? We can stay back and find our way," I suggested nervously.

I never liked all the attention on me, let alone thousands of Fae I didn't know existed until a week ago.

Holt rubbed my arm and brought his mouth to my ear.

"I'm not letting you walk all the way to the palace by yourself. Don't be nervous. I'm with you," he whispered, and I instinctively turned my face to rub my cheek to his.

"Okay," I said quietly, still nervous, but knowing he was behind me helped ease my nerves.

There was screaming and clapping, and people were dancing in the streets. I had no doubts he was good to his kingdom, but they seemed to revere him in a way I didn't expect.

One little girl stepped up to the horse before we could pass her.

"Is that your girlfriend, Prince? I was hoping I could become the Princess one day!" she shouted, placing her hands on her hips.

I laughed at the display of attitude, and Holt jumped down from the horse. He picked a nearby flower and walked over to her. He got down on one knee and placed it in her hair.

"She's not my girlfriend, yet," he looked back at me, smiling smugly. "Do you think she should be?"

The girl eyed me with a look that was far older than she appeared to be. "Well, she is pretty. I like her hair. I guess she can be your girlfriend. Marco down the street said he'd be my boyfriend anyways, so it's okay."

She jumped up and wrapped her arms around his neck in a tight embrace before running down to play with her friends. He jumped back up onto Thunder and wrapped his arms around me to grab the reins.

"Was that your way of claiming me?" I asked him over my shoulder.

"Oh, you'll know when I claim you, Prisoner," he whispered back, sending small bumps all over my skin.

We carried along to the edge of the village, where we handed over the horses to a male who was already waiting, surely hearing the commotion we caused on our way in.

Everyone looked so happy to see us, but he looked somber. Like he was pleased to see the princes but also like something terrible had happened. Holt was too excited to be home to notice, but I saw the man's face, and Cree also seemed to notice. He turned his head to the side and studied the male walking away with our horses.

"Thank you, Hugo," Holt said before dusting himself off and making his way towards the palace doors.

I was right in my assessment of the palace. It was bigger than the Sun Palace, which says a lot because our palace was the size of a mountain. Made of interconnecting gray stones, some darker than others, creating a pleasing pattern. An assortment of towers with small slits and large walls seemed to go on forever.

Where my mother seemed to favor gold, silver was used here. There was a drawbridge with water beneath it, and I realized that the water ran all the way around the building, then, the smell of salt hit me.

He said it was on the far west side of the land, but I didn't realize there would be a great expanse of water at its border.

I never really thought about what was beyond. But now I was struck by the movement of the water, and the crashing waves against the stones that surrounded it. The sound was serene.

I felt Holt's presence behind me.

"It's beautiful, isn't it?" he asked.

"It's more than beautiful. It's powerful. I could stand out here and watch it for hours," I muttered.

He didn't respond, so I looked over at him, and he was looking at me the way I was at the water.

"I agree," he said, smiling before placing his hand on my back and guiding me across the bridge.

The large silver doors opened before we reached them, and people moved about, preparing for the princes' arrival. A small older female ran up to us, her brown and gray hair curled slightly at the ends, coming just past her ears.

She wore a simple navy blue dress with a dark gray apron wrapped around her waist that accentuated her tan skin. She looked to be in charge of the others running around as she had just finished yelling directions at them.

"My princes, we weren't sure when you'd be back. We actually didn't know when you left, but you should have sent word that you'd be bringing guests! We've been a bit busy, but we could have had a banquet planned for your arrival. It could have been grand enough—"

"It's fine, Zyanya," Holt cut her off, smiling at her and bringing her into a big embrace. Her feet lifted off the ground and he set her back down softly, and she knocked him on his shoulder.

"Oh, enough of that, you," she said, trying to scold him, but she clearly cared a great deal about him and was happy he was home.

Cree came to kiss the female on her cheek, and she blushed at the tattooed Fae.

"And how in the nine hells did they convince you two to follow them here? You two look far too innocent to be hanging with these scoundrels," she said, eyeing my sister and me.

"Oh, you have no idea," Cree said, patting Camila on the head.

She shot him a look sharp enough to cut, and he laughed at her before introducing us both to Zyanya.

"This is Camila, the less innocent one," he said, pointing to Camila.

"This is Xio, the slightly more innocent one," he said, pointing at me.

"I'm Zyanya, I run the palace staff here," she responded.

She held out her hand and I shook it anxiously, worried she would feel the sweat pooling in my palm.

She pulled me into a hug before pulling Camila into one too.

"Anyone who can put up with them is good in my book. Let's get you two some food. I'm sure you're hungry after your travels. You two should go see your mother. She's in her chambers," she said, a quick look of that somberness the male outside had shot across her face.

"Why is she in her chambers? It's nearly lunch?" Holt asked.

Worry started to grow in my gut. Something was definitely wrong. I wasn't sure of what, but all the signs were there.

"I want to introduce her to Xio and Camila. We'll come back for food when we're done," he said, offering me his arm.

"I think you should go by yourselves, Holt. She might not—"

"Zyanya, what reason would she have not to want to meet our guests?" he asked.

She looked down at the ground. "You're right, do as you wish, Prince."

He looped his arm in mine and guided us to her bedchamber.

Cree and Camila followed behind us. I looked over my shoulder, their faces were tight with worry, and I turned my gaze back to Holt. He was greeting everyone we walked by cheerfully with his most genuine smile. We rounded a corner, and I spoke up.

"Holt... I think maybe...."

We came to another large silver door, and he pushed it open before I could tell him that we should wait behind. The room we entered was dark, a sitting area outside of the bedchamber beyond it. The curtains were drawn, and only one lamp was lit.

"Mother! We're home," he started, "why are you sitting in the dark?"

He used his magic to light the other lamps in the room, exposing his mother in the corner of the room.

His mother was astonishingly beautiful.

She had long brown hair that flowed down to her hips in tight waves. Her skin was lighter than Holt's but still a deep golden bronze color, and, she was dressed in all black. Her deep blue eyes shot up to us, full of tears.

Her eyes were puffy, and her cheeks glistened in the lamp's light. Holt stopped abruptly before reaching her, his shoulders dropped, and his whole posture seemed to loosen.

"No," he whispered, "no, it's not possible. I went to get the flower to save him!" he roared, with the realization that she wore the colors of mourning. "The doctor said he still had nearly a year, that the flower would help him before the worst of it came!"

His mother burst into tears and ran to him. She was petite, but her arms were lined with muscle as she wrapped them around him, laid her head on his stomach, and sobbed.

He held his mother while she soaked the front of his shirt in tears.

She looked up at him, lip still quivering. "It happened a few days after you two left. He...He sent you away to find that flower...He didn't... He didn't want the two of you to see him...."

She burst into tears again and clutched her chest.

Holt said that losing your soul-bound could create such pain that it could be felt physically, and his mother was a testament to it. Holt kept shaking his head in denial about what his mother was saying.

"Wait, you're saying that he knew he was going to die soon?" Holt whispered.

"He loved you two too much to let you see him die. He is the one who told the doctor to tell you about the flower," she swallowed a sob that bubbled up her throat. "After you told me you were going to find a cure, I went to find him. I was so excited that there was finally something that would save him. He explained that he couldn't bear the thought of you two watching him die. He wanted you to remember him as he was. I disagreed with him. I knew you would want to be here, but he was so stubborn. We fought about it before I tried to run and find you and Cree. I knew he'd be angry, but I couldn't let him make that decision for you," she paused and wiped her eyes. "By the time I made it to the gates, you two were already gone, I sent someone to try and stop you, but you were too far already."

Tears began to fall from Holt's eyes as he sat down and hung his head between his legs.

The Queen finally noticed we were there when he sat down, and she ran over to Cree.

I was so focused on Holt that I forgot that the King was just as much a father to him. He stared blankly into the distance while the Queen hugged him, sobbing as she did with Holt.

"I don't understand," Cree said gently, "why wouldn't he want us here?"

Camila wrapped her fingers tight around his.

"We didn't get to say goodbye," Cree said between heavy breaths.

"You did. You just didn't know you were saying goodbye. The day before he had the healer tell Holt about the flower. You all spent the entire day together," she said, looking over at Holt too. "He felt strong that day, but when he returned to our bedchamber that night, he fell sicker than he'd been before. He knew it was coming," she finished reaching up on her tiptoes to wipe the tears from Cree's face.

"He told us how much he loved us, that he was proud of us," Holt said quietly.

Cree ripped his hand away from Camila and stormed out of the room. She went to follow him, but she stopped at the doorway, looking back at me.

We knew grief, but our grief was different. We didn't know how to console grief this fresh. Our grief was for parents we didn't know. Of course, we knew who they are now, but it was different.

His was for the male who raised him as his own son, stood up for him when people said he should be cast out, and showed him what it was to be Fae.

That kind of grief was all-consuming. There was nothing we could have said at that moment to help them, and it hurt me to know their hearts were breaking.

Camila and I still stood in the doorway, a large painting of the Storm King and Queen next to us. The artist had great skill. The emotions of the two seemed to leap off of the image, they looked so incredibly happy.

The King was quite handsome, his ebony skin and cropped black hair complimented by his deep gray clothing. His strong jaw was lined with short stubble, the curve of his lips identical to Holt's.

There was no denying this male was the King.

A gasp caught my attention from across the room. The Queen's eyes fell on me, assessing. She turned her head to the side like she had a realization as she also looked over at my sister, and her eyes grew wide.

I'd been traveling with royalty for some time now, but the Queen was a different kind of royalty. The weight of her gaze had me fidgeting with my fingers and shifting on my feet.

"You two..." she started to say but looked back at her son, who was still working through his emotions. "Why don't we go get some food? I haven't eaten today, and I think Holt could use some time alone."

I looked over to Holt, unsure if I should stay or go. He gave me the best smile he could manage and nodded his head.

He told me his mother was kind and that she would accept us with open arms. I nodded and followed her out into the hall beyond her bedchamber.

She turned the corner and stopped us in our tracks. As small as she was, she was an intimidating figure. She walked a circle around the both of us, inspecting us from head to toe.

"You are Adelina and Jasper's daughters," not a question, a statement, like she knew there was no room for her to be incorrect. "You look just like them. Do my sons know who you are?"

"No, well, they didn't at first, we actually didn't know," Camila started rambling, the Queen making her just as nervous as I was.

"They know now," my voice cracked slightly, and I took a deep breath. "We have been in the human lands, Zuma, for the last ten years. She sent us there to protect us. She bound our magic and wiped our memory. Holt and Cree found us on their journey, and Holt broke the bindings she placed on us."

I could see the wheels in her head turning while she tried to figure out what to say next.

"Our mother left us a memory, she told us about a prophecy. Holt said you'd be able to help us," Camila finished my thought.

The Queen gasped and stumbled a step.

"The prophecy," she whispered to herself. She shook her head and stilled, taking a deep breath.

"Come, let's eat. We will figure all of this out after we have full bellies," she linked her arms with both of us and started to walk down the hall, her eyes still swollen from crying.

"You have a beautiful home, your majesty," I said, trying to fill the silence.

"Call me Chara," she said with a sweet smile, "it's ancient, but it does the job," she finished with a wink.

I studied her features, Holt was double her size, but he had her round eye shape. He had a similarly shaped nose, hers much more petite, but there was no denying this was his mother.

We seemed to be distracting her enough from her grief. It helped ease some of my nerves to know I was able to do this for Holt.

I wondered where he was right now and if he was coming to terms with what this meant for him.

We walked into a small eating hall, the windows stretched from the floor to the ceiling, navy blue fabric draped across them.

A gray wood table sat in the middle of the room, and a lightning bolt emblem was carved into the center of it. It was an intimate space, not the great hall I expected.

"I like to eat here when only a few people are partaking. I enjoy the view of The Meso, the sea," she said, standing in front of the window.

I came up to stand next to her and look at the view. The landscape took my breath away once again.

I could now see the white sand beach that lay behind the palace. The waves crashed, and foam rippled onto the white sand, making it appear gray.

If I were the Queen, I'd spend every meal here. She chuckled at my wide-eyed expression.

"I take it there are no beaches in the human lands?"

"No, there isn't," I said quietly, still watching the waves crash.

She looped her arm in mine again and sat me down at the table. Camila was already digging into the spread that was stretched across the table.

We had absolutely no table etiquette, let alone any knowledge of how royal Fae were supposed to act with other royals.

I kicked Camila's leg under the table to stop her from continuing stuffing food into her mouth like some kind of wild animal.

She looked over at the Queen, and we sat and watched as she gracefully lifted her plate, and a few of the royal staff came and placed different foods on it.

She smiled warmly at the staff and gave her thanks, and they backed away with a bow.

Camila and I both replicated the Queens moves, hopefully selling the facade that we had more etiquette than the poor human girls we'd been for the last decade.

She nodded at us, lifting the middle-sized fork from the row of cutlery we had, and began eating.

I eyed all of the silver cutlery at my disposal and tried to find the same fork she was using.

Zyanya walked in and jumped back when she found us three in the room.

"Your majesty," she bowed. "You left your room? I was just coming to tell them to bring the food to you?" she asked while she ran her eyes over the Queen in a motherly way. She seemed to take care of everyone here.

"No need. I'll be taking my lunch here today," the Queen responded.

Zyanya accepted the answer and left the room.

"We're very sorry for your loss," I told her genuinely.

"Thank you, Xio. This is a welcomed distraction. As you can see from Zyanya's reaction, I haven't left the room much. With Holt and Cree gone, I've been festering in my grief for...too long. I'm happy for the company."

We all began eating the food on our plates, and my mouth watered with the delicious flavors running across my tongue.

"You were friends with our parents?" Camila asked eagerly.

Holt mentioned they were all very close. Sadness ran across her features as she thought of her lost friends. She was the only one left of the group now that everyone else had passed.

"I was. Your parents were some of my favorite people. We ran Maya together and met every few years formally for our tournaments. They were very competitive, like all Fae," she laughed. "But they were so kind and warm. I met you once when you two were young. Your mother was very protective of you. She didn't let many outside of your palace meet you. Her power was unmatched but also a curse for her."

"What does that mean?" I asked.

"Your mother was a Mente. I have a touch of it myself, but nothing like what your mother was capable of. She knew that one day you'd be the key to save us all, she didn't go into the details of it with me, but she hid you from the world for that reason."

She took a sip of the wine that Zyanya brought in and set the cup back down.

"Is that how she was able to leave us the memory?" Camila questioned.

"It is. While I see flashes of possibilities and have very accurate intuition, her power was much more. So great that she could manipulate the mind and memories, bring them into the physical world, yes. Her visions of the future were much more clear than mine, though still only possibilities. Which leads me to the prophecy."

Camila and I looked at each other, and both took a deep breath. This was it. This would guide our next steps.

"I have it in the library. We can meet there in the morning after breakfast and work through it together. It's rather indirect from what I remember, but I'm sure we can figure it out together," she smiled, standing from her seat.

"Yes, that sounds great," I responded, standing up and pushing my chair in.

Some of the royal staff came in to clear out the dirty dishes. We walked out of the room and realized we didn't know where Holt or Cree were or where we'd be staying while we were here.

"Go to the beach, follow that hallway, and take a right. There will be some stairs that lead you out into the courtyard and to the beach," she said, giving me a knowing look.

There's that touch of the Mente power she mentioned earlier.

She turned to Camila. "Go to the training arena. It's on your left, right before the stables."

She went to turn away from us and tossed her hair back over her shoulder to look at us.

"I'm delighted my boys found you two," she said with a sweet smile.

I could see the grief of her lost love start coming back over her as she walked back to her dark chamber.

"Well, that was a lot to decipher," Camila said with a chuckle.

"That's putting it lightly," I responded, "I'm going to go to the beach. Something tells me I shouldn't ignore her commands."

We both laughed and turned to follow the directions the Queen gave us.

I rounded the hallway, it was lit with silver sconces, and people quickly made their way up and down. I took a right and found the stairs into the courtyard.

Spending so much time in the forest this last week raised the bar on what I found beautiful. But whoever designed this garden was highly talented. Flowers of every color covered the ground, and there were benches and gazebos throughout that had vines and other flowers climbing up them to offer privacy.

The stone path turned to sand, and I made my way to the beach, passing a few Fae enjoying the garden.

Holt sat in the sand with his trousers rolled up and his shirt removed. He stared out into the horizon like it would have the answers to why his father made the decision he did.

He looked defeated, like nothing would ever be the same for him. I supposed it wouldn't.

I slid off my shoes and left them by the gardens before coming and sitting in the sand beside him.

He didn't look at me, but his fingers wrapped around mine, and we sat silently, listening to the waves.

"I don't understand," he whispered, "why send me on a pointless journey to save him when I could have been there for him before he passed?"

I didn't have an answer, so I squeezed his hand tighter. He looked over at me, and the devastation on his face nearly brought me to tears.

The male I came to know was always so bright, witty, and powerful. But right now, he had nothing left in him to give. I wasn't sure what I could offer him, but I would sit out here on the beach with him until the morning if he wanted me to.

"He was so strong, the power he had was gifted from a God, and it still wasn't enough. I thought I still had time. There was so much he wasn't able to tell me. I have so many questions on how to run the kingdom and how to become the Fae he was. I wanted him to meet you," he said, shifting his toes in the sand. "He would have loved you, and now he'll never know that I found you."

"Where do we go when we pass?" I asked him

"Before the Gods were murdered, we went to Xibalba, the underworld. We were judged by Itzamna and sent to live in an afterlife in peace or turmoil. But no one knows now. That's the part that is really hurting me. Do we just go straight into the pits? Do they have to fight it out for spots in peace?" he asked, dragging his hand over his face and plopping his back onto the sand.

"I just hope he's no longer in pain, wherever he is," he finished before letting out a long breath.

I laid next to him, and the sand shifted as we turned to face each other. This grief was heavy, but I'd do what I could to help carry the burden.

"I'm here for you. Anything you need, say the word, and it'll be done," I said, my eyes moving between his eyes and lips. He smiled gently at the suggestion, but this wasn't a time to make any type of dirty joke, so he just nodded.

"Your mother is beautiful," I started, and his smile widened slightly. "She ate lunch with us and agreed to help with the prophecy in the morning. If you're up to it, we're going to meet in the library after breakfast."

"I'll be there," he said before laying his hand on the side of my face. "Did you tell her who you were?"

"She knew before we could even explain," I said with a smile.

He chuckled at that. I imagined his mother knew most things before people were able to get them out.

"She also told us a little more about my mother. It's nice to talk to someone who knew her when she was alive."

My chest tightened at the thought.

Grief was fickle. When unexpected or expected, it could tear your heart from your chest. No one was safe from it, but what was grief if not love?

It was a manifestation of all the love you wished to give the person who passed, all the love they gave you while they lived.

Grief was just love without the physical connection, and all that love doesn't disappear.

It has nowhere to go, so it bubbles up in your chest to the point of pain.

"Grief is the price of love. It won't ever stop because you will never stop loving your father. But, it'll change. It'll become easier, lighter. It leaves a void, yes. But, if you fill it with the good memories and make new memories for him, the void will be smaller," I whispered gently.

Saying that to him made me a little sad that I wouldn't be able to take all of the advice myself. I didn't have all of the good memories of my mother.

I would definitely be making new memories for her, though.

"The sun shines after a storm," he muttered.

I was his sun. He was my storm.

I never minded the rain.

I moved closer to him, and we laid in the sand, limbs intertwined until the storm started to part and the sun began to shine.

CHAPTER 24

CREE

I stood in the training arena, punching a wooden pole until my knuckles bled.

It was wrapped in a thick cloth for practicing sparring, so it took longer than it would have if I was punching a tree.

Which I did a few times on the way to the arena.

I savored the pain.

Anything but feeling what I was feeling right now was welcomed. I didn't heal my wounds and let the blood drip down to the floor.

Movement at the arena entrance caught my attention, I knew Holt would find me out here eventually, but I didn't want to talk.

Not yet.

"Go away," I muttered, "I don't want to fucking talk."

The footsteps stopped, so I went back to hitting the pole.

"Oh," a soft female voice whispered.

I looked up to find Camila walking out of the arena.

"Camila!" I shouted louder than I meant to, "I thought you were Holt. I wouldn't have been as much of an asshole to anyone else."

She gave me a look that said she didn't believe that for a second, which I might have deserved.

I was an asshole, but I had so much anger in me that I didn't know what to do with it.

I had a good life here, but sometimes I was just so mad at the things I couldn't control. My father taught me more than one lesson on controlling my anger. So I tried to think about what he would have said to me while another wave of it came for me at the thought of him.

'Cree, anger solves nothing. That anger of yours will consume you and destroy everything around you if you let it. You need an outlet. Make it work for you,' he'd say before bringing me out here to train with me until the anger lessened, which usually took hours.

He never complained, just encouraged me to work through it. Sometimes Holt would join, but he never had the rage I did.

I think I might have been born with it.

Whoever my parents were, they must have been some rageful Fae.

"You can stay. If you want to," I mumbled.

The truth was that I wanted her to stay.

I wouldn't tell her that outright, but she somehow knew me well enough already to know that's what I was asking.

She picked up a sparring sword and started swinging it around her body. Twirling and ducking around an invisible opponent gracefully. She spun to me and put the sword to my heart playfully.

She looked down at my fingers and sighed. "Why haven't you healed yourself yet?"

Would she judge me if I told her I liked the pain right now?

"Pain is better than sadness. Isn't it?" she followed up, taking my hand in hers.

I should have known she'd get it. We were more alike than either of us ever wanted to admit.

"Show me how to heal," she stated.

Not a question but a demand. I hesitated, and she looked up at me with her best *'did you not hear what I said'* look, and it had me smiling slightly.

"Yes, Viper," I smirked. "Healing magic is difficult. Everyone has a little bit, but mastering it isn't easy. It's why we still have healers. They study for years to be able to do things like fix complicated bone breaks and heal large organs. I let some of my magic up to my fingers. But, instead of willing it into the shadows or darkness to hurt, I will it into something to heal. It's hard to put into words. Just try it," I said, offering her my bloody knuckles.

Camila lifted her hand and willed the bright light of her powers into her hand, a wrinkle of concentration pulled between her brows before the bright yellow light turned pink, then red.

She placed it on my hand, and the skin started to fuse together, but I stopped her before she let the scars heal.

"I want to remember," I said.

She nodded and held my hands a little longer before releasing them and looking at the bloodied pole I was punching earlier.

I didn't realize I had split some of the fabric. They'd definitely need to replace it if they didn't want the others to cut their hands open.

"Do you want to talk about it?" she asked me, not making eye contact like I was an animal that would be scared off.

"I just don't know what to say, really. He was my father. He raised me. I'm having," I sighed, "I'm having difficulty understanding why he wanted to leave that way."

It was almost painful for me to get the words out. With Holt, it was easy. I didn't have to say everything. He just knew what I was trying to say without me actually having to explain my feelings.

"I don't get it either," she replied.

I knew she also meant the situation with her own parents. Their mother saved them but also caused some pretty terrible things to happen to them by doing so.

"I just wish I could have said goodbye. He's the third," I hesitated looking away from her. "The third parent I never got to say goodbye to."

I had to swallow down a small whimper that was trying to escape my throat.

"I can relate," she said with a smile. "I don't think we'll ever fully understand our parents' motives. Can't doubt they loved us, though."

She shrugged before picking the sword back up and twirling around.

Camila was as good at this as I was, but we were both trying.

I appreciated her effort; we broken Fae had to stick together, or we might just fall apart entirely.

I picked up another wooden sword and came for her while her back was turned, but she heard my footsteps and whirled around, blocking my hit.

She instinctively pushed her power into the sword, so used to using her daggers, and it shriveled up into ash and fell in front of her.

"Shit," she spat before I moved in closer to her and placed the sword to her throat.

"Yield," I said close to her ear.

"I hardly think you could do much damage with that," she said confidently.

One of the most terrifying Fae in Maya with a sword to her throat, wood or not, didn't stop her swaggering confidence.

I wrapped my shadows around the sword and let them harden into a sharp blade, I saw goosebumps prickle over her exposed skin, and she swallowed hard.

"Yield," I said again.

Her eyes locked with mine, but I found no fear there.

Just some sort of...Hunger? Reverence? I couldn't be sure.

We'd had our moments, but neither of us had taken a step past our quips and general fuckery.

I was too damaged, far too damaged to let anyone in.

Camila made me want to, though.

Would I just hurt her? Would I lose her forever if I made a mistake?

I swallowed as well before I heard someone clear their throat at the door.

Holt and Xio stood in the entryway, and Camila and I jumped away from each other like two teenagers caught by their parents.

"I just came to check on my brother," Holt said, "I showed Xio where your rooms are. She can take you to get settled in," dismissing them in a very princely way.

Camila ran over to Xio, and they exited the arena.

"So. Care to share?" he asked, flashing me his teeth in a knowing smile.

"Not particularly."

I turned to put the sparring sword back where I pulled it from so I didn't have to look at his stupid smile.

"I think she's good for you. There are not too many who can go toe to toe with you and still put up with you after. She pushes you," he said.

Nine hells, did I know it.

It infuriated me initially, but the more she did, the more I couldn't help but respect her for it. She looked at me and saw a shadow bastard, sure, but she also knew I was capable of more, and she called me out on it.

"I'm just, I'm too fucked up. Even before Father and now? Now it just seems impossible," I muttered, inspecting my knuckles.

She did an excellent job for her first healing. None of the wounds reopened. I traced my finger over them, remembering the feel of her magic caressing my skin.

"You are not fucked up. You just think you are. You just get so caught up in the darkness of the world that sometimes you forget there's light," he said.

We sat in the spots we used to sit in as kids when our father would let us watch him train with the others.

"Why'd he do it?" Holt asked.

The question I'd been asking myself repeatedly since our mother told us what happened.

"I don't know, but I think he just wanted us to remember him when he was at his best. I keep thinking about the day before we left. We would have known he was saying goodbye if we had been paying attention. It just felt so good to be able to spend the day with him how we used to. I didn't even try to analyze why we were doing it."

That day was one of his best since we discovered he was sick. We rode through the kingdom together and out into the plains surrounding it. We stopped at a river we used to play in as kids and drank the water while he recalled different stories of us two there.

He told us how proud he was that those little kids turned out to be what we are today.

He told us he loved us more than he had in the last year.

When we returned to the palace, all of our favorite foods were ready in the Queen's dining room. We ate together and laughed with our mother for hours while drinking wine.

I looked over at Holt, who seemed to be recalling all the same things I was.

"That was a good day," he whispered and swallowed. "I'm almost glad that was our last memory."

"Me too," I said, putting my hand on my brother's shoulder.

Maybe we could understand why he did it. It eased some of my anger, but not all of it.

"I'm still angry," I declared.

"Me too."

We sat silently for a bit longer and I could almost feel him here, telling us to keep light on our feet or to remind us that defending ourselves was just as important as attacking.

"Mother just gave me this," he said, pulling out a folded piece of paper with the King's royal seal on it. "I haven't opened it yet. She said he left it for the both of us."

He handed it to me, and I ran my finger over the dark gray wax he used to seal the letter. I broke the seal, and the signature feel of his magic overwhelmed both of us.

His voice floated to us from the letter, the words he wrote being spoken into the air around us.

I'm sorry, my sons. I wish I was a better Fae. I wish I could have told you everything, that I would have been strong enough to have you here when I passed into the next life. I couldn't let you see me like that. Your mother has told me exactly how she feels about me taking that decision from you. But, I hoped that it set into motion the fates you hold. My sickness, Jasper's sicknesses, were not of the natural sort. They were curses put on us by a great evil coming for Maya. Part of our curse was that we could never tell anyone. I didn't know Jasper's curse was the same as mine until I was cursed too. I worked around the curse in my last moments to get this letter to you.

I was there, at the Sun Palace, when she came for the Sun Queen and the princesses. I flew out by myself to discuss how our crops were not bearing the same fruit they once did, seeing if hers were doing the same. I was worried about famine then. I don't know who she was, the one who came, she was covered in smoke. She cursed me to live the next ten years, knowing that she was coming for us, knowing I wasn't able to do anything to fix it. If I had told anyone, I would have died where I stood. I saw Adelina get the girls out, though. They will be the key to fixing this. Them and the two of you are going to save all of Maya. I tried everything to break the curse, to find a fix for the crops, to no avail. I sent you so far to find that flower because it only grew near the human border. I hoped that fate would draw them to you somehow if you were close enough to them. Find the prophecy, it must be fulfilled, or we are all doomed.

Nothing has made me prouder than being your father. I would have given up all my power to stay with you two and your mother. Please take care of her. Losing me will be more difficult than anything she's been through. She didn't know about my plan, but she will help you. She loves a puzzle, and this might be the most important one in our existence. I know that you will fix this, the last four descendants.

Cree- Don't let your anger consume you. Remember what I always told you. Let some light in, and allow yourself to be happy. You deserve it.

Holt- The kingdom falls to you. I have no doubt you will make a great King. Don't forget to make room for what brings you joy.

You two are all I am and more.

Love,

Father

His magic slipped away, leaving his words on the paper glowing until they faded into regular black ink. We sat there staring at the paper, rereading his words over and over until they were burned into our minds.

"I don't even know what to say," Holt muttered, "this whole time, he knew his life had an expiration date. How was he so happy?"

"He had us," I responded, hoping we made the last ten years of his life everything he wanted. I looked back at all the times we made things difficult for him and cursed us for being so stupid.

We got off the dirt floor and walked out of the arena, but I looked back at it one last time.

The old memories of our father, the new memories of Camila, and the letter co-existing in one blissful moment, my chest warmed more than it ever has.

I didn't hate the feeling.

Chapter 25

Camila

Xio brought us to two joined bedchambers. They were exquisite, their design matching the grandness of the rest of the palace.

Shaggy rugs covered the marble floor, and an enormous bed sat in the middle of the room. The bed was covered in thick blankets that ranged from silver to deep navy blues with enough pillows for a small army.

Chara brought us some dresses she said she'd never worn before and told us we could have all of them. She said she'd send her seamstress to us tomorrow so we could have some more riding clothes made for us. She knew we'd need them before we needed the dresses.

Each room had a bathing chamber filled with soap, salts, and oils that I couldn't wait to get my hands on. We never had such fancy things, and I was ready to experiment with each and every single one of them.

I ran the water into the giant silver tub. Two people could have fit into this thing, three if they were small.

The water was steaming hot, just the way I liked it. I dumped every salt into the water that was available, the smells all mixing together to make something heavenly.

I dipped my body in and groaned at the pleasure it brought me.

The salts helped relax my muscles, which had been tight after riding a horse for weeks straight. I could feel the built-up dirt the river and springs didn't remove peeling away from me with the help of the salts.

I dunked my head under the water and cleaned my hair with some concoction that smelled like lavender. I worked all the tangles out of my hair with my fingers and rinsed out the lovely lavender-smelling cream.

My skin began to wrinkle, so I grabbed the towel next to the tub and dried myself off.

I left the towel in the bathing room and walked over to where I laid the dresses out, naked. I hadn't been free to move around naked in some time, and it felt amazing.

I picked up a deep purple dress, the fabric was velvety smooth, and the sides of the dress were removed, allowing for panels of skin to show. It had silver trim running down the plunging neckline and the sleeves gathered with a silver cuff at the wrists.

It was beautiful, more beautiful than anything I'd put my body in.

I was so entranced by the dress I didn't hear that someone entered my room until I heard footsteps approach behind me.

"Camila, I just wanted—" Cree's voice stopped abruptly when his eyes landed on my naked body.

Every inch of me was exposed, including the scars that Lord Wayward's guards left on me.

They ran across the back of my thighs, multiple lines thick and raised. I quickly grabbed a folded blanket at the end of the bed and tried to wrap it around me.

I turned to find Cree still as a statue, breathing heavily with shadows gathering around his fingers.

"Who did this to you?" he asked, calm, but laced with anger.

"Oh, it happened in Zuma," I answered quietly.

I didn't let anyone see my scars. Anytime I spent time with someone naked, the room was dark, and I was conscious of if their hands ever ran over the back of my thighs.

The only person who saw them was Xio, and that's because she was the one who helped clean the wounds.

"Why?" he said shortly, unable to get out more than one word through the anger pulsing around him.

The shadows were still moving around his fingers, licking up his arms.

"I wouldn't bow to him. He wanted me to kiss his feet," I answered.

The room exploded into darkness for a few seconds, covered in the shadows of his power. When they cleared, he was directly in front of me, and I gasped.

I had felt the darkness of his magic before, but this was different. It felt like he could begin and end a world with it.

"It was a long time ago," I said, trying to find the right words to calm him down.

I didn't understand why he was so angry for me.

"Actually, in a way, it led me to you," I admitted for the first time out loud.

He looked at me through hurt eyes like I was saying it was his fault, and I quickly started explaining.

"We were running that day because we stole from him. We had a solid plan to wipe out as much of his treasury as we could and run for the hills. We had people in his estate helping us with the plan, and everything went smoothly until a guard saw us in the garden. We took care of him and got out over the walls, but a servant must have been nearby then. There wasn't supposed to be anyone there. They told the guards that they saw a girl with brown and gold hair slipping over the walls. I was the only one who fit that description, so they came for us. Thankfully, I heard the commotion before they made it to us, and we got out into the forest and crossed into Maya. I was stealing from him because I wanted revenge for what he did to me. Had he not," I hesitated, not wanting to anger him more, "done what he did to me, we may not have found Maya. We might not have been forced to steal food from your camp," he was still staring down at me, but his gaze softened slightly. "The thing you said about scars, I never let anyone see them. I was never proud of them. I hated them for reminding me how he made me feel in that street. I've never felt so ashamed as I did, bleeding naked in the market. Now, I don't hate them as much. I'm trying to be proud of them. Because they led me...they led Xio and me here," I finished, already feeling a little too vulnerable.

"Every inch of you is perfect. I hate the bastard for what he did to you. You should have killed him. I'll kill him. But you are perfect, Mila," he said, caressing my jaw with his thumb.

"I did kill the guard who did it. He was one of the guards that followed us into the forest when we were escaping. I didn't even feel—" I stopped, unsure if I should share this with him.

"Good. He deserved to die. You shouldn't have an ounce of regret for what you did."

My shoulders sagged slightly. I thought he might see that darkness and turn away.

That wasn't the case. My darkness matched his.

He looked like he might kiss me, and I found myself really wanting that.

But he shook his head slightly and backed up a step leaving the space in front of me cold and empty.

"I was just coming in here to escort you to dinner. I did knock, but I guess you didn't hear me. I'm sorry for the," he stopped, searching for the right word. "Reaction."

He ran his hands through his hair, embarrassed at the slip in his control. I dropped the blanket and stepped into the dress I was admiring, he watched me carefully, and I walked to where he stood.

"Can you help me with the buttons in the back?"

I lifted my hair to allow him access to my neck, and in some primal way, it felt like a submission. Letting him know he didn't scare me with his outburst. I felt him step closer to me and start working on the buttons.

His fingers grazed the skin on my neck and back, and I let out a small gasp.

He finished, and I let my hair down. He didn't move from behind me but ran his fingers down the skin that the dress left exposed. His breath skimmed my ear, and my chest was rising and falling rapidly.

He hesitated for a second, then placed a trail of kisses up my neck. The contact broke the trance that had me frozen in place.

I whirled around and stood on my toes to wrap my arms around his neck, my mouth met his, and he let out a growl.

His lips parted, and I let my tongue move into his mouth. He was breathing heavily, and he backed me up until the back of my knees hit the bed and he caged me in with his body. I ran my hands down his strong arms and traced a trail down to his abdomen.

"Camila! Dinner!" Xio cracked the door and yelled before closing it.

We stared at each other for a few moments, only the sound of our heavy breathing filling the air. He sat up, pulled me with him, and fixed my dress before checking his clothes for any sign of what we were about to do.

"Chara will come next if we don't go down there, so let's avoid that," he whispered before looping his arm in mine and guiding us out of the room and down to the hall we had eaten in earlier.

I wasn't sure what to think about what had just happened. I knew I couldn't give myself entirely to him right now.

But maybe I could give a little.

Chapter 26

Xio

I wore an exquisitely beautiful light gray dress that Chara brought to my chamber before dinner.

Fashion here was a little more risque than I'd grown used to in Zuma, but I couldn't deny the fact I looked great.

The dress's fabric sparkled, and it reminded me of the sun on the sea every time I moved. It flowed down to the ground loosely, and the sleeves were sheer and billowed out at the wrists.

My sister wore an equally beautiful dark purple dress that complimented her skin tone.

Tonight, we really did look like royalty.

We sat around the table together while Chara told us embarrassing stories about her boys growing up. Some Holt had already shared with me, but some it appeared he kept to himself.

I encouraged her along through the story she was telling now.

"You're kidding," I burst out laughing.

"I'm not! Even as toddlers, they were always trying to one-up each other. All you saw were naked little butts running through the hallways with all the nurses stumbling over each other to grab them before they made it out of the palace. Arlan is the one who caught them. We all fell into a pile of laughter at the front entryway," she said through tears the laughter brought to her eyes.

She wiped them, and everyone settled for a moment at the mention of their father.

They told us about the letter they had received from him, but we didn't ask any questions yet. We wanted to give them some time to work through it, but we didn't have much of it.

"Do you feel any differently after the letter?" Chara asked, eyeing her boys with only the kind of consideration a mother could accomplish.

"I feel a little better. I still wish he would have gone about it differently. But, I also understand why he did it," Holt said.

"How much hell did you give him for it?" Cree asked with a slight smile.

He was still feeling pretty down about everything. He didn't laugh much when we told stories, but we could tell he liked hearing them.

"You know I gave him enough," she said, flipping her waves over her shoulder with bravado, but her eyes fell on the empty chair at the table where he should have been.

"I'm going to retire for the evening," she said, rising from her chair, and we all stood as one. "I'm so glad I was able to meet you two again. I look forward to getting to know the Fae you've become," she said to me and Camila as she rubbed the side of our arms gently.

She smirked knowingly when we both looked at her sons.

Nothing got past her.

"My boys, we will get through this together. Today with you two has been the best day since he passed. I love you both."

She stood on her toes to kiss their cheeks, but they still had to bend down to meet her halfway.

Chara left the room, and two of her handmaidens trailed her back to her bedchamber.

I really liked her. Her presence put me at ease the way I imagined my own mother's would have.

If things had been different, would we have grown up together? Would we all be a little less damaged?

What-ifs were a slippery slope I couldn't let myself slide down. I had to believe our fates were what they should be, or else I wouldn't make it.

"Well, I'm exhausted. I plan on stretching my entire body out on that bed. Did you feel yours? It feels like you'd be sleeping on clouds," she said, rising and stretching her arms above her head.

Cree watched her like he wanted to say something, but he didn't.

They both arrived at dinner slightly disheveled and late. They weren't fooling anybody. Whatever they were doing, I hoped she was taking the advice she tried to give me, even though I wasn't taking it myself.

She slid out of the room, leaving us three. Holt was smiling at me, and I back at him. Cree realized he was left with us and quickly got up and made his way to the door.

"I'm going to go...check on my horse," he said before quickly exiting the room.

We watched each other silently for a while. The sun set quite some time ago, so the room was much darker than when we started dinner.

"Walk with me on the beach?" Holt asked, offering me his hand.

"I'd like that," I responded before allowing him to guide me out of the palace and into the courtyard.

The courtyard was just as beautiful under the starlight.

There were new flowers I didn't notice before. Where some of the brighter flowers had puckered themselves up, large black and gray flowers were peppered throughout them fully bloomed.

They sparkled slightly when we moved, and Holt caught me looking at them.

"My mother had them planted so we could enjoy the garden at any time of the day. They're called estrellas, stars," he said while we made our way into the sand.

We both slipped off our shoes and left them in the garden, walking hand in hand down the shore. The moonlight shone on the sea, casting silvery waves that trickled past our toes. We walked for a long time in silence, enjoying the company and the sight.

There was not a single other soul on the beach, and the awareness that we were genuinely alone hit me. We walked over to what looked like one of the gazebos from the garden, but there was no roof.

It was meant to be used at night to see the stars and listen to the sound of the waves.

I looked over to see Holt removing his shirt and laying it on one of the benches in the gazebo. He walked to where I stood in a few solid strides and offered his hand to me.

"Trust me?" he asked.

I wasn't sure why he was asking that. He knew I did.

I nodded and took his hand, but he walked back onto the beach instead of walking further into the gazebo.

I felt a breeze coming from behind me as a large shadow loomed over my shoulder. Holt smiled smugly as I took in the sight of his colossal eagle wings.

The last time I saw them this close was when he removed the binding my mother had placed on me. I didn't get the chance to look at them up in detail when he shot us into the sky, but now I could see how truly magnificent they were.

At first glance, I thought they were just brown, but now I could see how many different shades there were.

Deep brown, but also warm golds and white feathers buried beneath them. He stretched them wide as I ran my fingers across the huge feathers they were covered with.

A shudder ran through him as I got closer to the base of the wings, where they met his back. I smirked, making sure I remembered that for the future.

"They're stunning," I said while going to run my fingers down the wing on his other side.

"The last time I flew with you wasn't particularly enjoyable. I'd like to rectify that if you let me," he asked gently while I came to stand back in front of him.

"Over the sea?" I asked.

I couldn't get enough of the water. The chance to fly over the waves was something I'd never turn down. He nodded, and I eagerly jumped up to wrap my hands around his neck.

He placed one hand behind my back and the other behind my knees and my smile was so big I could barely see.

He looked at me with so much admiration you would have thought I was the one about to fly us around. He bent his knees slightly and began to beat his wings once, twice, and suddenly we were shooting off the beach and over the water.

The stars above us no longer twinkled but were streams of light shooting past us. My head was still buried in Holt's chest while I adjusted to the odd feeling of being in the air. I pulled my head away from him and looked out into the great expanse of water.

The waves moved and crashed fiercely this far away from the shore, some creating a tunnel of water before falling back into the sea. Another one started to form, and Holt shot down to the sea.

My breath ceased in my chest as the water started to curve above us and then beside us, creating a wide funnel around us.

From above, the waves seemed to dissipate quickly, but this one seemed to stay much longer.

The deep blues of the water gave way to lighter blues and greens, with streaks of color and white running between them.

This experience, there wasn't a word for it.

The tunnel finally began to wane, and we shot out of it while the sea lightly sprayed across our skin.

The saltiness of the ocean found its way into my mouth since the smile on my face was still stretched from one side to the other, but I didn't even care. There was nothing that could stop this moment from being beautiful.

He shot back into the sky, and I reached my hand toward the moon. It felt like it was close enough that I could touch it and run my fingers through its craters.

He slowed down, and we floated in the sky for a few moments, staring into each other's eyes. My heartbeat was still raging, but as I looked into the thunderstorm that lived around his pupils, I couldn't help but let out a deep breath.

He kissed me gently before shooting back to the gazebo on the shore we had left earlier. He set me down carefully and wrapped his fingers around mine. We walked hand in hand into the structure.

He sat on one of the stone benches and pulled me into his lap. I placed my legs on either side of his, straddling him.

His beauty never ceased to amaze me. I watched a few of his curls shift as the wind blew. The color of his eyes when he found out his father had passed turned dark, nearly black.

Now, they were a lighter gray, and in the moonlight, they sparkled as he stared down at my lips.

"Thank you for today," he murmured gently, "this isn't what I was expecting to bring you into, but thank you," he said, rubbing my cheek with his thumb.

"I hardly did anything," I answered because I didn't feel like I did. I wasn't sure if I had the right words or if I lingered in his presence too long when he needed space.

"You did exactly what I needed," he said, pulling me closer to him, lining up my chest to his and his lap to mine. "You're everything, Xio. I don't know how I lasted two centuries without you. When I laid my eyes on you, I knew I wouldn't ever let you go. Sorry about the prisoner thing."

I wasn't sorry.

"But I knew in that very moment you looked up at me with so much passion in your eyes that you had to be mine. I was so worried you would try and escape. I told myself that if you wanted to leave me when we got here, I'd let you, but after our moment in the springs, I knew you felt the same way. You were made for me, Xiomara. You're the calm in my storm. You're my soul-bound," he finished.

I couldn't breathe. I couldn't move. I stared down at the male who took me prisoner, saved my life, and protected my sister and me.

I couldn't deny how I felt.

My soul knew his, we may not have known each other long, but my heart was his. I still couldn't get any words out, and he smiled at my sudden loss of the ability to speak.

"I'm not asking you to marry me right now. I know you still have a lot to work through. The whole saving the world thing may get in the way of the extravagance that is Mayan weddings. But I'm yours, Xio. There's no one else for me. I'll prove to you every day that I deserve you, that the Gods chose right. I'll protect you with everything I am until Maya is safe and at peace again. If you'll let me."

My heart was beating in my ears, and my breath was still coming in short pants. I knew this was what I wanted.

Damn the world, this God-like Fae was mine. From now until forever. I touched my forehead to his and lingered close to his mouth.

"Yes," I whispered gently.

"Yes, you'll marry me?" he asked smugly, and I smacked him on his shoulder.

"Well, I'll marry you after we save Maya. But you're still mine until then," I said with a shrug. "I feel it. I feel all of it."

He had been so still during his side of the conversation, but me claiming him let loose the beast that lived within him.

The entire gazebo was lit with lightning, moving around us, replicating the energy that always seemed to float between us.

His eyes glowed bright, and I let my magic join his. The gazebo was bright, with intermingling flames and lightning surrounding us.

Neither came close enough to touch us, but it danced around us, moving as fast as my heart was beating.

His mouth found mine. This kiss...this kiss was everything. This wasn't some random man in the back of a pub like I'd had before.

This kiss held power, held passion, held purpose.

I moaned, and he moved his hands to trace the skin on my back the dress I wore left exposed. His skin was warm against mine, even though the breeze from the sea made it cool here.

I couldn't take it anymore. I needed to feel more of him.

Our kiss grew more and more passionate by the second, exploring each other's mouths truly for the first time. I had every ridge and dip of it memorized already.

It's like he said, we were made for each other. Here at this moment, the fact couldn't be denied.

I moved my hands from around his neck and slid them down to pull off his shirt. He helped, and I traced the lines of his muscles until I reached the top of his pants.

He went still as a rock and brought my gaze back in line with his.

"You're sure?" he asked, "once this starts, I don't know if I'll have the power to stop it, Xio. I need you to be sure right now."

I was never more sure of anything in my life.

"I believe I remember a mention of making me scream? I see no audience?" I said smugly, looking around us and stepping away from him to remove my dress.

It took two quick moves because of how little fabric was holding it up. He remained still for a few moments longer as he took in the sight of all of my skin.

Every inch of it was exposed, the last time in the springs, I felt the desire to cover it up, but now I stood firm and confident.

I knew the power this body held, and he did too. He moved so fast that I didn't see him come for me as he laid me down on the bench. He fell to his knees and hooked both my legs over his shoulders.

I felt the warmth of his body on my inner thighs, and that alone felt like it could send me over the edge.

But then he settled his face right at my entrance and claimed me with one long flick of his tongue.

I moaned louder than I meant to, and the sound of my pleasure had him going back for more. He moved in smooth and quick strokes, sucking and tugging, before bringing his finger up to where his mouth lay against me and pushing it inside.

The gazebo left the stars exposed, but I saw stars that weren't there. Everything ceased to exist but Holt and me on this beach.

He sent me over the edge quickly, and I needed more, more now. He swiped his tongue one final time before climbing over my body and kissing up to my neck.

I sat up and placed my hands on his pants, sending flames across them, singeing them right off his body.

He jumped up and looked at me with his mouth hanging open, shocked at the control of my power.

"Little something I've been working on," I said with a slight shrug, I moved him to sit on the bench, and I went to straddle him once again.

This time, the lack of clothes made this maneuver all that much better.

I sank onto his Godly length and screamed just as he said I would.

I tossed my head back with my eyes closed, unable to move for a moment, as he filled me more than I'd ever experienced. He took my nipples in his warm mouth while I adjusted to him and he ran his hands over my hips.

"Eyes on me," he groaned around my nipple.

I did as he commanded and my gaze locked in his, a different kind of storm brewing in his stare.

I brought my body up and back down in long even movements, keeping my eyes on him. His hands gripped my hips tighter while he began to thrust into me as well.

Just when I thought I couldn't take anymore, he brought his fingers between us, small waves of electricity running over them before he rubbed the bundle of nerves in smooth circles with his thumb.

I yelled his name over and over again until both of us were overcome with unexplainable pleasure. We fell onto the ground in a pile of limbs, breathing heavily. Every inch of my body was tingling.

I couldn't think, couldn't move.

This was transcendent.

There's no way anyone else in all the world could experience what we just did. The Gods couldn't have chosen a better partner for me.

I looked over at him. His eyes were still closed, still lost in the pleasure we had just experienced. The realization that I had burned his pants off came back to me.

I wasn't thinking about the fact we would have to make it back into the palace. I was too lost to him to think of anything else.

A slight cough came from the beach, and we both jumped up.

"Uhh...Mother sent me. She said to bring you some pants, she saw a flash of your bare ass running up the beach into the palace. So...I'll just leave it here on the beach," Cree said before we heard footsteps running away quickly.

We burst out laughing. His mother said she only had a touch of Mente abilities, but she just saved her son a lot of embarrassment.

"I hope that's all she saw," he muttered while helping me back into my dress.

I grabbed his pants off the beach for him, and he slid his powerful legs into them. We walked down the beach into the gardens. Before we made it back into the palace, we stopped to look at the estrella flowers one more time. I turned to him, and he held me tight in his arms.

"Mine," I whispered, squeezing him possessively.

He squeezed me back.

"I am yours. You are mine," he whispered back in my hair and laid one more passionate kiss on my lips.

We made our way to his bedchamber and spent the rest of the night in each other's arms.

Chapter 27

Camila

Last night was the best sleep of my life.

I didn't know what the beds were made of, but I was convinced they were imbued with some sort of magic.

I wasn't even upset when the sun shone in my room. If I slept in a bed like that every day, I might become a morning person.

Probably not.

The Queen, Chara, she asked us to call her, said to meet her in the library after breakfast, so I asked some of the handmaidens to point me in the right direction.

Xio never returned to her room last night, and I had my suspicions about where she was. Her and Holt seemed inevitable the longer I was around them. I didn't feel there was a point in telling her to be careful anymore.

THE SUN, THE STORM, & THE SHADOWS

She was already deep into it with him, figuratively speaking. Although, now I was guessing physically too.

I turned a corner and ran smack into Cree's large form. He looked to be deep in thought himself.

I hoped he would return to my chamber last night, but he never did.

He looked as if he'd been up all night, his hair a little more unruly than usual, shadows under his eyes.

"Good...morning" I said awkwardly.

Why was I like this? Always one step forward, three steps back with us. Not that I was really sure where we were taking those steps half the time.

"I was just making my way to the library. Is that where you were heading?" he asked, placing his hands into his pockets.

He was still wearing the clothes he had worn last night, and they were dirtier than they had been at dinner. My guess was that he stayed in the training arena all night. This thought had me scanning him for more wounds, but I didn't find any.

I didn't answer his question, so he looked at me with his eyebrows drawn together. "Camila?"

"Oh yes, that is where I was going."

We walked in that direction side by side, slower than our usual pace. We passed many palace staff on their way to begin their day, each one smiled brightly at us as we walked side by side.

"Were you up all night?" I asked, breaking the silence.

He sighed, not making eye contact with me. "I couldn't sleep. I wasn't lying when I said I felt a little better after the letter. But, I just couldn't sleep."

I didn't want to admit that I stayed up waiting for him, but the words came out before I could stop them.

"I thought maybe you would have..." I trailed off, and he stopped and turned me towards him.

"I didn't think you'd want to be around me while I was," he paused, "less than unpleasant."

"I don't know if you remember, but you've been less than pleasant most of the time I've known you," I said jokingly, "I'm just as fucked up as you, don't forget. Broken things and all," I finished, raising my brow at him.

"You just seemed to be in a good mood at dinner. I didn't want to bring you down," he replied.

He swallowed and looked down at our feet. I was in a good mood, but the darkness within me was always lingering nearby. Just as it was with him.

"Some days are better than others. Next time, don't think for me. Let me decide. I'll turn you away if I don't want your unpleasantness," I shrugged and continued walking to the library.

"I have no doubt about that," he laughed.

He pushed the door to the library open, holding it for me to walk in behind him.

There were rows and rows of books on shelves that ran all the way up to the ceiling. Silver ladders were placed throughout the space so the books on the highest shelves could be reached.

I was never much of a reader. The libraries in Zuma were reserved for the elite and wealthy, but if I had access to a library like this, I could see myself becoming one.

I ran my finger over a section of books that looked to be spell books, and I stilled.

A faint memory of my father and mother teaching Xio and me to read in our own library rolled through my mind.

I read a short word, and they both jumped up and down in excitement, lifting me in the air and shouting about how proud they were of me. The first new memory I had since we visited our palace.

It gave me hope that more might come. Cree looked back at me, wondering why I stopped so abruptly.

"You okay?" he asked.

He studied me, looking over my body for signs of injury just like I did this morning.

"Yes, I just had a flash of—" I stopped.

I wondered if I should share this with him when he was in such a bad space. When he wouldn't be getting any memories of his parents.

"You had a new memory?" Cree asked, his face softening as he realized I wasn't in any physical pain. "What was it?"

"Just of our parents teaching Xio and me to read in our library. It was just a flash, but, it felt good. The more signs I see that they loved us, I don't know, it just was nice," I shrugged, and he took a step towards me with a genuine smile pulling at his lips.

"Camila, you don't have to be scared to share those things with me. I'm happy that you have the chance to learn about them, even if I don't," he said as if reading my mind.

The sound of the door opening reached us from the other side of the room and we took a step back from each other.

"Good morning," Chara sang, floating in, no longer dressed in black.

She wore a beautiful dark gray dress, not much brighter than the black, but not the clothes of mourning she wore the day before. It swished with every step toward us she took.

Cree brought his face down to her, already expecting the kiss on his cheek she was coming for. She smiled at me and rubbed my back while she passed between us to the table where books and scrolls were waiting for us.

Holt and Xio came through the door laughing together, looking very, very happy. It seems like my guess about her whereabouts were accurate, judging from the glow that was coming from both of them.

I placed a hand on my hip and gave Xio a knowing look. "Have a fun evening?"

It was my turn to act in the motherly role, even if I wasn't very good at it. I'd be asking for all of the details later. They both bit their lips to try and hide their smiles, and Cree and I rolled our eyes at them before standing with the Queen by the table.

"Good morning, Mother," Holt said to Chara before kissing her cheek and sitting at the other side of the table.

I would need to take some pointers from Chara. She seemed to have these two trained in a way I didn't expect.

"I had Luis pull all the old prophecies and tellings from the Gods. I have an idea of which one your mother might be referencing, but I think it would be beneficial to take a look at all of them to see if we can find anything," Chara said while opening an old dusty scroll. "This is the original. It was a prophecy from the God of wisdom, Itzamna. He was also the creator, the one who helped make our world and the people within it. He didn't interfere much with us, allowing the Gods beneath him to have more power."

That must have been before he went crazy and killed all the other Gods.

"He believed his creation was just and that we had the power we needed to defeat anything that came about."

She rolled her hand across the scroll.

"This is in the language of the Gods, but it was translated to our tongue," she opened a large book bound in silver and gold. "This is the translation...

The world I built is just and true, but free thoughts can be dangerous. There is no good without evil. No light without dark. No dark without light. For during the day, there are shadows, and even the night has the stars. One of my creations will try to eclipse the others, but all my creations are strong in power, magic, and wit. For when the rising and setting suns find themselves in storms of shadow and rain, an even greater power will be born. When the east falls, ten summers will pass before they must act in the eleventh. All sides must join, the Jaguar, the Eagle, the Serpent, for all were made equal. No one greater than the last. The mountains hold a weapon, while the Grasslands hold a message. All hope will be lost if the Hearts of Maya do not succeed."

Chara finished and passed around the book for us all to re-read.

"He couldn't have just said, *Hey, here's what's coming for you, meet it here and kill it before it kills everyone*," I asked, partially joking, but how easy that would have made things.

"He never allowed himself to directly interfere. You'd think eminent danger would be an exception, but apparently not," Chara responded.

"The rising and setting suns, I'm assuming that's us? Why our mother thought we'd be important in this fight?" Xio asked Chara.

"Yes, Xio, you were born as the sun was rising. Camila, you were born as the sun was setting. You are the rising and setting suns," she said confidently.

"Your tattoos," Cree muttered. "That's what they are. Rising and setting suns."

"Holy shit, you're right," I responded.

Having it pointed out now, it seemed so obvious. The half circle with lines protruding from either side, it looked just like the sun setting or rising over the horizon.

The fact my mother knew this would happen from the moments we were born saddened me. She knew her kingdom would fall at some point and that we'd have to save it. It's why she protected us so fiercely, not allowing us to be too far from her side.

"And we are the storms of shadow and rain," Holt said, looking at Cree. "You were always destined to be my brother."

I could have sworn I saw silver lining Cree's eyes before he blinked, and it was gone.

Chara smiled sweetly at her sons, one made of her blood, one made of her choice. She loved both equally.

It was apparent. She knew Cree well enough that he wouldn't have an immediate response to what Holt had just said.

"The Descendants were referred to as the Hearts of Maya when each God chose a Fae to carry their blood. You four are the remaining Hearts," Chara said confidently as she drew her gaze across each of us. "You have less than a year until whatever is coming makes its appearance. Your father died on the last day of summer," she murmured, a shadow of grief running along her features.

"This also says we're going to have to partner with the Serpent tribes if we're to take it literally. You two are from the jaguars," Cree said, pointing at Xio and me. "And we're from the eagle. The Serpents are the last division of our country."

Holt looked at his mother. "It says they have a message. They live in the Grasslands. I don't know what they would know that we wouldn't."

Chara was the Queen during the war between the Serpent tribes and our people. However, she looked just as confused as we did.

"I'm not sure. I know they were not all inherently evil. When their original leader fell during the war, a new one arose. They were the one who agreed to the treaty so quickly. I don't think they wanted any more death, not that that makes them a great person," she said.

"And the mountains," Xio started, "that would be back where we just came from, near the Sun Palace?"

"Yes, the mountains surround the palace. Whatever weapon they speak of would be somewhere in the general area," Cree responded, "we're going to have to split up at some point."

He was right.

We had less than a year to find the weapon and the message. Not to mention we needed to become efficient enough in our magic to beat this force that only four Descendants could stop. There was certainly more to decipher here, but the main points of the prophecy were figured out.

"My intuition tells me that Cree and Camila should go to the Grasslands, and Xio and Holt should go to the mountains. You should leave in a fortnight, no sooner. I don't know what you'll find or how you'll find it, but who goes where feels important," Chara said, not looking at anyone in particular, but staring out the windows that lined the back wall of the library.

I wondered how her Mente power manifested and if my sister or I would have it. She mentioned that the extent of my mother's power was a blessing and a curse, so I wasn't sure if I wanted it.

"Zyanya has planned a great feast for your return. It will happen a few nights from now. It seems she has invited the entire kingdom," she chuckled. "You will have to decide before then if you would like your identity to be made known or if we should introduce you as someone else. I will stand by either decision but know you should be proud of who you are. My seamstress should be visiting you later today to fit you for gowns of your own for the feast," she finished, and removed herself from the table, and we all stood as she left the room.

"You should know that she uses the word feast very loosely. She really means a night full of wine, food, dancing, and debauchery," Holt laughed and looked over to Xio, anticipating what they would get into at this feast.

Cree moved to another section of the library where another table was located, but this one was covered in different textures.

I followed him over and realized it was something like a map of Maya, but instead of being drawn on paper, it was built directly into the table, showing the peaks of mountains and miniature versions of the palaces.

Cree ran his finger over the small castle on the east side of the map. "This is a replica of Maya, it took the King a century to complete, but he was so proud of it."

I noticed how sometimes he referred to him as the King and sometimes as Father. I wondered if it was a conscious decision or just a slip of the tongue.

"It's amazing. I've never seen anything like it," I said while walking around the table to inspect it further.

The map the King built was made with great skill. Every tiny detail seemed to be an exact replica of what we've seen thus far. Just as they said, the Sun Palace rested on the east and the Storm Palace on the far west. Small villages like the ones we visited were sporadically placed between them, but most of the area was the Grasslands, where the Serpent tribes lived. They explained they were nomads and had no real stronghold.

We'd have to track them down to reach them, which could take a while, judging from the size of the lands they reside in. A jagged line ran through the middle of the table, which must have signified the boundaries between the two kingdoms before the Sun Palace fell.

Cree was calculating already, we had a fortnight to come up with our plan, but I could see the wheels turning in his mind.

"What are you thinking?" I asked.

"It would be so much easier if they stayed in one place, but they could be anywhere between here," he said, gesturing to the grass between the kingdoms. "I'll have some scouts see if they can find anything before we leave," he finished, his mouth tight as he thought about the best action plan.

"But Camila, this is going to be dangerous. We don't fully know what the Serpents are capable of or what their numbers have grown to. We're going to have to trust each other if we want to come out of this alive."

His gaze on me was so intense I shifted on my feet. Did he still think that I was scared of him? Sure, he had great power, dark power, but I was never afraid of it.

Just in awe of the sheer quantity he held.

"I trust you," I said quietly.

He knew this was no small thing for me to admit. If there was one thing I lacked, it was trust in others other than Xio. We only ever had each other, and she was the only person I knew would never hurt me. Everyone else was capable of it.

For whatever reason, I did trust Cree more than I trusted others. Even Holt, who had been much more pleasant than Cree had been over our time together.

"Do you trust me?" I asked, not looking at him.

If he had said no after I admitted that I trusted him, I would have been more embarrassed than I'd like to admit.

"I do. For some reason, I do," he responded.

I looked up to find his face tight with confusion but no signs that he was lying. He did trust me, and it looked like it confused him just as much as it did me.

I eyed the mountains. I didn't want to leave Xio. There's never been a time when we were apart in all of my memories. Even the ones that were starting to come back, she was glued to my side. I knew Holt could protect her, but it didn't help the worry growing in my gut.

"We have time. We'll formulate a plan. We'll be able to stay with Holt and Xio until about here."

He pointed at a spot where the path to the mountains split from the way to the Grasslands as if being able to read exactly where my mind was going.

"We will all be okay. Neither of us will let anything happen to you two," he reassured me.

"More like we won't let anything happen to you two," I said.

The comment caused a small smile to form on his face, the first real one I'd seen this morning. We actually had gotten really good at controlling our powers. Nowhere near them, but you won't win anything if you don't have confidence.

Holt and Xio were still at the table we sat at earlier with the Queen. They were quietly studying the other books pulled from the shelves by the librarian.

"I think that's enough studying for the day," I said loud enough for them both to hear me, "we have a fortnight to figure it out. Our brains need a rest."

I took the book from Xio and placed it back on the table.

"Let's go train," I said, wiggling my eyebrows at Cree, knowing he needed this as much as we did after today.

"You did have a day or two off. I'll figure out where they put our weapons and meet you all down in the arena," Cree said before drifting off into the hallway.

I gave Holt a dismissive look, which I'm sure he wasn't too familiar with. I doubt anyone but his mother dismissed him, being a little prince and all. He looked at me confused, so I turned my chin to the door, and he finally caught on to what I was asking.

"Oh... I'll go help Cree," he said before running into the hallway to catch up with him. My sister missed the entire interaction while she tried to stack the books neatly for the librarian to easily put back.

"Are you going to make me ask?" I questioned her.

We had some good laughs about some of our other sexual encounters. The humans we tangled with never seemed to know what they were doing. Something about Holt told me this would not be the case.

She eyed me thoughtfully. "Camila, it shouldn't be possible to feel the way it did. It was like, an out-of-body experience. I don't even have words. I'm pretty sure I died and came back to life. My body is still tingling," she said as a shudder ran through her at the thought of her night with the Descendant of Chaac.

"So better than the pub boys, is what you're saying?" I joked, and we both laughed.

"But it wasn't just sex. It was so much more. It's like we were made for each other. We both felt it. We both admitted the pull we felt. He thinks," she hesitated a moment, "he thinks we're soul-bound like Mother and Father were, and I'm pretty sure he's right."

Holy shit, soul-bound.

I didn't even know everything that entailed, but it sounded intense.

When she told me our parents were soul-bound, she said it was as if the Gods picked them for each other, that it was their fate. That nothing could stop them from finding each other.

"How do you feel about that?" I asked.

Xio was more trusting and optimistic than I was, but this seemed like a lifetime commitment. I wasn't sure she was ready for such a thing.

"I feel," she loosed a breath. "I feel good. I don't know how to explain it, but it's like my soul knows his. Even if I tried to deny how I felt, it wouldn't matter. He asked me to marry him. Well, eventually."

She looked so cheerful. The idea of marriage made me want to run as far as possible. But, it seemed to have the opposite effect on her. So I could get on board with her.

"Well, I'm happy if you're happy," I responded, and she pulled me into a tight embrace.

"Care to share how you feel about Cree?" she asked.

"You mean general disdain?" I responded jokingly.

She gave me that look she always gave me, telling me she knew me better than I did.

"I don't know, Xio, we're both pretty fucked up. I don't think either of us is ready to tie our souls to each other or whatever it is you're doing," I joked again, and she rolled her eyes and dropped the topic. "So...are you engaged?"

"I don't know if I'd call it that, but, I'm his," she responded proudly.

We made our way to the rooms where the seamstress was waiting to take our measurements. She sounded so sure.

I hoped one day I could be so sure about my...situation.

Chapter 28

Xio

Tonight was the night of the feast, and I was excited for some time with Holt. The last three days had been so crazy that we'd barely been able to see each other, outside of the small funeral service they held for Arlan, the Storm King.

It was a beautiful service on the beach in the courtyard. Everyone invited brought a trinket to send with the King to his afterlife. We placed the items in a boat, and Holt used his powers to drift it out to sea and lit it on fire with a flash of lightning. They sang a song called 'The Death Song,' but it was beautiful.

Not a sad morbid song but a piece full of life. Holt, Chara, and Cree spent some time alone together after that.

I'd spent most of my days in the library trying to find any information I could about the weapon in the mountains, but I hadn't had any luck yet.

Holt spent time catching up on his princely duties he missed while he was away, and now that his father was gone, he was helping his mother fill in some of the spaces his father once did.

There was talk from the council, a few trusted Fae who helped run the kingdom along with the royals, that Holt should take the throne.

As Chara is not a Descendant, the crown should rest with someone that had God's blood. We had to explain the entire situation about my parents, the prophecy, and the looming end of the world. They agreed to delay the coronation a year, but even that was pushing the boundaries. We didn't even have a full year, so we agreed. If we weren't successful, there would be no kingdom to serve.

My sister and I sat in my chamber, preparing for the feast with the handmaidens Chara sent to help us with our hair and makeup.

We decided to tell everyone who we were, so this was even more important than just a feast for us. It was telling Maya that we weren't dead and would protect them with everything we had.

"One last time, you're sure?" I asked Camila.

We were both nervous, but she was much warier than I was. While she was proud of our lineage, she also was worried that people would want answers we didn't have.

I understood that, but it felt more important to me that they knew that we were alive, especially in these difficult times. The famine was taking a toll on the people, some hope would do them well.

We went back and forth for the last three days but decided to announce it tonight. Chara was elated at our decision since she knew our parents so well she wanted us to embrace them.

"Yes, I'm sure. You're right, I'm still nervous, but this is what's best," she said, trying to sound as confident as she could.

She looked beautiful tonight.

The handmaiden working on her makeup did a damn good job. They lined her eyes with kohl and applied deep red lipstick to her lips. They also applied some sort of shimmery powder to her lids I wasn't familiar with, but it was beautiful.

My makeup looked similar, but my lipstick was a lighter shade of red that complimented the red dress the seamstress had made for me. The powder on my eyes brought out every gold fleck of my eyes. I stared at myself in the mirror in awe of how far we'd come from struggling humans to two of the most powerful Fae in Maya.

I removed my robe and grabbed the dress I'd be wearing tonight. The fashion ideal here was less was more, and I embodied that tonight.

The dress was made of a shimmery red fabric that was slightly sheer, but there were so many layers that it covered enough. It was backless like the dress I wore before, but instead of the billowing sleeves, this was sleeveless.

It was held up by two panels of thin fabric on each of my shoulders, and extra material ran over my shoulders, creating something like a narrow cape on both sides of the open back. The gold embellishments were my favorite, reminding me of my mother and home.

A gold chain ran around my waist and across my bare back, holding everything together, but smaller golden chains ran down the length of it, creating the illusion of something like sun rays.

I felt powerful, and I'd need every bit of power tonight.

Camila finished putting her dress on, the fabric similar to mine but in a deep orange color. Rather than backless, she chose the same missing side panel design she had worn before.

She had small golden gems that ran down the skirt in straight lines, also creating the illusion of sun rays. I wondered if Chara pictured us tonight and chose the other dresses we wore before accordingly.

Chara had been incredible these last few days. I looked forward to spending more time with her when we weren't in such a time crunch.

Having her as my mother-in-law would be such a gift, and I found myself smiling at the thought of me and Holt's wedding.

Holt said they were extravagant here. I'd have to ask him about that later tonight.

I reached my hand toward Camila. "Ready?"

She wrapped her fingers tightly around mine and nodded.

"I'm ready," she responded.

We stepped out of my bedchamber to find Holt and Cree waiting in the hallway.

My breath caught in my throat at the sight of Holt in his finery. He looked so delicious I wanted to skip the feast and head right back into my room with him for a different kind of meal. His gray trousers were perfectly tailored and hugged every muscle in his legs. His matching tunic complimented his broad shoulders, and intricate designs were stitched into the trimming around his collar and cuffs in the same shade of red as my dress.

He walked up to me and placed a kiss on my forehead, an act I'd grown to love more than anything.

The casual displays of affection were never something I was a fan of, but I couldn't get enough with him. He offered me his arm, and I looped mine in his.

"You look absolutely astonishing," he whispered as he took in my newly enhanced face and hair.

I allowed the handmaidens to pin my curls back, creating a bun to accentuate the back of the dress, but I still had some of them framing my face. Camila opted for leaving all of her hair down but swept it to one side.

"You don't look too bad yourself," I joked, pulling my red lips into a smile I couldn't help.

Camila looped her arm in Cree's, they looked like they were having a conversation with their eyes alone, and I didn't want to interrupt it.

Cree wore a similar style to Holt but in all black. Which was expected of him. As I walked closer, I saw faint auburn stitching on one shoulder of his tunic, matching Camila.

He looked almost as good as Holt, almost.

They led us down a maze of hallways until we were on the other side of the courtyard, where the great banquet hall was located.

Chara was waiting for us at the door, looking ever the Queen in another gray dress. She wore an intricate silver headpiece that was in the shape of great eagle wings. Diamonds and gems lined the wings, and they sparkled in the light in the hall while small jewels and beads dangled from the tips of each wing.

The mourning process was gruesome, but it seemed like she was working through it. I was sure she still cried through the night, but she was trying, and that was all that mattered.

"You all look so beautiful!" she gushed as she came to inspect all four of us. "I knew my seamstress would do some of her best work on you girls. I want one for myself!"

She stepped to Holt and fixed his collar, then to tried to make Cree's hair appear like it was styled. As soon as she turned her back, he shook it out, and Camila slapped him on his arm for ruining his mother's work.

Chara turned back to us and sighed at Cree. "I knew you'd do that," she said, rolling her eyes. "Alright, remember the plan?"

"Yes, they'll announce you three. We'll accompany you to the dais, then we'll make our announcement," I said as I tried to run through the lines I came up with over the last few days.

I had a glass of wine while we got ready to help with my nerves, but now I wished I had two. Although a slurring returned princess might not have been the best idea.

"Correct, we'll be right there with you the whole time. After your announcement, we'll open the floor to dancing and advise that the food is ready," she reassured me.

She'd been the Queen for hundreds of years, so this was just another day for her. I tried to channel some of her queenly energy when the doors opened, and we began to walk.

The hall was ridiculously big. It was its own section of the palace alone. The design was open, with great windows and gray and silver decorations.

I took a deep breath when I realized just how many Fae were in the space. It had to be thousands. The entire kingdom was here, Zyanya made sure of it.

I heard whispers as we walked. "Who are they?" "Have they finally settled down?" "Where did they come from? I've never seen them before."

By the time we made it to the dais, I couldn't remember a single one of their faces, and my nerves were starting to overcome me.

Chara stood in front of her throne and sat. Holt and Cree followed in the smaller thrones and us in the chairs beside them. The entire room bowed and waited for her to release them.

"You may rise," she said firmly, and the sound of everyone rising simultaneously reached my ears. "My boys have returned, and we will have a great feast to celebrate them."

The crowd roared and people clapped and celebrated. She raised her hand, and every single one of them went quiet.

"They have returned with two guests, who I'm sure you noticed as we walked in. Their beauty is unmatched. They will make an announcement for all of you."

People clapped, but not as eagerly as they did for Holt and Cree. They were all wondering what this announcement was, I was sure.

I stepped up out of my chair, and Camila followed me. I looked back at Holt as my nerves started to consume me, and one small smile from him had my entire body relax.

He was with me. I could do this.

"My name is Xiomara, and this is Camila," I started, "we are the daughters of Queen Adelina and King Jasper of the Sun Court."

Gasps sounded around the room, and people in the back shifted to get a better view of us.

Chara raised her hand again, and everyone fell silent.

"We have been missing for the last ten years. Our mother hid us because she believed we would be the key to saving Maya from the famine and the evil it comes from," I stated.

"We have the power of Kinich in our veins," Camila boomed.

I lifted my trembling hands, and let flame and light twist around my fingers while Camila did the same.

"We will fight with Cree and Holt to banish this evil. We are here to stay. We will protect the people of Maya the same way our parents did. We will not fail," I finished.

I was pretty sure I forgot some of the lines I rehearsed, and I tried to remember in the few beats of silence that rang out after I finished my speech.

Suddenly the entire room went crazy. People hollered and clapped the way they did for their royals.

They shouted. "Princess, Princess! The Descendants have returned!" as we stood there with shocked faces.

We knew the news would bring hope, but this kind of reaction I was not expecting. The noise started to fade, and Chara, Cree, and Holt came to stand beside us.

"We will defeat what is coming for our people together," Holt said, and the room burst into noise once again.

Someone fell to one knee, resting their fist on top of it, with their gaze on the floor. Suddenly waves of people all fell to the ground in the same gesture.

Every single person was now resting on one knee. They all were silent as the sound of my heartbeat sped in my ears. I looked over at Holt, who was smiling proudly.

He placed his hand on my back. "It's a sign of respect. They're saying they trust you with their lives."

"Tell them to rise and celebrate," Holt whispered between my sister and me.

Camila and I held each other's gaze for a second before stepping out from beside the others. I held her hand in mine.

"Rise, and celebrate!" we said together, and everyone rose and began cheering again.

Holt grabbed me by my hand and led me to the table behind the dais that held the food for us. "You were incredible," he whispered into my ear, his warm breath sending prickles down my spine. "If I didn't have to show my face for a while longer, I'd drag you back to my chamber right now."

I stilled. *They'd seen enough of us, haven't they? We could slip out...*

"Oh my gosh, that was amazing, Xio!" Camila came barreling next to me, jumping up and down in a very un-princess-like manner. "I can't believe you did that. Your voice didn't shake one time! I'm starving."

She grabbed a plate and pilled various foods onto it. Holt was watching the two of us, amused, and he began to place food on a plate. He handed it to me filled with fruits, cheeses, and various types of meat.

"Eat so we can dance. We've got a long night ahead of us," he said suggestively.

If it was up to me, we surely would.

I stuffed my face with the delicious food, and someone brought me a glass of wine.

I didn't know how to dance like the Fae, but maybe that wouldn't matter too much with some wine. I wanted to savor this free moment where everything didn't rest on our shoulders.

Tonight we were just us, and I was going to take that advantage.

Chapter 29

Cree

Camila looked ridiculously beautiful tonight.

Rip my heart from my fucking chest, beautiful.

I couldn't stop watching her. While we were walking in together, I could hear people whispering about how she looked in her dress. It took all my power not to cast the entire room into shadows so no one could see her anymore.

I didn't know what exact emotion that was, but I felt it.

I sat next to my mother on the dais, watching the night unfold.

Camila had been asked to dance by so many Fae I could hardly keep track of her. She politely accepted each time but didn't let them get too close to her.

I knew she was still cautious. She wasn't used to this many eyes on her, this many people wanting to know who she was.

She was worried about the announcement. I could see it in her eyes.

She let Xio make most of the speech, but she stood up there and didn't waver one bit.

The power in her voice when she told the room to rise nearly brought me to my knees. She was meant to be a queen one day, and while raised by royalty, I was still just a bastard.

Yes, the King and Queen were my parents, and most of the kingdom even referred to me as one of the princes, but I never claimed it.

It didn't feel right. I loved the family that found me, and I may have had some random God's blood in my veins, but I didn't know who they were.

Camila deserved the world, not this broken version of a sort of royal.

Each time she finished a dance, I saw her scanning the room looking for me, but someone else asked her to join them before her eyes met mine.

She picked up on the Fae dances pretty quickly. I wasn't expecting her to move with such grace.

"Stop pining. Go dance with her," my mother said, pointing her eye toward where Camila was about to finish a dance.

"She deserves more than me," I grumbled.

My mother knew the darkness in me well. She never tried to change me, she would encourage me to see the good in things, but she never told me I was wrong for how I saw the world.

"You are more than enough, Cree. But it's just a dance. I'm not asking you to propose to her."

I sighed and watched Camila twirl and move.

She placed a hand to her chest. "Wait...are you... scared?"

Knowing that if she made this into some kind of competitive dare, I would be forced to listen to her. The smile on her face gave her away, but she knew I was well aware of all her tactics.

Damn it all. I was scared. I was terrified of Camila.

The way she made my heart jump had me wanting to remove it altogether.

"Holt is dancing with Xio," she said, pointing to my brother, who was spinning Xio around him with a smile splitting his face.

I'd never seen him so happy, he was always smugly confident, but this sort of happiness was new.

I wanted it, but I had no idea how to get it.

How do you let someone have so much power to hurt you?

Give someone access to ruin your life more than it already was ruined?

That mostly applied to me.

I rolled my eyes. "Stop that."

"I have no idea what you mean. I think I'll retire to my room. It would be a shame if the music had to stop right now. As I walked out the door, leaving you an opportunity to go get your girl," she said while standing, not allowing me the opportunity to tell her to stop.

My girl, why did that make the breath catch in my chest.

She made it to the edge of the dais, and just like she said, the music stopped. The room parted for her to make it to the door, looking back at me and winking before descending the stairs.

My mother, ever the instigator.

She never in my two hundred years steered me in the wrong direction, though, so I wouldn't stop listening to her now.

I rose and followed behind her, weaving around Fae to get to Camila. Her back was turned to me, but I made it to her before my mother made it to the door.

Which I was positive she made sure of. She exited, and the door closed behind her. The music started up as soon as the door shut.

Someone was trying to get Camila's attention for a dance, but I may or may not have tripped them with my shadows, so they couldn't make it all the way to her.

"Not gonna happen," I muttered while reaching for her hand to turn her around and face me.

She whirled around with a small polite smile on her face. When she realized it was me, it grew wider than it ever had. For me, anyway.

For the first time, I noticed she had dimples as the slight divots in her cheeks appeared and her smile stretched across her face.

She had definitely had some wine, but she looked just as devastatingly beautiful as she did at the beginning of the night.

The wine caused some redness to rise into her cheeks, and damn, did it make me feel something in my gut.

"Are you, on the dance floor?" she asked while studying me for some sort of fatal injury I was sure to have at the suggestion I was going to dance.

"I couldn't watch another male dance with you. I think I may have cracked the arm of my throne," I muttered.

Someone else tried to get Camila's attention since we were still standing here talking instead of dancing. I growled at them and they quickly turned on their heel.

I pulled her close to me and started to lead her into the dance of the song playing. Holt and I had to take so many dancing lessons growing up I could do this in my sleep, it was never my favorite thing, but I was good at it.

Camila looked up at me with her brows raised. "Cree...you can dance."

I let a small smile loose, although it may have been bigger than I wanted it to be.

"Being raised by royalty will do that to you," I said smugly.

I turned her into a spin and quickly brought her back to my body. She gracefully followed my moves, and the bottom of her dress twirled and swished with every movement of her hips.

It was mesmerizing.

Just a dance, my mother said.

This felt like something else entirely.

I brought my hands down the sides of her dress, the exposed skin sending sparks into my fingers.

As the song ended, I spun her in one final move. She twirled on her toes before ending with her arm raised above her head.

I was so entranced by Camila I didn't realize the people around us had stopped and watched as we danced. I bowed slightly and proceeded to get back to the dais.

I felt highly exposed for some reason.

Like allowing them to see me smile down at her was some sort of vulnerability. Before I made it to the dais, Holt stepped into my path, stopping me.

"That was cute," he said, with his arms crossed. "Change your mind?"

He didn't have to remind me about what he was referring to.

He knew I knew. I told him I was too fucked up for her.

"I didn't change my mind. I just," I huffed," Mother told me to dance with her."

Blaming her would be much easier than saying I was ready to rip Camila's clothes off and claim her in the middle of the dance floor.

I needed to get a hold of myself.

"Yeah, I saw that move she made. Always the meddler," he said, laughing. "But you know if she is pointing you towards her, it's no mistake."

Yes, I did know. I couldn't stop thinking about it.

"How do you do it with Xio?" I asked him.

"Do what?"

Of course, he didn't know what I was asking, he knew me so well, but sometimes he forgot that we weren't made from the same stone.

"All of it," I said shortly, not knowing how to put it into words.

"It happened quickly, didn't it?" he laughed at himself. "She's everything. There's nothing I wouldn't do for her. I just allowed myself to feel it all. It's scary. If she ever left me, I think my very soul would shatter."

Yeah...not reassuring.

"But it's more than worth it. We balance each other out. Xio makes me feel like I could take on the entire fucking world, and I do the same for her. When I look at her, I know I have a purpose beyond all of this. I was made for her. Her for me. Even our power feels more when we're together."

Well, damn, if that wasn't poetic. I looked over to where Camila and Xio now danced together.

"Yeah. You're fucked, brother," he placed his hand on my shoulder. "You've got the look, whether you want to or not. Just remember what father said," he finished before going to get some more wine.

Father told me to let some light in and allow myself to be happy.

I wasn't sure how to go about that, but the first step would be getting Camila alone.

Chapter 30

Camila

Holt had mentioned debauchery, and I was starting to see why.

Fae started pairing off and disappearing. Some were nearly doing the deed on the dance floor. This type of public display was something I wasn't used to.

Every human was a prude compared to this.

Xio sat in Holt's lap on his throne while he whispered something in her ear, she chuckled and whispered back, and they both blushed.

I decided to get some air.

The banquet hall was joined with the courtyard on its far right side. The doors were already open, letting fresh air into the untamed behavior that was happening in the room.

Xio mentioned some flowers out here I hadn't had the chance to see yet, so I went on a search to find them.

I followed the path near one of the gazebos, and the flowers I was looking for sparkled in the moonlight.

They were so dark and gloomy compared to the flowers that bloomed during the day, but they were even more beautiful in this light.

Black and gray, but they glittered in a way that had me walking toward where they ran up the gazebo ahead of me. I jumped back when a figure moved within the structure.

I was so struck by the flowers that I forgot to stay aware of my surroundings. I moved to turn away, not sure I wanted to interrupt what may have been happening out here.

Before I could move, the figure stepped out of the gazebo into the moonlight.

Cree stood a few feet away from me, and my heart fell into my stomach.

"Oh, I'm sorry. I was just looking at the flowers. I'll leave you and whoever—" I stumbled on my words.

I didn't know what else to say, so I tried to escape, but I somehow made it in the middle of a bunch of flowers when I admired the estrellas.

"Camila, stop it," Cree said firmly, grabbing my arm and forcing me to look up at him. "I'm not out here with anyone. I was actually...I was about to come and get you."

He looked back at the flower-covered gazebo, and I followed his gaze. Small flames were lit inside like he had plucked the stars from the sky. I looked at him, slightly confused.

This seemed much more romantic than I would have expected from him.

"It's stupid. I just thought...You looked so beautiful tonight. My mother got into my head. We can go back inside."

He tried to move us away from the entrance, but I pulled my arm from his grasp and sidestepped him into the gazebo.

He had candles set up all around the gazebo, and he plucked some of the estrellas from outside and laid them sporadically across the benches and the floor.

"I'm broken, Mila," he muttered from behind me.

I turned to face him, and he looked more nervous than I'd ever seen him. He fiddled with his pants, and his forehead started to look increasingly sheen.

"But, I want you to know that I want to try and be better. We have a hell of a journey ahead of us. We can take it slow, help each other through all the bullshit. But, I want you to let me be there for you, and I want to ask you," his Adam's apple bobbed. "To be there for me."

This was real. Cree, the dark, tattooed, scary, shadow bastard, he was laying his heart out there for me to take.

Sure, we both had some issues, we were broken individuals, but maybe together, we could make each other whole.

It scared me to my bones, but I knew he felt the same way.

We could do this together, fight together, and survive this cruel world together.

I took a moment too long to respond, and his face sank, thinking I didn't want this.

"Cree," I said, placing my hand on his face, making him look me in the eye. "Together, we'll do this together. Through anything that comes."

He shuttered, actually shuttered at my words.

He was worried I would turn him down. I could hear it in his voice.

That was the worst part for the both of us, the fact that we could hurt each other. The vulnerability. We gave each other the ability to bring more darkness into our lives, but, what if we brought each other light?

What was it the prophecy said—

"Even the night has the stars," he whispered as if knowing exactly what I was thinking.

He placed his forehead on mine, and we sat there for a long moment taking each other in.

His scent, so strong now, earthy but something else. I shifted closer to him. Something almost cold, like frost over a campfire, woodsy and warm, but also cool and absolute.

He looked down at me with amusement. "Are you sniffing me?"

"If I said yes, would that be weird?" I asked through embarrassment.

"No, smell is a pretty prominent thing with the Fae. We can sense changes in emotions, amongst other things," he answered with a sly smile. "Though we are typically a little more subtle..." he said, drawing it out as if to say it was just the slightest bit weird.

"Oops," I said, shrugging slightly.

He pulled me close to his body. "I like it."

"You smell like flowers in the summer, like warm lavender," he said, sniffing me dramatically before I slapped him on his arm.

He swept me off my feet and I wrapped my legs around his waist.

He looked me in my eyes, but it felt like the gaze bore straight down to my soul.

I wouldn't be mentioning anything about my soul to him right now. I wasn't sure how all that soul-bound stuff worked, but I knew we weren't there, not yet.

"I promise you can kick my ass if I'm an asshole from now on. I'll even make it easy for you," he finished smiling smugly.

"No need. I'll be putting you on your ass again any day now. I can feel it," I said, pridefully raising my chin.

My power only seemed to get stronger. I could do more every day than the day before, and I was damn proud of it.

"We'll see about that," he muttered before breaking into that beautiful lopsided grin of his.

I brought my face to his and claimed his mouth with mine. I parted my lips for him and couldn't stop myself from raising my hips when his tongue swept in.

I felt it everywhere, he moved to lean me against one of the gazebo pillars, and my back met the cool hard stone.

I ran my fingers through his hair and down the back of his neck before sliding my hands into his tunic, asking for it to be removed.

He used the leverage from the pillar to prop me up on his hips for a second while he removed the shirt, and I felt every glorious inch of him line up with me. His skin glowed in the moonlight, accentuating all of his tattoos.

I ran my hands down his chest and noticed again how blank the lower left side of his chest was.

"Why don't you have any tattoos here?" I asked.

He stilled for a second.

"That, is a conversation for another time," he answered before kissing me and distracting me enough that I forgot the question altogether.

He slid his hands into the gaps of my dress on the side, and fire ran through me, not just the fire of my power but the fire of the passion between us.

A snap of a branch outside the gazebo had us pause as we heard footsteps and giggling coming toward us. He looked at me, knowing that this type of behavior wasn't something I was used to after spending ten years away from Maya. He would stop this if I asked him to. I knew he would, but I didn't want that.

"I don't care," I muttered against his mouth, and he let out a growl of approval, but shadows started swirling around us, creating more cover than the gazebo offered.

"I had to watch you dance with too many Fae tonight. Nobody is allowed to see what I do to you," he breathed against my neck, and then he moved.

He moved so fast I could barely keep up as he removed my dress and then his pants, exposing his tattooed legs, and hoisted me right back up onto the pillar.

He kissed me with the passion of the attraction and the hate we experienced since we met. There was nothing gentle about it.

This was no lovemaking after the admittance of love between two.

This was teeth and nails and ferality.

He used his Godly strength to lift me up and placed each of my legs on his shoulders, leaning my back against the pillar. He gave me no chance to adjust to the new height before his mouth was on me.

It took one drag of his tongue to have me moaning his name, he licked and sucked, but I needed more.

I needed it all.

"More," I gasped, and he brought me back to line my entrance with him.

THE SUN, THE STORM, & THE SHADOWS

He claimed me in one deep thrust, and I could barely keep myself up. Every muscle in my body tightened and loosened simultaneously to the point I had absolutely no control over my limbs.

My eyes were closed, and my head was thrown back. He brought his hand to my face and grasped it to pull it toward his.

"Are you okay?" he asked.

I was more than okay. I was in pure bliss. There was no way this was real.

"More," I muttered again, the only word I could form, and he obliged.

He pumped in and out of me at such a rate that vibrations were ringing between us, his hands gripped my ass, and I watched his arms push and pull.

His biceps were bulging, and his shoulders were rock-hard as he moved me along his length. I finally gained the ability to move my arms, and I ran them all over his body.

I ran them up his back and pulled his mouth to my neck. He licked, kissed, and sucked it, giving me exactly what I needed to push myself right into oblivion.

My muscles tensed around him, and I let out a scream that had to be heard across the kingdom.

He savored every last drop before dropping me onto the floor and trying to climb over me.

But I had enough of him taking control for the night.

I somehow willed my legs into moving and flipped us over and onto his back. The candlelight sparkled around us in the swirling shadows, casting golden light onto his glistening skin.

The maneuver had him reaching a space inside of me he somehow hadn't reached yet, I gasped again, and he ran his strong hands up my sides before finding my nipples.

He rolled them in his fingers, hard, and it took all I had to move my body. I ground my hips along his length, and we quickly found a rhythm as he also moved his hips to match each drag of mine. I let out a moan that I felt in every inch of my body, and Cree tensed beneath me.

"Fuck, Camila. Make that noise again," he whispered.

He dug his fingers deep into my hips, before he took his hand and smacked it across my ass hard enough to welt, leaving behind the sweet bliss of the sting. I screamed instead, and suddenly I wasn't moving anymore. We came together, both of us grunting and moaning with the pleasure we were overcome with.

I fell onto his chest, and we breathed heavily for what felt like an eternity.

"That was," he muttered like he too couldn't believe what we just experienced. "I have no words."

"Me either. I've got nothing left," I said against his neck, and he wrapped his arms around my body again.

We decided to take it slow, but I had a feeling that was going to be easier said than done.

"You are..." he tried again to form some words.

"You too," I whispered back to him before he drew his shadows back in, and we stayed on the gazebo floor, staring into the night sky.

Chapter 31

Xio

I sat in the library and huffed a long breath. Last night was indeed a long night, but it didn't go as planned.

Holt and I stayed up all night drinking wine and exchanging stories from our pasts, learning everything there was to know about each other.

Well, as much as we could fit in a couple hours before we inevitably got too drunk and passed out.

I now knew that while he often wears gray because it's the color that symbolizes his kingdom, his actual favorite color was navy blue.

His father taught him everything he needed to know about being the King one day, which was something I tried not to give too much thought to.

While, technically, I was born to be the Queen of the Sun Court, I in no way was ready to confront that.

Arlan also taught him how to build things with his hands. Just like the replica of Maya he built here in the library.

Every time I thought I had him figured out, he'd tell me some other tidbit of information I wasn't expecting.

He told me about the weddings in Maya, which were far more intricate than the boring ceremonies in Zuma.

The wedding had to be outside in the elements, most likely on the beach. We had to be surrounded by earth, water, air, and fire. Flowers for each of the four main Gods would adorn the altar with offerings for them to bless the union. Even though they were gone, this part of the ceremony still remained.

We'd have to be barefoot, wearing white ceremonial garments. The attendants would form a circle around the altar, joining hands.

Different glyphs and symbols would be painted on our skin, and when we accepted each other and kissed, the symbols adorning our chests would become permanently inked on our bodies in gold and silver.

Our union marked for life. After that, the feasts and celebrations lasted for days, all of the kingdom coming to join on the last day of the festivities.

I was looking forward to it more than I wanted to admit. I couldn't allow myself to think about it too much, as we had so much to figure out before that happened.

We couldn't stop talking and never even got to the more erotic plans we had for each other. But waking up in his arms, with my head on his chest, was more than enough for me.

Holt sat across from me, trying to find anything he could on the weapon from the prophecy.

We only had a week to figure out how to go about this.

"Anything?" I asked him, and he held up his finger for me to give him a moment to finish what he was reading.

That sparked some hope before his shoulders fell, and he shook his head.

"I wonder if we're looking at it too literally? Maybe it's not a actual weapon. What else is in the mountains?" I asked him

"Our history says that is where the Great Ceiba tree lives. Where the Gods stood when they created Maya. I'm sure plenty of your Alux friends live there, but they can't be wielded as a weapon," he replied.

"Maybe we should start there? If that is where Itzamna stood, maybe it'll give us more clues to follow?" I asked, just trying to grab onto anything at this point.

"It's guarded by magic, so we won't be able to just stroll up to it but we can try. Some stories say that is where he killed the other Gods. But we can't be sure since none lived to tell the accurate story."

"How do we know he was even the one to kill them?" I asked.

"He was the only one strong enough to wipe out all the Gods. We've all just assumed it was him. Before I was born, the Gods used to come and visit their Descendants once a year. The festivals were extravagant for their return. We'd set out offerings for them, and we would sing and dance all night. That was when there were also more Gods. While Kinich, Chaac, and Ixchel were the main three outside of Itzamna, there were also other smaller Gods that would visit their Descendants in the villages between kingdoms. Every Fae celebrated across Maya, but one day they never came. Never in all of our years did that happen. People started to whisper of Itzamna killing them after that," he finished.

I didn't think I could believe anything I didn't know to be entirely factual.

"Well, I still think we should go there. Hopefully, we'll find something useful," I responded, and he moved to my side of the table.

He pulled the chair I was sitting on to face him and caged me between his arms with either hand on the armrests.

"I'll go anywhere you go," he said darkly, the look in his eye telling me he was at least a little disappointed that we fell asleep last night.

"Is that right?" I responded before trailing my hands up and down his body.

"No time for that," we heard his mother say as she glided into the library.

She always moved as if her feet weren't touching the ground. The elegance and grace only achievable by centuries as the Queen.

"I mean, we have a little time," Holt said quietly enough for only me to hear, or so he thought.

"Nonsense! You need to go down to the village. We are expected at an orphanage shortly. Xio, you can come as well. The people are curious about you after the feast. Actually, where are your sister and Cree? I told him what our plans were last night."

As fast as she made her way into the room, she was gone again to search for the missing parties. Holt took a step closer to me, about to take advantage of the fact we were once again left alone.

"Now, Holt!" we heard her yell from the hallway.

I didn't know how those two got away with anything. She always knew when he was up to something.

"We should listen to her before she comes back and drags us by our ears," I said jokingly, but Holt seemed to have a flashback of her doing something similar and straightened.

"You're right. Let's go."

He offered me his arm, as he always did when we strolled around the palace.

"So what do you do at things like this?" I asked him.

We'd shared a lot about ourselves personally, but I still didn't fully understand what his role as the Prince was and what his role as the King would be.

We passed lots of people throughout the hall, all smiling and greeting the Prince and me.

He finished smiling and waving to one of the royal staff carrying a bag of oats before answering.

"I will help hand out new toys for the kids, and we'll bring them some sweet treats to enjoy. We try to go as often as possible, but it's been some time since we've visited with everything going on lately. The kids enjoy having us there, and the people in the village like to see us when we visit. It makes them feel more connected to us, and we try to listen to any concerns they might have outside of when we hold court. So, it's a long day. Worth it, though," he explained as we turned around the corner to find Chara near the entrance with Cree and Camila.

Somewhere along the way, Chara acquired a beautiful crown that looked like intertwining twigs cast in silver.

They looked like they, too, were just scolded for not being ready when expected. They both seemed oddly okay with it, though. I hadn't checked in on her this morning because I assumed she would still be asleep when I went to the library.

"Interesting," Holt said with a small smile playing on his lips. "What you been up to, brother?"

Cree ignored him in favor of opening the door for us all to walk out. We descended the steps, and a carriage was ready to take the five of us down to the orphanage. The carriage was beautifully crafted, and everyone in the village recognized it. People cheered and shouted for the royals as we passed by.

It was amazing to see someone in power so respected. It was never like that in Zuma, the people who held power were cruel and feared. I wondered if that's why the Gods decided to create the Fae in favor of a better creation.

Thankfully, I was dressed for the occasion already. I was getting used to the luxury of having the handmaidens help me each morning.

I wore a beautiful silver dress today that matched the lighter shades of Holt's eyes.

Which definitely wasn't on purpose—definitely not.

Although soon, we would be back to wearing riding gear and sleeping in a tent, so I shouldn't be allowing myself to become so comfortable with it.

Chara cleared her throat. "Know that the shock of your return has probably settled now. They may have questions about where you two have been."

I thought she was talking to Holt and Cree, but Chara's eyes were locked in with mine when I looked up. I didn't think about the fact we might have to talk about that while we were here today. Sure, making the announcement was one thing, but getting into the details was entirely different.

"Do you want my advice?" she asked, and I wanted her advice more than anything right now.

I wished I could lean on my own mother. Chara's warm personality has made me comfortable enough with her to almost feel a mother-daughter relationship forming between us.

"Yes, please," I answered.

She sighed. "While I always say that the truth is the best way to earn trust, I don't think you should explain it all quite yet. I think you should simply tell them your mother hid you to protect you and that you will use your gifts to help Cree and Holt stop the famine. We don't even understand everything yet. It could only cause more issues if we try to explain."

Relief filled me. I thought she would tell me to spill my whole life story, and I wasn't quite ready for that. Holt put his hand on my leg and squeezed, letting me know he was there. Like always.

"Days like this can be exhausting, but the joy the villagers get from it is more than worth it," she finished, just like Holt said.

They really were the epitome of what royalty should be.

Cree and Camila were engaging in some very intense eye contact next to us. From the look of it, they definitely crossed some lines they set out for themselves last night.

As much as they said they weren't ready or weren't good for each other, they sure seemed to find their way back each time. I wanted to bridge the conversation about the soul-bounds, but I knew that would only scare Camila.

I'd let her bring it to me. It kind of only made sense that the remaining Descendants were destined for each other. The carriage stopped abruptly, and the door was swung open.

Chara stepped out first, and the village children all ran to hug her and ask her to play. Cree and Holt went next, and the children also swarmed them.

Cree tried to hide his smile, but I'd gotten to know him enough to see that he didn't hate the idea of helping the children.

Even if his exterior screamed that children would be appalling to him.

We stepped out next, and all the children turned to us and started whispering to the other royals, asking who we were.

Holt whispered into one of the small girls' ears, and her smile grew wide as she ran over to me and hugged my legs as tight as she could.

The rest of the children followed suit, jumping up and down and pulling on me and Camila's hair until the Queen announced it was time for them to have their snack.

Holt led us through the children over to a cart that looked like it came from the palace full of cakes and sticky pastries.

"What did you say to her?" I asked him.

"That is between Cora and me," he responded with a wink before grabbing the toys from another cart.

He knew the small girl by her name. It was almost too sweet for me to handle.

I found myself thinking about what a little girl with his eyes and my smile would look like.

We really needed to figure out how to save Maya.

Chapter 32

Cree

I wouldn't say it out loud because it went against my scary shadow personality, but, the days we visited the orphanage were my favorite.

As an orphan of sorts, doing anything to make their lives a little better made me happier than I liked to admit. I had my favorites here, the ones with similar dispositions to me.

The ones who didn't jump up and down when we arrived, or stood back and watched the other kids play with the new toys.

I tried my best to connect with them, which frequently led to us hiding behind the orphanage while I showed them how to fight and use their magic.

They always wanted to see mine, infatuated with the things I could do with the shadows. But they were getting good, especially Michael and Lucia.

They had the potential to join the Warriors, and I was proud of how far they had come. Their parents died in a fire when they were young, but they were old enough to remember.

They came here and didn't talk to anyone. They didn't engage with the other children and refused to leave each other's side. I could feel their sorrow, pain, and anger on my first visit back after they arrived.

All of the things I understood well. I explained to them that I didn't lose my parents the same way, but I didn't know mine, which made me angry.

We'd been working through it together for a while, and now Lucia had the most beautiful little smile I'd ever seen.

Well, second most beautiful.

I'd have to let Camila in on my secret today, which made my stomach turn slightly.

I wasn't really sure what she saw in me. If the darkness attracted her to me, would this make her look at me differently?

I couldn't be sure.

But as Michael, Lucia, and the rest of the other orphans gathered by the side of the building waiting for me, I didn't have much more time to think about it.

Camila was handing a little boy a wooden horse from the toy cart.

The sun was pouring over her, highlighting those strands of gold in her hair. She looked happy. The more I thought about it, the more I realized that she probably felt the same way about the kids that I did.

I walked over to the toy cart and snatched the bag of sparring weapons I had placed there earlier.

I grabbed Camila by the wrist, dragging her with me to the side of the orphanage.

"Where are we going?" she asked, confused as to why I didn't explain before pulling her away from the toys.

Probably could have warned her, but there was too much going on in my mind to try and explain.

Last night was incredible, so incredible that I woke up this morning positive it was a dream.

I told myself that I wouldn't go back on my word and try to be a better person for her, but it would take me more than a few hours to achieve that.

We made it to the back of the orphanage, where my band of misfits was waiting for me. There were about eight of them, and they all looked up at me, confused as to why I was bringing her with me.

I always ensured no one followed us back here, just in case they disapproved of me teaching them how to use their magic to fight.

"This," I hesitated, "This is my...Camila," I said awkwardly.

Yes, we told each other we would be there for each other and help work through the bullshit, but what exactly did that make her to me?

Camila took the opportunity to step forward and smile at each one.

"Hi, I'm Princess Camila. Who are you all?"

My cock jumped slightly at the use of her title, odd.

Each one told her their name, some more reluctant than others, and she listened to each one telling them how happy she was to meet them.

She might not have been confident in her skills with the people, but right now, I could see she'd make a great queen.

She looked back at me, questioning why we were back here with her eyes.

I stepped to her and whispered into her ear, "the particularly troubled," and that was all I needed to say.

She knew what I meant.

Camila was troubled herself.

I walked a circle around my little tribe, pretending to inspect them.

"I see you all have been training since my last visit. You look like you've all put on a small child's worth of muscle. Impressive. Keeping our meetings a secret still, are we?" I asked them, and they all nodded like the little warriors they were sure to become one day.

"Now, don't you worry about the princess here. She's one of us, and she'll keep this secret with us, won't you?" I asked her, raising my eyebrows in a fake threatening fashion.

"Absolutely, we stick together," she responded, and damn, did it make my heart skip a beat.

I knew she would know exactly what to say to put the kids at ease. They all sagged slightly before straightening back into the form I'd shown them to stand in before our sessions started.

"Why don't we show her what we're made of, warriors?"

The smiles on their little faces grew wide, and Camila crossed her arms against her chest, pretending to believe they couldn't do much. This only encouraged them more.

She knew that people like us would rise to any challenge we were faced with.

They got into formation and started to show all the moves we'd been practicing over the years.

A few of the newer ones didn't keep up with the older ones, like Michael and Lucia, but they moved with just as much ferocity.

"Excellent!" I boomed, "now, let's get out our weapons, shall we?" I asked, tossing the bag of wooden swords at them to grab their favorites.

They all grabbed their swords by the hilt, and I paired them off for two-on-two battles.

While I favored my sort of magic, they didn't have that to access.

They had the average power, which was still very powerful, of force to use to their advantage.

I'd shown them how to throw it into their swings and knock opponents down with a flick of their fingers, and they were displaying everything I taught them so far. Camila brushed my side and smiled up at me, she knew how hard it was to pull yourself out of the darkness, but these kids were doing their best.

"You surprise me, shadow bastard," she whispered while watching them fight with all the ferocity of the Storm Court Warriors. "Although I should have known you'd have a soft spot for the orphans. You did admit that to me at some point if I remember correctly," she said with a shrug before going over to assist one of the smaller girls with her swing.

Camila fixed the girl's stance and showed her where to swing so she got the most power out of the blow possible. The girl nodded along as she assisted her and did everything she said to do.

Up until now, she wasn't able to land a blow on the boy she was fighting. She stepped forward, shifted her weight, and brought the boy down in one swing of her sword.

"Ha! I told you I'd get you one day!" she said, jumping up and down and doing a little victory dance around the boy on the floor.

Camila laughed and helped the boy up from the ground.

"First rule, don't underestimate her power because she's a girl."

She winked at him before gathering fire in her hands.

The boy looked shocked. But within seconds, his eyes turned to something a little more like admiration as she walked away from him and returned to my side.

"I think he might be enamored with you," I told her with a slight chuckle.

"He can get in line," she said, directing a wink at me.

Now that had me looking at her just like the little boy.

I had to walk away from her before I kissed her in front of all these small children. They would look at me like some soft Fae, and I couldn't have that.

I watched as Michael and Lucia battled. Neither of them had won yet, and they were both starting to sweat profusely. Lucia sidestepped and tried to dive under Michael's arm, using his height to her advantage, but Michael anticipated the move and blocked her.

Lucia spun out and used some of her force power to try and knock him off his feet, but Michael just jumped out of the way.

Lucia tried again with the same maneuver but directed the force just high enough to where he would be when he jumped to avoid it, and he came tumbling down to the ground. She quickly brought her sword to his neck and smiled smugly.

"Yield, big brother," she said, and he rolled his eyes at her.

"I yield," he muttered before she helped him off the ground, and they looked at me.

"How old are you two now?" I asked.

"I turn 18 next month. She just turned 17 last month," Michael reminded me.

They'd be out of the orphanage soon. It was hard for kids to leave the orphanage with no family to help them, some just ended up on the streets.

We tried our best to ensure this didn't happen, but we couldn't save everyone. But these two, I could do something about.

"When you age out of the orphanage, I want you to come to see me. If you would like, I'd enlist you into the Warriors. There will always be a place for you among them as long as I'm Commander," I said.

Both of them were quiet for a moment. Maybe I shouldn't have assumed that they would want that, is a life fighting what a child who lost their parents would want—

Suddenly I felt warm bodies around me.

They both had their heads buried in my chest, and Lucia looked up at me with tears flowing from her eyes.

"We would be honored," she said before burying her face back in my chest.

I patted them both on their backs, and they stepped back. They immediately picked their sparring swords back up and started to engage in another battle.

The warmth in my chest was almost uncomfortable, and when I turned away, Camila was standing nearby watching the encounter.

She looked proud.

Proud in a way that only the King and Queen, my mother and father, had looked at me. It almost made my knees buckle, but I somehow made it over to her.

She knew I wouldn't want her making a big deal about what I just did, so she simply smiled and placed a brush of a kiss on my chest. Which was as high as she could reach without me meeting her halfway.

The kids all let out a long "oooooh," and she told them to mind their business and keep training before she made them fight her instead.

She would be the end of me, but, I think I'd fully embrace that ending.

Chapter 33

Holt

The last week flew by in a blur.

We would have to be leaving the palace in just two days now. Xio and I weren't any closer to figuring out what the weapon was, but we both decided our plan to find the Great Ceiba would be a good start.

Cree was able to send some of his scouts out since we returned, and they had a general idea of where the Serpents might be. But being nomads, they could be somewhere else entirely by the time they made it out into the Grasslands.

I savored every moment I had with Xio in the palace.

Watching her with my mother was something I never even knew I wanted.

She was incredible, not many others could keep up with my mother in a game of wit, but she did it gracefully, and I could tell my mother liked her.

She mentioned how much she would miss us when we were gone. It broke my heart that I would have to leave her alone in the palace, but she had such a sound support system here that I knew she'd be fine.

I just needed to figure out how to ensure she had a future longer than a year.

Xio and I found our way to each other's chambers every night since the feast. Sometimes coming in with only a few hours until morning, and other nights we spent the entire night exploring everything there was to us.

Physically, emotionally, and spiritually, it was overwhelming, but in the best way possible.

I knew she'd been practicing her magic every day, but I was still worried about taking her out into the potential danger.

She could handle herself, I had no doubts about that, but everything in me screamed to protect her and not let her into harm's way.

Unfortunately, we didn't have a choice much longer. I sat on the beach, watching the waves roll in, thinking about my father.

I wondered if he always felt like this, with the pressure of an entire kingdom on his shoulders. If we succeeded, I would have to fill those shoes, and it scared me more than I'd like to admit.

Sure, I'd been training for it since I could talk, but training and doing were not the same. I wish I could speak to him, ask him how he did it.

He always seemed so happy when we were together, like he knew every decision he made was the right one.

I had enough confidence for more than one Fae, but the confidence to make the right decisions for tens of thousands? I wasn't sure I was capable.

"He didn't always know if he was making the right decision," my mother said from behind me, as always that intuition of hers found me exactly when I needed it.

I didn't know how she did it, but she was there anytime Cree or I needed her. It used to drive me crazy when I was young, when I just wanted to stew in my anger. Now I was grateful for it, so grateful for it.

She sat next to me, digging her toes in the sand the same way I always loved to. She was wearing black again today.

I was curious to know if it was because she was missing my father or if it was just a choice in fashion. She stared off into the rippling waves with puffy eyes, and I found my answer.

She'd been so strong since we'd been back, but I knew a lot of it was just a mask she wore. No matter how much she tried to hide it from us, this type of pain didn't go away so easily.

"He would worry himself to the point of stomach ache sometimes," she started, smiling slightly at the thought. "We'd sit up all night discussing the matters of the kingdom, even after we met with the council. He put on a brave face for everyone, but this type of power isn't something that comes easily," she finished, finally looking me into my eyes.

Her lip quivered slightly, and I brought her into my chest for a hug.

"I miss him," she whispered into my chest.

My mother was so small, and now she also seemed so fragile. Which was never a word I'd used to describe her in the past.

"I'm just worried I won't be as good at ruling as he was," I murmured, "what if I make the wrong choice? Even now, how do I know what I'm doing is putting me on the right path?"

I expected some kind of reassuring message she was always so good at.

"You won't, you don't," she said, looking up at me with those big blue watery eyes. "But Holt, all you can do is trust your gut, trust the people around you to help guide you. He lives within you, and you will be even better than he was," she said confidently, pushing some of the curls out of my face that the wind blew onto my forehead.

The confidence she had in me was reassuring enough.

Between her and Xio, they always knew what to say to make me breathe a little easier.

"Xio is your soul-bound," she said, not a question but a statement. "I only say this because I know you are already aware. I knew it the moment I laid eyes on her. Keep each other safe, Holt. You two will do great things together. Follow your hearts. They won't lead you astray."

"The Alux said something similar to her," I laughed.

All the years of her trying to tell me that the Alux were real came back to me.

"Did they now?" she asked, mocking me, "I'm glad you finally believe me, although I can't think of any scenarios I lied to you before, interesting."

Just like that, we were both laughing, helping each other out of the darkness that could consume us if we allowed it.

"I've had Zyanya ensure that Thunder and Night will be ready when you leave. They've stocked all your supplies, so you should be good for a few weeks. I picked out a couple horses for Xio and Camila as well, just as strong as yours," she reassured me.

Although I would miss riding with Xio, having two horses for all our things would be best.

"Thank you, Mother. I'm going to miss you greatly," I told her while placing a gentle kiss on her forehead.

"You'll be back, and the throne will be waiting for you," she said before standing and dusting the sand off her.

She left me on the beach, feeling a little lighter and ready to take on whatever came for us.

Chapter 34

Camila

It was time for us to leave the palace.

The time we spent here was a gift. A short few weeks of peace before we had to go out into the world and face the dangers that came with it.

The Queen mentioned a few days ago that she picked out some horses for us to travel with, and Xio and I were walking down to the stables to meet them.

We'd have to leave shortly after, so as I walked down the path to the stables, I looked at the training arena where Cree and I had our first real moment together.

I would miss this place, the palace where Cree grew up.

He was still perplexing, but seeing him in his world helped me understand him better.

My boots met the dirt of the stables, and I looked up to find the two horses Chara picked out for us.

They were magnificent. Two mares like she knew how much we loved the power of femininity.

It was also abundantly clear which horse belonged to who.

The horse to the left, Xio's horse, was light silver with a crisp white mane. Long hair fell around her hooves, which moved in the wind as it breezed through her legs.

My horse was astonishing, black just like Night, but her mane had streaks of silver in it, just like I had streaks of gold.

They were powerful horses, almost as big as Holt and Cree's stallions.

I ran my hands through her silver streaks. "What's her name?" I asked Hugo, the same male who had met us when we entered the palace.

"Her name is Vela," he said, patting her on her side.

"Like the constellation?"

"That's the one," he said before moving over to Xio's horse.

How fitting, Night and Vela, night and the stars.

"Your mare's name is Gale, like the wind," he said to Xio, "If you're going to ask where it comes from, too," he chuckled while getting the saddles we'd be using to ride.

Chara picked these out specifically for us. She really was a wonder.

While Hugo got Vela and Gale ready, we met the boys outside the stables.

They were giving last-minute instructions to Alex, who commanded the warriors in their absence.

We met him at the funeral, and he was extremely intimidating. He fit right in with Cree and Holt's general ambiance of large-killer-Fae. His complexion was lighter than Cree's but still warm.

He had short, dark blonde hair that you'd think was brown until he stepped into the sunlight. His eyes were a similar shade to the Queen's blue but much deeper than hers, almost navy.

Subjectively speaking, he was an attractive male.

We came to stand next to them while they wrapped up their conversation.

"... they'll need to be ready. We have just less than a year to ensure all the ranks are properly trained. Less than that, really, if we want to get them moved to wherever they should be. We will send a messenger hawk from one of the villages nearby as soon as we have that information. You are acting Commander. We are trusting you to get this done," Cree finished saying.

From what he told me, he was the Commander of the Warriors since they always knew Holt would have to become King one day.

He and Holt would work hand in hand in a battle, but Cree was the one who commanded them.

"Yes, Commander, it will be done. I swear it," Alex swore, placing his fist on his chest and pounding it twice before marching away to act on his orders.

Commander Cree, that made my skin prickle a bit.

"It's time to go," Holt exclaimed.

We'd be able to travel together for a few days, but then we'd have to split up.

I still wasn't looking forward to it, but I knew it was for the greater good. Even Cree seemed less than enthusiastic about leaving his brother.

Hugo brought our horses out to us, our bags strapped and ready to go. I grabbed my cloak from the bag on the left side and closed the bag back up.

I felt a shadow come up behind me, and I knew that shadow anywhere.

"So you met Vela," Cree stated, running his hand through her mane. "Chara picked her, but I knew you'd like her," he said, coming over to help me fix my cloak.

"Seems a little on the nose," laughed. "But I do like her a lot. Don't tell Night, though. He still hasn't fully forgiven me for scaring him with my flames."

Cree didn't respond immediately, and I turned to find him deep in thought.

"Are you ready?" he asked, "for the journey, where it will take us?"

He knew I was nervous, but our mother trusted us, so I had to.

"I am. We can do this," I reassured him while also reassuring myself.

Chara was heading towards us with Zyanya in tow, they were coming to say goodbye, their mouths pulled down in frowns.

She was going to miss her boys, but, part of me felt like she would miss us too. With the loss of her husband, having us with her had helped distract her from the worst of it.

"I had all of your favorites stocked, princes," Zyanya told Cree and Holt. Cree flinched slightly at the title but allowed her to finish. "We're going to miss you," she said before stepping back and letting Chara step forward.

"Be safe, but be courageous. You all have everything you need within you," she eyed us all gently. "Follow your hearts, and trust your guts. Lean on each other. You don't have to do any of this alone."

Her eyes finished on Cree and me, like the last part of the message was aimed toward us, which it was.

We trusted each other, but we both had the type of personality that wanted to protect others by doing things alone when possible.

We wouldn't be able to do that on this journey.

"I love you all dearly, although our time has been short, Xio and Camila. I already feel as if we're family, as if you're my daughters. Which I know is a lot. I don't want to pretend to take the place of your mother, but I do feel a mother's love for you already."

She gave us both a deep hug that brought tears to my eyes before releasing us and moving to Cree and Holt.

"My boys, remember everything your father and I taught you. You are our greatest blessing. I have every confidence that you will prevail, and I already can't wait for your return."

They both bent down to hug her, and watching her love them brought even more tears to my eyes.

We all mounted our horses and headed out of the village and to the outer gate.

The journey ahead was unknown, but if there was anything I knew, it was that the power of my mother and father ran through me.

I was Princess Camila of the Sun Court, daughter of Jasper and Adelina, Descendant of Kinich, and I would not fail.

Chapter 35

Xio

Our journey out of the palace and to the first place we were making camp at went much faster than I thought it would.

The location was wide and flat, leaving plenty of space for us to be comfortable. Although I did already miss the bedchamber I'd stayed in for the last few weeks.

I was able to pack a few extra changes of clothes this time, so I was thankful for that luxury, at least. The nights were getting colder than before, with autumn coming fast.

Holt assured me that the winters in Maya were nothing like in Zuma. It got colder but not by a lot. Nothing like the frigid tundras I encountered over the last decade.

My sister and I always struggled through them worse than most. Now I knew we weren't ever made to endure them.

We opened our packs to find that Zyanya packed all four of us a tent each.

"That won't be necessary," Holt said, pushing my tent back into my bag.

Well, that solves that.

Cree seemed to know that Camila would want to make that decision on her own as he eyed her with her hand on her tent.

She told me about their moment in the garden, and it seemed we both had embraced the Fae part of us that didn't mind doing such an act outside of a bedchamber.

"I won't use it today, but, if you annoy me, I'm glad I have it as an option," she said while putting her tent back in her bag.

And that was that.

Holt and Cree set up the tents for us, and Camila and I built a fire using our magic. Thankfully, Zyanya also packed us some of the foods we'd come to love in the palace since they wouldn't rot in a day, but soon we'd be back to eating the same old thing as before.

This time, we had more weapons. I had Holt supply me with a beautiful golden bow. I thought he had it made for me, but he didn't make such a claim.

It would come in handy for hunting game when we got tired of nuts and dried fruit. I'd been a little rusty in my archery skills after not using them for some time, but I'd been training with it over the last couple of weeks, and it was a weapon of beauty.

My magic melded with it seamlessly, it was now my second favorite weapon I owned.

"We have two days until we have to separate. The goal is to find whatever it is within two months' time. We've got a lot of ground to cover in the mountains. You guys may have it a little easier finding the Serpents but figuring out whatever message they have hidden won't be easy," Holt said, sitting down next to me by the fire.

"My scouts said they were located northwest, but that's all we know. We will calculate the best way to go about finding the message. I'd prefer to just ask them if they know what the fuck the prophecy is referencing. Doubt it'll be that easy, though. I'm sure we'll be bloodied before it's all said and done," Cree responded, cracking his knuckles like the sound of getting bloody wasn't all that unappealing.

"Two months sounds like such a long time," I said sadly.

Camila watched me with sad eyes. "But I'm glad we won't be alone," she mumbled.

"If my sister gets hurt, I'll kill you," Camila said to Holt.

She had always been intimidating, but she seemed to have mastered the Fae level of intimidation in our time in Maya.

"I'd die before I let that happen," Holt said seriously, and the heaviness of our situation fell around us.

We hadn't even really discussed the possibility of us not making it out, not wanting to breathe life into the thought.

"Will you two stop at Sun Palace at all?" Cree asked us.

The thought of being so close to our home and not having time to stop there hurt a little. I knew we were on a mission with a time constraint, but if somehow we were able to find the weapon quickly, I would have liked to make it back there.

"We'll assess that as we go as well," Holt responded, knowing how I felt about it, "enough of the somberness. Let's play a game," he said, taking out a jug of ale and popping the cork out of it.

"A game?" Camila asked.

I didn't know where he was going with this, either.

"Yes, a drinking game. For one of our last nights together before we have to split up, I wouldn't want to play tomorrow when we can't afford to feel the effects of it the next morning," Holt responded.

"What do we have to do?" I asked him, liking the idea of getting my mind off what was happening.

"It's simple, we go around the fire, and you have to ask for a truth or a dare. You have to drink if you can't complete what you ask for. Cree goes first, so you guys can get a feel for it," he said with a wink tossed at me.

Cree rolled his eyes. He apparently was familiar with whatever game we were playing.

"Dare," he said quickly.

"You..." Holt trailed off, trying to think of what to dare him into. "Oh! You have to fly up past that tree," he said, pointing up to the top of a tree to our left. "But as soon as you get that high, you have to extinguish your wings and free fall to the ground," Holt said with a chuckle.

Things had been so serious that I forgot how utterly ridiculous they could be when they were together.

Cree looked as if he might not take the dare, but after a few moments, he got up, and his wings appeared on his shoulder blades.

Camila was just as excited and intrigued as Holt was.

I was the only one worried that he'd hurt himself, it seemed.

A few mighty flaps of his wings had him flying up above the trees.

I rarely got to see his wings at all when we were in the palace. It was still as astonishing as the first time.

"Make sure you get all the way up there!" Camila yelled, not allowing him to cheat his way out of the dare.

He made it to the top, and he let his wings vanish from his back as he fell down all the way to the bottom of the tree.

"Shit!" he yelled before his shadows softened the landing a second before he hit the hard ground.

"Drink! That was not part of the deal," Holt exclaimed while he and Camila fell into laughter. I chuckled at the two of them holding each other up from toppling onto the ground howling their amusement.

They had fallen into such a brother-sister camaraderie since I told her about us fully accepting what we were to each other.

It made me happy that she had someone else to confide in, along with Cree and me.

"I couldn't help it! My magic defended me without me even thinking about it!" Cree yelled back at them.

They didn't care and threw the jug at Cree before he drank three big gulps.

"Xio! You're up," Cree yelled at me, trying to get the attention of himself.

"What do you choose?" he asked me.

"Truth, I don't want to break all of my bones," I answered him back.

He pondered what he should ask me. I'd been a pretty open book, so I didn't think there was much he could ask me I hadn't already shared with Holt.

"How would you prefer to die?" Cree asked.

"Gods, Cree! Why so morbid?" Holt questioned, seemingly upset with the question of my future death.

I just laughed at him. Death seemed to be everywhere these days. I knew I couldn't hide from it. It didn't necessarily scare me anymore. Not that I wanted to leave any of them anytime soon.

"I want to die of old age with my children all around me to celebrate my life after," I said proudly.

I'd had some time to think about the best way to go. Everyone was quiet for a moment with the deaths we experienced all returning to our memories.

"Camila, what do you choose?" I asked, moving on from my answer.

"Easy, dare," she replied, and I had to think about what could possibly be a good dare for my sister.

"Okay!" I lifted a branch and let some fire gather in my hand. "You have to make it all the way to that tree over there," pointing to another tree, trees being the only thing around us. "And back before the branch falls to ashes."

"Done," Camila said, getting in a stance to run as fast as she could.

I let the fire in my hand reach the branch, and she was off.

The wind blew her hair every which way, and she made it to the tree, but by the time she turned around, the branch had almost already burned through.

She panicked for a second, and suddenly a burst of yellow exploded from her. A huge winged jaguar came roaring through the yellow light, and she slid back to where we were standing.

All three of our mouths hung open. Our jaws might as well have been brushing the very ground before us.

Holt had tried to instruct us into our animal forms for weeks without any luck, and Cree wasn't sure where he came from or if he even had an animal form.

This was the first time either of us had successfully accomplished the task.

"Oh, my Gods! Camila!" I shouted, running over to her and running my hands over her fur. She looked just like our mother in the memory, but her coat was black rather than the golden spotted shade of our mother.

She was incredible, mighty, and powerful.

Camila started beating her wings, and I had to take a step back. She floated off the ground before another burst of yellow flashed, and she was back in her Fae form.

"How did you do that?!" I screeched.

I needed her to tell me exactly how she figured it out. If she could do it, I could do it.

"I have no idea," she said through heavy breaths. "I just panicked when I saw the branch was almost gone, and suddenly I was covered in fur, and my claws were digging into the dirt," she explained, still trying to catch her breath from the ordeal.

"I knew you could do it!" Holt said before picking her up off the ground and spinning her around, just before Cree grabbed her from him and attacked her with a long passionate kiss.

"You are incredible," he said while she blushed, looking into his eyes.

They both looked over at us and jumped back from each other like they just remembered they weren't alone.

They weren't fooling anybody.

I had to admit I had the tiniest inkling of jealousy, but I was too happy that she figured it out to let it show.

"How did it feel? To be an animal?" I asked her.

"It didn't feel weird. It felt like that was the only form I had. I was still in there. I just felt more...wild," she answered.

Gods, I couldn't wait to do it myself.

"That is so freaking cool," I said, spinning her around me. "Do you think you could do it again? Or just the wings like Holt?"

She concentrated hard, but nothing happened.

"Not yet. Maybe I need to be in a panic? Maybe I should try a free fall from up top of the tree like Cree?" she asked far too seriously.

"Oh no, that won't be necessary," Cree answered before she could get too into the idea.

Camila just shrugged and went to sit back down in her spot like it had never happened.

"Well, I think I won the game, no?" Camila asked us all, and we just agreed.

I didn't think there could be a winner in a game like this, but she won it easily.

We all looked at the sky for a bit longer as the stars glittered, and the moon shone on the site. We retired to bed not too long after that, the idea that I might be able to fly soon at the front of my mind.

Chapter 36

Camila

Today was the day we'd have to separate. I sat on a log while the others packed our site up with sweat dripping down my forehead, my face tight in concentration.

And nothing.

I hadn't been able to shift again, which drove me crazy. Cree had to stop me from trying to purposely throw myself into some sort of panic multiple times.

After he threatened to, rather seriously, tie my arms and legs together, I decided I'd stop. For now.

It wouldn't be the first time he put me in binds, so I figured I should take the threat a little seriously.

We were all moving a little slow this morning, the fact we were going our different ways thick in the air.

"Alright. We're all packed up," Cree said gently, "you might want to go," he stopped, looking at Xio, suggesting I say goodbye to my sister.

I nodded and went to my sister, who was pretending to open and close her saddlebags repeatedly.

She turned to me with tears already lining her eyes.

"I don't want to," she muttered before pulling me into a hug. "How will we do this without each other?"

I didn't have an answer. We'd always been there for each other.

The rock, the mother, the sister, the confidant, I'd never known a life where she wasn't just an arm's reach away from me.

"I don't know," I whispered back to her, "but we have to, and we won't be alone," I told her, looking over to Holt and Cree, who appeared to be going through their own brotherly goodbye.

"You're right. I know you'll be safe with Cree," she said.

"And you with Holt," I replied before bringing my forehead to rest on hers.

"We are powerful, Xio," I whispered.

"We will not fail," she whispered back, as she held my arms and I tightened my grip on hers.

We both brought our magic up to the surface of our skin simultaneously. Letting the light and flame dance with each other around our bodies, creating a bright orb that resembled the sun.

We both drew our power back in and stepped away from each other.

"I love you, Camila. Please be safe. Listen to Cree," she said to me, knowing my love for stubborn, hard-headedness.

"Psh, better tell him to listen to me," I replied, "I love you too, Xio. I'll see you in two months."

She nodded, and we both turned to mount our horses.

"Holt, remember what I said?" I yelled at him, and he nodded once at me.

He'd protect Xio with his last breath. That brought me some sort of assurance, but not enough.

"Be careful, Xio. Watch out for my brother," Cree said to her, and she too nodded, knowing if she tried to speak right now, no words would come out.

We came to the point the paths separated, and we followed them without looking back, moving into a trot.

It felt like I had left half of my heart back on that path.

I swallowed a sob trying to escape me.

Inhala, exhala. Inhala, exhala.

Everything was going to be okay.

Our mother believed in us, and so would I.

We would not fail.

I repeated this over and over until the sob no longer climbed up my throat.

Until I believed my own words.

We were no longer on a trail but deep on the plains of the Grasslands.

Cree knew I needed time to think about things, so we hadn't spoken in a while. He needed time too, so we both sat in comfortable silence.

"We're going to have to make camp somewhere around here. Nowhere is particularly safe, but maybe over there could work," he said, breaking the silence and pointing to the base of a hill. "The hill can offer us some coverage,"

We both guided our horses to where he was pointing. The sun had already begun to set. We pushed it longer than we normally would have, wanting to dwell in our thoughts.

Neither of us wanted to stop riding. It gave us both some sort of peace. There weren't many trees around like when we were in the forest, so Cree tied our horses together.

"They won't be able to get far from us like this, but I'll have to keep watch anyways," he explained.

"Don't you mean *we*?" I asked him, already trying to do everything himself.

He looked at me like he was ready to fight me on this, but I stopped him before he could reply.

"Do you plan on staying awake for the next two months, or what," I said, raising my eyebrows asking what exactly he was thinking.

He looked at me blankly like that was precisely what he was suggesting.

"Shifts, Cree. We'll take shifts," I said before pulling out our tent.

"Fine," he muttered, "shifts it is," he said, taking the tent from me and setting it up for us.

He finished quickly and returned to where I had made a small fire. We didn't want to draw too much attention, so we only used it for a little bit before extinguishing the flames.

"I've got the first shift. Get some rest. I'll wake you up for yours," he said, pointing me to the tent. I gave him a look saying I hardly believed he'd wake me up.

"If you let me sleep all night without waking for my shift, I will stab you," I said with my dagger in hand, making my way to the tent.

"That makes me sort of curious, for how exactly you'd accomplish that?" he said like the thought amused him.

I turned quickly and threw my dagger at him. It landed a hair away from the hand he was resting back on, and he yanked it away quickly.

"Forgot you could do that. I'll wake you up," he said before turning back to survey the area.

We all trained during our time at the palace, but many times, we were alone or with whatever warriors were training when we showed up.

When Cree and I trained together, it was always one-on-one combat. Outside of my little murder-escape attempt, he really didn't know how skilled I was with a blade.

A decade in the human lands with nothing else to do but train was plenty of time for me to become an expert.

The tent already had our furs laid out and a jug of water in it for me to rinse off with. I cleaned myself the best I could before pulling the covers over my body and going to sleep.

"Camila, Camila, I promised I'd wake you up, but you don't seem to want to, so," I heard Cree say while I was half asleep.

I opened my eyes to his body over mine, trying to shake me awake.

"I'm up," I said, rubbing my eyes. "You can get ready to sleep."

"I can take the next shift and wake you up later if you want?"

I'd be lying if I said that didn't sound amazing, but I wasn't going to let him do that. We said we would lean on each other, so that's what we would do.

"Nope, I'm fine," I said, grabbing my daggers and going to take the next watch.

He laid down in the spot I left warm and pulled the furs over his body. I opened the tent flaps, and the starry sky stared back at me.

Out here in the Grasslands where there wasn't much else, the sky went on forever. I could see further than I ever could in the forest or in the palace.

I was amazed at just how much untouched land there truly was here.

I wondered where Xio was and if she was looking up at the same sky I was right now.

Chapter 37

Xio

We traveled for four more days before we could even see the mountains.

I let out a sigh of relief when I saw their peaks. The first step of doing anything was getting there, and we were close.

Holt explained that searching every mountain could take weeks to months, but I'd worry about that once we got there.

These nights with Holt all to myself had been wonderful. We hadn't grown tired of each other yet. I could picture myself doing this with him for the rest of my life.

I missed my sister so much that it hurt, but being here with Holt made me feel alive.

I laid in the tent trying to sleep but could not get my mind to sit still for the life of me.

The last time we were in the forest, Cree was attacked, and I was all too conscious of that while Holt was out there by himself.

I pulled my pants back on and left the tent.

"It's not time for you to be awake yet," he said with his eyes still watching the forest around us.

"I can't sleep. We can switch if you want?" I asked him.

My shift to stand watch wasn't for hours, but there was no point in both of us being awake if one of us could be getting some rest.

"I'm not tired either. We can watch together," he said, patting the empty spot next to him.

The air was chilly, so I grabbed the blanket I used in the tent and wrapped it around our bodies.

We sat in a little cocoon of warmth, watching for any movement, but the forest was silent.

I looked over at Holt, my protector, my lover, the other half of my soul.

There was no light that he looked bad in, but the moonlight always made him look, more. He was beautiful. His brown skin illuminated in the silvery light was almost too much to look at; it made his high cheekbones even more prominent than they already were.

His hair was so black and shiny that it looked silver in this light, like his eyes. His gaze was still out on the forest, but he licked his lips mindlessly, which was enough of an invitation for me.

I crawled into his lap, wrapping my arms around his neck, and traced kisses down his jaw.

"Xio, how am I supposed to stand watch with you doing that to me?" he asked with a slight smile on his lips, not able to keep the serious tone he meant to.

"I don't know what you're talking about. I'm just offering you compensation for your services."

"Oh, do tell, how much are my services worth?" he asked, giving up on trying to stop me.

I kissed his lips and swept my tongue into his mouth before pulling it back into my own.

"Well, it is quite late," I started, running my hands down his arms. "And you're out here all alone, not a single other Fae here to help you." I slipped open his shirt and kissed his collarbone. "That's got to be worth a decent amount, no?" I asked before pulling his shirt off his body.

I ran my fingers lightly down his abdomen, and his body tensed at the touch as I got closer to where he wanted me.

"I think, we'll need to open these. To give you your proper compensation," I said, running my finger over the waist of his pants, placing kisses where my fingers touched.

"If you insist," he said, shifting enough to unbutton his pants. "This is dangerous work, you know," insinuating that his services were worth a good bit of money.

I'd show him exactly how much I thought they were worth.

As soon as he unbuttoned the last button, his length sprang free, already hard and ready for me.

I took it in my hand, and he let out a low growl with anticipation. He tried to move towards me, but I pushed him onto his back.

"None of that. I'm the one benefiting from your protection. You just lay back and keep watch," I demanded, and he listened immediately, smugly placing his hands behind his head.

I moved back onto my knees and put one of my hands on the ground beside his thigh. He watched me move and work as I licked him with one long flick of my tongue from base to tip.

He groaned at the feel of my wet tongue before I took him into my mouth.

"Xio," he let out, a plea for more.

I wasn't going to deny a future king.

I wrapped my other hand around his base and moved it while I slid my mouth up and down.

"Fuck," he let out, another encouragement I took to heart.

I sped up, moving faster, and let my other hand join, working him with both hands and my mouth. It only took a few pumps of all three combined before he tightened, and my mouth filled with his warmth.

I swallowed it down and looked up at him, devastation and pleasure mixed in his features. I kissed back up his abdomen until I reached his jaw.

"Will that do, your highness?" I asked him before he flipped us over and laid me on my back.

"I think you paid too much. I owe you a little something back," he said while peeling my pants from my body.

The act already had me soaked, and he groaned his approval at what he found.

And then, he paid me back.

We finally made it to the base of the mountains.

We picked the area furthest from the palace and decided to work our way back. We were entering something more like a jungle rather than the forest we came from in the middle of the kingdoms.

The air was warmer than it was in the forest, still not summer warm, but warmer than what autumn was bringing the west.

Holt told me that we might see some jaguars out here. He assured me that they wouldn't hurt us and that all the animals of Maya lived together simultaneously.

Only hunting their source of food, which was not Fae.

I wasn't even scared.

I just wanted to see them. I felt connected to them through my mother. I also thought seeing them might encourage the jaguar within me out of my skin.

Holt kept telling me that it would happen, that it took him some time to be able to control it willingly. When I asked him how long, he said a few weeks.

In the lifetime of a two centuries, a few weeks seemed like a day in my life.

I kept trying. I could feel it within me, a beast of tooth and claw ready to come out if only I knew how to call to it.

Now was one of those times, which were pretty often, that I wished I had my mother to ask.

I hoped if we could make it back to the palace, I could find something to help.

There had to be some sort of book about Kinich and his powers, but I wouldn't be able to get my hands on that for some time.

We worked our way through the jungle, the path here nonexistent. In some spots, we had to get down from our horses and burn our way through. We tried to avoid this as much as possible, not wanting to damage the jungle.

But we almost made it to the other side. Holt also explained that there would be a place to stop for the night outside of the jungle. The foliage here was too thick to find a spot big enough for our tent.

The air was so wet here it almost felt like it was raining.

Otherwise, I would have been fine lying right on the ground. This jungle felt like it was a part of me. I breathed better here and thought better here.

I loved it.

Unfortunately for me, the region we were traveling through wasn't going to take much longer to get through, and I sighed as I saw the edge.

I looked back and took it all in, I ran my hands on a tree limb hanging near where we were walking, and I swear I felt the connection down to its roots.

I wondered if my mother ever spent much time here before we made our way out of the jungle and found ourselves at the bottom of a great mountain.

The sun would be setting soon, so there wasn't much point in trying to scale the mountain now.

"There are some caves over here. We will probably use those more often than not while we're here," he said while pointing to a spot a little way down from where we stood.

The cave we found was reasonably shallow, which was good. It meant we only had to watch our fronts, not our backs, for anything that might come for us.

I could still see the jungle, so I was glad to have another day to ogle at its beauty. We quickly set up and ate, creating a small fire in the back of the cave.

We didn't want the cave to fill with smoke, so we only used it for a little bit before we extinguished it, and the only light left was the stars. Holt took the first watch last night, so it was my turn to take the first watch.

He kissed my head and went to lie behind me on the bedroll. I watched the jungle, not really sure what I was looking for, but my eyes were drawn to it.

Suddenly a flash of gold and black caught my attention just outside of the cave, in the direction of the jungle.

I looked back at Holt, who was already asleep and tiptoed to where I saw the flash of color. Something in me told me it wasn't dangerous, but I didn't see anything. I didn't want to move too far away from the cave, so I turned to go back.

Before I could make it, a jaguar came from behind a rock. It moved with such grace and power in each step it took.

Its shoulders moved in waves as it crouched low to inspect me, its tail slightly waving behind with its wings tucked in tight.

I stilled, while not scared, it was a wild animal, and I didn't want to accidentally scare it away.

It moved close to me, its yellow-green eyes burrowing into my soul.

It brushed against my leg, and I swore I could feel something like a sentient.

Like this was not just some wild animal, but a creature of great wisdom, something that had been around for a long time and had learned from its life.

It walked a slow circle around me, maintaining contact with my legs before sitting in front of me.

I don't know how I knew, but I knew it wanted me to sit with it. So I did, we locked eyes, and mine began to glow, my power recognizing its own.

Holt said that jaguars were one of the animals revered in Maya. That they held great power and were a symbol of might and authority.

Right now, I felt every bit of that to be valid. We held our gaze for what may have been hours or minutes. Something in my mind opened, and I felt a different kind of power unlocking.

I took a deep breath as all my memories came rushing back to me, every sweet moment with my mother. Every skinned knee my father mended.

The day he died.

The love they had for us, the feeling was so overwhelming I doubled over and had to hold myself up with one arm.

The jaguar laid down and brushed its head against my arm, grounding me as everything ran right into me, over me, around me.

I couldn't breathe for several seconds. I don't know how I remained quiet, but I did. When I looked back into the jaguar's eyes, I was no longer looking at him.

I didn't even know how I now knew it was a him.

But I was looking into his mind.

I just got my mother's power.

I was a Mente.

Chapter 38

Xio

I sat outside the cave with the jaguar for hours. I never went to wake Holt up for his shift to take watch.

I had no idea how this power worked.

As Chara said, hers just manifested as strong intuition and flashes of visions.

What I was experiencing was far more significant.

I could look into this animal's mind and see all of his memories. Just as Chara said my mother could, I saw him walking through the jungle daily.

I saw my mother in the jungle with other jaguars, interacting with them. I saw him watching the mountains.

I saw when Holt and I traveled through the jungle and picked this cave to make camp in. It was an odd feeling. I wasn't sure how it would work on a Fae.

I sighed and thought to myself that I should probably go back to the cave and wake Holt, and that the jaguar should get back to whatever he was planning on doing.

As I thought this, the jaguar nudged my hand and sprinted back into the jungle. Like, it read my mind.

Or I spoke into his mind.

Chara mentioned that my mother could manipulate a mind and memories, but I wasn't sure if this was what she meant by it. I trekked back into the cave to wake Holt.

He still slept so peacefully. I knew he was tired. Our traveling had been pretty gruesome the last couple of days.

We pushed ourselves hard to get here, hoping we'd find the weapon faster. I knelt next to him and shook his arm a little to try and wake him.

He stirred a little before grabbing me in his arms and pulling me in for a cuddle.

"I just saw a jaguar," I said to him, and his eyebrows shot up.

"Did you go back into the jungle alone?" he asked.

I shook my head. "No, it came to me. But, Holt, I have all of my memories now. He helped me. I don't know how to explain it, but he helped unlock my Mente power. The power from my mother."

He sat up quickly and held me by my arms at my side, inspecting me like any of this was something he could see physically.

"How? How'd that happen?" he asked.

"I don't know, we looked into each other's eyes, and it's like the dam in me holding my memories and power back just burst open."

"I wonder if your mother knew that power would manifest, that you'd be able to bring your own memories back when it did? Can you do it for Camila?"

That was the first question I asked myself when my memories came flooding in.

It didn't feel fair that I knew everything about our past and she didn't.

"I think so. I was able to look into the jaguar's mind and see his memories. I don't know how it works for Fae, but I think I could do it," I said, and he looked at me, really looked at me.

Like I was his savior, like I was something to be worshiped.

"Try it on me," he said confidently, straightening his back like he wasn't even scared I would somehow turn his brain into mush.

"I'm not sure that's a good idea."

Sure, I had this power, but I had absolutely no idea how to use it or control it. What if I just wiped out his memory completely?

"How else will you figure it out if you don't practice with it?" he reasoned.

He had a point.

"Okay, if you start to feel your brains turn to soup, tell me right away," I said jokingly, but I hoped he took it seriously enough to know I sort of meant it.

He nodded and closed his eyes.

"Okay. I'm going to try and look into your mind. I won't mess with anything. Just look in. Think about something you don't mind me seeing."

He lived a long life before he met me. I didn't want to see him with other females or anything else, particularly unsavory.

"Ready?" I asked him.

"Ready," he responded with a nod.

Now I just had to figure out how the hell to look into his mind in the first place. With the jaguar, I felt a connection.

I definitely had more of a connection with Holt, so it should have been easy. I closed my own eyes and tried to find me and Holt's connection.

My face pulled tight with concentration until, it was there.

I could see our souls.

They were connected like a bridge of pure light. It moved and flowed in one and out of the other in a never-ending loop of pure energy.

I followed that bridge until I reached his mind. He was thinking about the first time he met me. When Cree and him had us on the ground for trying to steal from him.

He thought I was beautiful, but his heart skipped a beat when I looked into his eyes. He felt the connection between us but didn't understand why.

When he noticed I was human, he grew even more confused, but he knew he needed to bring me with him.

He wanted to protect me and claim me.

He never wanted to punish me.

He just didn't know...

The memory changed to our conversation after we tried to escape from the village. He remembered a conversation with Cree earlier in the day. He told him to stop thinking with his cock and to toughen up. Cree saw how Holt was looking at me and not treating me like a prisoner. After his comment about our inability to escape him, he felt sick to his stomach.

He knew what I was to him, but he couldn't tell me...

The memory changed to our time in the springs at the Sun Palace. When he was telling me about soul-bounds, he was worried I would be scared.

He was worried it would make me run away from him again. He noticed the way I looked at him and how comfortable I was with him.

He noticed my confusion about it.

He thought it wasn't fair that he had an explanation for the feelings, but I didn't.

He watched me as I washed my hair. I didn't know he was watching me.

When I turned around, he was already washing his own hair...

The memory changed again to the first time we had sex. He watched me as I bounced up and down on his lap. This memory had more feelings than any of the others. It was almost like I could feel it in my body.

I could feel our souls connecting on a level they hadn't yet before. He thought that I was the most beautiful thing he ever saw in his life.

He thought there was no way it was possible to feel the way he did, that his entire body was on fire.

He thought he was in...

I snapped out of the memory. I felt like I saw more than he meant for me to. I opened my eyes to see Holt rubbing his temples like what I did caused him pain.

"Are you okay?" I asked him, rushing over to him to check for any signs of an ailment.

"I'm fine, Xio. I promise. It was just a weird feeling to have you in my head, that's all," he chuckled, trying to reassure me he was okay, but I still wasn't sure.

I grabbed his face to check his eyes to ensure I didn't pop any blood vessels. But he just stared at me intently.

"You saw our souls, too?" he asked.

I didn't realize he could see that. I must have somehow shown it to him.

"I did. They're connected. Like you said. We're truly soul-bound. Not that I had any doubts before," I responded, scruffing his hair up a bit.

I loved when his curls fell into his face.

I loved the way he watched me as I interacted with him.

I loved—

"I love you, Xio."

I took a deep breath as he brought my gaze back to his own.

"I know that you saw that in my memory. It was true then. It's true now. Love doesn't even feel like a big enough word for what I feel for you," he admitted, tears began to well in my eyes.

"I've waited over 200 years for you. The moment I looked into those gorgeous golden eyes, I knew you had to be mine. I knew why no one else was ever enough, because you were made for me, only you. I'd bend to your every command, my very soul belongs to you. I'm not worthy of you, but I'll spend every day for the rest of our lives showing how deep my love for you runs."

For the last ten years, I didn't think anyone loved me other than Camila.

Now this beautiful Fae, this kind, honest, strong, powerful, utterly gorgeous Fae, was telling me that he loved me.

I had my memories back, I knew the love my parents had for me, and everything just felt perfect.

Like tonight was the perfect combination of every terrible thing that happened to me and every bright thing that happened to me.

Just pure bliss, pure unadulterated bliss. In the face of all the darkness, all the evil that was coming. I would hold onto this moment with the Fae I loved.

I would come back to this very moment any time I felt less than.

Whenever I thought I wasn't powerful enough or just wasn't enough in general.

I would come back to this moment, and I would relish in every feeling.

"I love you, Holt. There's no one else. There's nothing else. You are my beginning and my end, the air I breathe. I will follow you anywhere you go. You are my fate."

He was on me before I could even take another breath.

His mouth crashed into mine, teeth hit teeth, tongue met tongue.

It was not a beautiful kiss.

It was ferocious, like the love that I felt for him.

It was the power of a storm, the power of the sun coming to make something else entirely.

He pulled me into his lap, and I wrapped my legs around his body.

We sat and held each other in the cave, in the mountains meant to save us.

But here in this cave, none of that mattered.

Nothing was coming for us.

The world wasn't ending because I had my body wrapped around my entire world.

Chapter 39

Camila

We'd been traveling for a week and hadn't found the Serpent tribes. We made it to the area the scouts had found them before, but there was no sign of where they went.

The grass was worn in some spots, and we found minor burns in the ground where fires must have been. But they were no longer here, and they certainly knew how to cover their tracks. Cree and I did one more lap around the site and decided to look on foot for a little bit. Thinking that being at a different point of view would give us some advantage.

"I don't understand how they could just disappear without leaving any kind of tracks," Cree muttered, frustrated, while crouched down to the grass to inspect it further. "It's like every single one of them just flew away, and that's impossible."

"Maybe they've just gotten good at it, being nomads for thousands of years?" I suggested, and he shook his head.

"No, there's no way they could be this good," he responded and stood up, looking into the distance.

We turned in the direction of our horses when suddenly an arrow shot into the spot we were about to step into.

My flames immediately gathered in my hand, and Cree's shadows wrapped themselves around us, creating a barrier of protection. We whirled in the direction the arrow came from, and three figures crested a hill in the distance.

I went to form an attack, but all three dropped to the ground on one knee, just as they did at the feast. My face pulled into confusion while I looked to Cree to see if he understood what was happening. He looked just as lost as I did.

"They're saying they won't attack us. That they respect us," he said, laced with confusion and question.

"Do you think it's a trick?" I asked.

The Serpent tribes were described in a manner that I wouldn't expect any act of respect for either of our kingdoms. As our people both fought against them hundreds of years ago.

"What's the move, Commander?" I asked Cree, and he let his shadows dissipate slightly before stepping in front of me.

"Rise," he told the figures, and they rose from their knees with a fist over their heart.

"What is the meaning of this?" Cree asked, stepping closer to them so we could hear what they had to say.

The closer we got, the more detail I was able to see.

They wore clothes in different shades of the earth. Their armor was ornate and detailed, but it only rested on their shoulders and chest with a thin shirt beneath it. All three of them had some sort of green stone jewelry adorning their bodies. Two of them had similar coloring to Cree, but the one in the middle was darker, like Holt, and they were covered from neck to toe in tattoos.

"We came to collect you. Our leader has a message he believes you will need to hear," the one in the middle exclaimed.

Cree and I stilled.

How did they know we were coming? Were the scouts compromised?

"We mean you no harm, Prince," said the one on the left side.

They knew exactly who we were.

"I'm no Prince," Cree exclaimed.

Still uncomfortable with anyone referring to him as one. Even though he was, in almost every sense of the word. All but one. And that small fact of blood was what held him back from claiming it.

They all smiled gently, not a menacing smile I would have expected from the Serpents, but a warm, knowing one.

"Oh, but you are," the one on the far right said.

Cree looked taken aback at the comment but ignored it in favor of getting more information.

"Where is your leader?" he asked the three Serpents.

"We will take you to him. Follow us."

We both still had our magic gathered in our hands, but we followed. This was exactly what we came here for, so we would take advantage of the opportunity.

We got to the top of the hill, and my knees buckled. At the base of the hill was something I didn't think I'd ever see.

Something I felt like most other things in this world were just a fairy tale.

Sitting at the bottom of the hill was a dragon.

A real-life fucking dragon.

Cree and I were both planted on the hill, unable to move or speak. It appeared I was not alone in the shock this brought me, which I selfishly appreciated.

"That's a fucking dragon," Cree muttered, "a real-life, huge ass dragon," he followed up with while walking down the hill cautiously.

"He's not exactly a dragon," one of the Serpents exclaimed, "he's a coatl, feathered serpent," he said proudly.

The closer we got, the more I realized this to be true.

He didn't have legs, and his dark green body was thin and long. His wings were covered in feathers of varying shades of yellow and green, as well as the tip of his tail. He turned his face to us, and I stopped moving once again.

His face was serpent-like but more square. Like it was chiseled out of stone, and around the crown of his head was a mane of feathers resembling a crown.

He was magnificent.

He opened his mouth slightly to expose the lines of razor-sharp teeth within it.

He was ferocious.

We got up close enough to touch him now, and the sheer size of his body was daunting. The thickest part of him stood as tall and wide as Cree, and he was long enough to stretch from the bottom of the hill all the way to the top.

Cree told me that Serpents were not meant to be evil creatures, and I wondered if this creature should be revered just like the jaguar and the eagle.

Just as Itzamna said.

"He will take us to where our leader is," the Fae with the darker skin started, "his name is Aapo," he said, pointing to the mighty Serpent.

He reached his hand out to us now. "And I am Eadrich. I am so pleased to meet you, Prince"

We both shook his hand. Still a little lost in the shock of what we were experiencing. Cree didn't even remember to correct him on the Prince title.

"Our horses," I said.

I just got Vela. I didn't want to lose her already, and I knew how much Cree cared about Night.

"That is why there are three of us. I will take you on Aapo. Kaax and B'atz' will take your horses back to our site. It will take a few days, but we give you our word that they will make it safely."

Cree and I looked at each other in a wordless conversation about whether or not we should allow it. I nodded.

"We'll allow it. Take good care of them, or there will be consequences," I said to B'atz' and Kaax with a glare.

Being around Cree had given me lots of time to study his most intimidating Fae glare. He nodded at me slightly, giving his approval of the use of his glare for our horses.

They beat their fist to their chest twice and went to retrieve Vela and Night.

"You can climb up his wing. You two can sit between his wings. It's the best place to sit if it's your first time," he said with a smile.

Aapo let his mighty wing down, and we carefully climbed up on it over his feathers. Doing our best not to ruffle them too much. His back was lined with small ridges and horns, making something like handles for us to hold onto.

I settled between two ridges and held the horns in front of me. Cree did the same thing behind me. Eadrich sat closer to Aapo's neck.

He gave him a command I didn't recognize, and suddenly the mighty beast's wings started to beat. His body began to slither across the grass before the wings lifted him right off the ground.

He continued slithering in the air as he moved faster and faster until the entire world was a blur. Cree held me protectively, but his entire body was tense with the closest thing to fear that he could experience.

Eadrich looked back at us with amusement written all over his face as he laughed at us.

I was sure we looked as if we were just struck by lightning.

Suddenly we were diving back down to the ground. The world started to retake shape as he slowed down, this area so similar to where we had just left. Cree said all of the Grasslands looked alike, and they certainly did.

Aapo slithered down between two hills like he was when he found him and nestled into the grass.

I surveyed the area, but couldn't see much past the hill. We slid down Aapo's wing and started to crest the hill. Aapo let out a great roar and started slithering away between the hills.

When we got to the top of the hill, my jaw hit the floor for the second time today.

This was not just a few rogue Fae.

This was a civilization full of hundreds, maybe thousands.

They had extravagant green tents around the perimeter, and the flat area between them was busy with movement. Someone let out a warning cry, and they all turned to look at us.

They all fell to the ground on one knee, just as the males who found us did. We didn't know how to go about this.

Telling a few random Fae to rise in the grass felt okay, but commanding a tribe? That felt like something only their leader should be able to do in a situation like this.

A male dressed in all black walked between the Fae, still kneeling.

There was no doubt he was their leader. He walked with his shoulders back and chin high, power exuding from him. The closer he got, the faster my heart began to beat.

There was something so familiar about him. He was tall like most males were, but even taller. His hair was straight and black, and he had it pulled back into a bun at the nape of his neck.

A few rogue strands hanging to his brows. He had deep tan skin and tattoos, just like the others we met.

But once he got close enough to see his facial features, the straight arrow-like nose, those black upturned eyes.

He made it directly in front of us.

He muttered the words that brought Cree to his knees.

"Hello, my son."

CHAPTER 40

CREE

"Hello, my son."

Words I wanted to hear my entire life, my whole body ceased to work.

I hit the ground hard, falling on my knees, and everything spun. My breathing came in heavy pants, my heart beating faster than should be possible.

My chest was so fucking tight I thought I had to be dying.

My shadows were swirling around every part of my body. A presence to my right moved into my eye line on the ground with me, knee to knee.

I had no idea who the figure was. I couldn't even see their face.

"Breathe, Cree," the faceless figure said.

"Breathe," the figure came closer.

The brown and gold around their head sparked something in my memory, but I couldn't hold onto it.

They placed their forehead on mine and both hands on either side of my face.

The feel of their skin started to pull me out of whatever attack my body was having on itself.

Their magic came to meet mine, and the shadows began to pull back into me.

My vision cleared, and I saw her.

"Mila," I murmured.

"Yes, Cree, it's me. I need you to breathe," she commanded, and my body listened to her.

The world began to be what it once was.

I stood back up, Camila grabbing my hand before I was fully on my feet. She stood next to me, her presence anchoring me.

"Who are you?" she asked the male who claimed to be my father.

"My name is Kan. Come, let's talk in my tent," he said while he turned around on his heel to the tremendous black tent that sat in the middle of the rest.

"Rise, my people," he bellowed before we made it into his tent.

As one, they all rose, and the sound of bustling bodies filled the space as we stepped into Kan's tent.

The tent was fit for royalty. Rugs of different textures filled the area, and a bed sat on the ground in the far right corner.

There was a large table and at least ten chairs around it. Kan directed us to sit on one end of the table, and he went to sit on the other end.

"Explain," I commanded, my shock turning to anger.

Anger at whatever this person was going to say. No matter the explanation, it resulted in him abandoning me as a baby.

I looked to Camila to find her giving him a stare that could kill.

"I need you to understand that everything I'm about to tell you will be a shock. Angering. But I want to start this all with the fact that I am so happy to meet you again. You may not believe that, but I need you to know that."

Not very reassuring, but I nodded all the same.

"200-odd years ago, I met a female. She was the most beautiful creature I had ever met. She had long dark hair and skin like cream. I was out scouting on my coatl, Ajtzak, for a new site, and she was by herself in the Grasslands. She was sitting on a hill crying, and something about her drew me to her. She was magnetic. She told me that she'd made so many mistakes in her life, and she just wanted to start over. When her gaze locked with mine I had to help her. She rode with me back to where the tribe was located and smiled a smile that could light up any night. I had lost my mate a few decades back and didn't think a smile would ever have the same effect on me. I gave her a tent next to mine to keep an eye on her, and we fell in love. It was fast and passionate, all-consuming love. She fell pregnant with you fast, like everything else that happened with us. We were so happy and so excited...but...a little while after you were born something changed in her. She grew worried. She said that her past was going to catch up with her and that she wasn't honest with me about who she was. She knew I would love her through anything because I truly thought I would. But what she told me, what she told me was unforgivable," he stopped, trying to gather his thoughts.

He was looking down at his hands like they would somehow be able to help him say what he needed to.

"She told me who she truly was, and why she lied to me. She was so sure I would understand, which is what shocked me so much. Your mother Cree, your mother is Ixchel, the Goddess of the Moon."

The world began to spin once again.

What he was telling me had to be a lie.

There was no way that was possible.

"That's not possible," Camila blurted out.

"She died long before Cree was born. You can't be who you say you are," she started to stand up and take me with her, outraged for me at the lies this male was spitting.

"It is not. Please sit down, Princess."

Camila's brow furrowed, we had yet to tell him who we were. She slowly sat down, staring at him through narrowed eyes.

"It is possible because she told me that she was the one who killed all of the Gods."

He said that quietly, like there were other people around who might hear.

That explanation was also not possible.

None of this was fucking possible.

"She fell in love thousands of years ago with the God you descend from, Princess," he said with his gaze on Camila now. "Kinich. He was a just God, but as an individual he was not the best. He never returned her desire, and it drove her mad. One day he agreed to," he hesitated, "a joining with her, and she thought it was the beginning of true love between them. But after, he told her it would never happen again. He just used her. This enraged her, her heart broke, and she wanted them all to feel the pain she felt. The main Gods had a stronghold in the mountains at that point. Kinich, Ixchel, Chaac, and Itzamna lived near the Great Ceiba watching over their creations. She gathered them all, telling them she had an important matter to discuss and she killed them all. The power she had through her rage was unlike anything she had ever held before. She left the mountain and grieved for the love she wanted and the loss of an intrinsic part of herself. The part that was just and fair, and kind, and beautiful. She started rumors that Itzamna was the one who did it after she and the others didn't show up for their offerings. She couldn't bear the thought that the Fae she loved would see her as a monster. She traveled throughout Maya for a long time in hiding, using a glamour to change her features slightly, until I found her. I had never seen her before, our people didn't give her any offerings, so we didn't know what she looked like. When she realized this, she saw a second chance with me. But, I didn't react as she thought I would. She thought I would understand because I loved her, but I couldn't understand how she could do such a thing. I was enraged, and I took you and left on my coatl. I left for a fortnight and I took care of you by myself during that time. Those two weeks were...they were perfect. Two of the best weeks of my existence. We bonded, and I loved you so much, so much that I couldn't let her have you. I couldn't let her hurt you the way she did the other Gods. I remembered how kind the Storm King and Queen were when we agreed on the treaty, and word reached me that they just had a son of their own. They seemed like they would be better parents to you than I could alone, or that your mother could. I would never let her have you. Ever. I would never let her hurt you. So I took you there, they were holding court, and I left you outside the throne room with a rattle my mother passed down and note with your name. You loved that rattle, always making noise with it into the hours of the night if we allowed it."

He smiled gently at the memory, and my heart softened and hardened simultaneously. He shouldn't have made that decision for me.

Sure, the life he left me in was great. But not knowing where I came from took a toll on me.

I wasn't sure it would ever be repaired.

"I never stopped thinking about you. I sent scouts into the kingdom periodically to check up on you. They told me how well you were doing, how the royals took you in as their own and raised you with their son as I expected they would. I also sent artists with the scouts a few times so they could sketch what you looked like for me."

He got up from the table and grabbed a stack of well-worn papers like he really did look at them often. He slid them over to me, sure enough, it was my face.

As a child, as a teenager, and as an adult. Some were of Holt and me doing whatever we did when the artists found us.

Some of them were just me by myself. I slid them back to him, not giving him any sort of reaction yet.

"But, when I returned without you, your mother was outraged. She nearly destroyed our entire tribe, but I hold great power myself that I also hid from her. I never embraced it because I didn't feel the magic I had in my veins was mine. It didn't seem fair that I had this magic while others didn't. I am a minor god. Kukulkan, the messenger God they referred to me as. Itzamna himself gave me this power. She didn't know who I was either because I never came to the mountain. I only assisted Itzamna with messages. When I released my power on her, she was so shocked that she fled. I don't know where she went, but she never came back. I always expected her to return and fight me, but she never did. After I found out the truth Itzamna came to me in a dream, for he is the creator, he can't be killed. She merely destroyed his physical form, but he is the very sky and earth. He can't be destroyed. He never interferes with matters of his creations, so he never came to me with the message of what really happened. But once I found out the truth, he gave me one last one, one last hope to save the world he made. The prophecy. I haven't heard from him again."

We sat in silence.

Taking the overload of fucking information my supposed father was throwing at us.

"That is where you get your power from, Cree. Your shadows are from your mother. The Moon Goddess, she only let the people see the lighter power in her, afraid the Fae would be scared of the darkness of her shadows. You also have my power in you, but from what I've heard, it hasn't manifested. Probably due to the fact you didn't know you had it within you. If you let me, I will teach you. But she is coming, Cree. She will be back by summer. I worry about what she will be when she returns. She was broken once, but," he hesitated, "I fear she has lost any light she once held. Looking back, we both loved the idea of who we could be outside of what we were. Our story shows that, in reality, you can never escape your true self."

He stared at me while Camila did the same.

Waiting for my reaction, but I had none. I didn't know how to process this.

I was no mere Descendant.

No orphan.

My mother was *the* Goddess of the Moon.

My father was Kukulkan, the messenger God.

Camila, Holt, Xio, and I would have to...

I would have to kill my mother. It was the only way to save us all.

About the Author

Mikayla D. Hornedo lives on the east coast with her beautiful family. She is married to the love of her life, Dom, who pushes her to be her best every day. She has two gorgeous girls who she hopes grow up with a love of reading, just like her. For more information about upcoming books, exclusive content, and news, please visit mikayladhornedo.com

Acknowledgements:

I just want to say thank you to every single person who has helped me on the journey to publishing my first book. I can't believe that a small dream of mine has manifested into an entire novel.

Thank you to my husband, Dom, and my two beautiful daughters, who have supported me from beginning to end. Thank you to all the other family who didn't miss a beat and helped in any way they could. I'm so lucky to have such a strong support system.

Thank you to my ARC team. This experience would not have been the same without all of your encouraging words and support. Not only taking the time to read the book but also posting about it on social media, telling your friends, and sending me so much love, it's almost unbelievable.

Lastly, thank you to all of the authors out there who have helped guide me in this process!